# THE BOOK LOVER'S TALE

## IVO STOURTON

D0492006

**BLACK SWAN**

TRANSWORLD PUBLISHERS
61–63 Uxbridge Road, London W5 5SA
A Random House Group Company
www.transworldbooks.co.uk

**THE BOOK LOVER'S TALE**
**A BLACK SWAN BOOK: 9780552773874**

First published in Great Britain
in 2011 by Doubleday
an imprint of Transworld Publishers
Black Swan edition published 2012

Addresses for Random House Group Ltd companies outside the UK
can be found at: www.randomhouse.co.uk
The Random House Group Ltd Reg. No. 954009

The Random House Group Ltd supports the Forest Stewardship Council (FSC®),
the leading international forest-certification organization. Our books carrying the
FSC label are printed on FSC® certified paper. FSC is the only forest certification
scheme endorsed by the leading environmental organizations, including
Greenpeace. Our paper procurement policy can be found
at www.randomhouse.co.uk/environment.

Typeset in 12/14pt Bembo by
Kestrel Data, Exeter, Devon
Printed and bound by
CPI Group (UK) Ltd, Croydon, CR0 4YY

2 4 6 8 10 9 7 5 3 1

# *Prologue*

IT WAS VERY KIND OF MY WIFE TO HAVE SENT YOU, CON-
sidering the circumstances. The duty solicitor looked
rather young. He was terribly excited when they brought
me in: I think his experience is more in the drunk-
drivers, rowdy-pub-crowds line. He was shaking a bit
when he gave me his business card, and when I told him
he'd misspelt 'solicitor' on it he went white as a sheet. Just
my little joke, but he didn't take it terribly well. Anyway,
thank you for coming out at such an unsociable hour.

Would you like a cigarette? Turns out this is the only
place they'll still let you smoke inside. I want you to
know, right from the off, that I'm guilty. I done what they
say I done. There's all kinds of things to straighten out,
mitigating factors and self-defence and provocation, and
with good luck and a little help from yourself hopefully
I won't have to go to prison or anything unpleasant like
that. What I really want to know is, can all that side of
things wait? There's something I want to explain to you.

What's happened to me, you see . . . what's been
happening to me . . . I have this feeling – well, this hope
really – that it might be a tragedy. I used to think you
couldn't do tragedy any more, because everything in the
modern world has this tendency to the trivial. It either
comes out half-baked as sentimentality, or burned to a

7

crisp as irony. If we want tragedy we have to go backwards out of our own age, to Tennessee Williams maybe, or even further than that, back before Joyce where the rot set in. It's like backing an occupied hearse out of a tight parking spot on a steep hill, backing yourself out of your own cultural moment; you're almost certain to get it wrong in the most awful way. Then this thing happened. I met Claudia at the end of spring, and ever since then things have been getting more serious, somehow. Everything just got more and more serious until eventually I found myself here, and in the police car on the way back from the airport I suddenly thought, this is all so serious, it's practically tragic. I can't tell you how exciting that was, even with all the fear and grief. Imagine if you were an ornithologist and you found a great majestic dodo, running fleet-footed from palm to palm on some heretofore unknown desert island. That's what it's like for me, to come upon a living tragedy.

But the story can't do it alone. With tragedy, you see, the story is only one half of the equation. The other half is the listening. You know that old riddle, if a tree falls in the woods and there's no one there to hear it, does it make a sound? Well, I never really gave a crap about the environment, but as far as people go, a tragedy only exists if there's a protagonist and an audience. I'm the protagonist, or at least I think I am, but nobody knows the whole story. In fact I've spent most of the last few months desperately trying to keep the whole thing secret. There's been no audience, no one who can feel fear and pity at my downfall. I know I could write it down, or tell someone else later when there's more time, or even give an interview to a newspaper or keep a prison blog or something, but this is fresh tragedy, it won't keep and I can't bear the thought of it going off. It's too awful, the first real tragedy of the twenty-first century, spoiling and curdling into melodrama. That's what will happen, if I don't tell someone right away. Do you remember Horatio's last speech in *Hamlet*?

> So shall you hear
> Of carnal, bloody, and unnatural acts,
> Of accidental judgments, casual slaughters,
> Of deaths put on by cunning and forc'd cause,
> And, in this upshot, purposes mistook,
> Fall'n on th' inventors' heads: all this can I
> Truly deliver.

It's such a wonderful ending, because you've just watched the play, you've seen Hamlet beg his best friend to give some meaning to his death by telling the tale to others, and then Horatio stands up and promises something which sounds exactly like the trailer of a crap Hollywood movie. You just know he's going to get it so wrong, elide all that moral ambiguity and soul-searching, all that insight into the nature of being, all that poetry, into a hodge-podge of lurid sex games and murders. And Shakespeare points it up for you so perfectly by having that one phrase, 'Truly deliver', hanging out there as a broken line, rhythm mangled, exposed in all its vainglory. You must think it rather pompous of me to quote Shakespeare, but I find the classics a real comfort when other things are so disturbed. It's been rather a relief to me, waiting for you in this room, to go over some of the old lines.

Anyway, it's not wholly self-indulgent, because it's helped me to decide what I want. The detective inspector (detective *chief* inspector!) wishes me to give a statement, and after we've spoken I shall do just that, with your kind assistance. Before then, however, I would be very grateful if you would listen in silence to the whole thing. I would like you to bear witness, you see. Just once, before everything gets muddled up, and people start arguing about forensics and legalities, before the papers start talking up my carnal and unnatural slaughters, I want to try and say what really happened. I have to tell someone. If things had gone differently it would have been the person sitting next to me in first class on the way to Rio, but you can't always get what you want. If you can bear to be my witness, it just might come across as a proper tragedy, just this once, before it becomes a news item on the internet and some journalist hacks my Facebook account and downloads a decade-old photo of me wearing bondage gear at a university party. Will you listen? I would be so grateful if you would listen.

# 1

THE FIRST THING I CAN CLEARLY REMEMBER JIM SWANSON saying to me is: 'I only have one question – why do we need this?'

I smiled at him and nodded to indicate that it was a fair question, an excellent question in fact.

'I don't mean to be aggressive,' he said.

Nothing in my manner had indicated that I found the question aggressive, but I got the impression that Jim liked to think that people found him intimidating. I could imagine him saying something like, 'I'm not such a bad guy, when you get to know me' to a new secretary, in the secret hope that she would assume he was terrifying. I smiled again, sensing that there was more to come.

'And I don't pretend to know about books or interior design or any of the things you guys know about,' he said. 'But I do know how much all this is costing. Money I know! So I just want you to tell me why I'm paying for it, quick, before the wife gets back. Shortest words you can, I'm not much of a reader.'

He smiled. It was clear that he was proud of his self-professed ignorance, and of the focus on business that had prolonged such ignorance through adulthood. This was part of the service I offered. I did not just select their books for them; I validated their life choices. When you hired Matthew de Voy of Manches Interior Design, you did not merely assure yourself a library filled with the most aesthetically pleasing, harmoniously toned, culturally fashionable and above all tasteful books available. You also got to employ a man who embodied in so many ways the snobberies that might have cornered you at odd moments in the playground of life, and pointed at you and called you names. I was ex-public school, of a good and impecunious family, with even the Gallic surname to suggest a Norman lineage; I had gone to Cambridge and studied English and got my first and attended all the parties; I had slept with the fashionable people in the fashionable postcodes; I had eschewed the professions, spurning the eager embraces of the law and banking to pursue instead the life of an aesthete, dilettante, womanizer, traveller and novelist; and, above all, I had failed.

Failure in my chosen life, or more precisely the exhaustion of my money, after which disaster all other ambitions beat a disorderly retreat, had made me an incredibly attractive prospect as a servant. The workaholic, East End trader types, to whom my life at its zenith must have been a kind of active reproach, were afforded now the rare opportunity of making me beg for meat from their table, generally an extremely expensive designer table also furnished by Manches Interior Design, of which my wife was the proprietress. I fully understood, therefore, the motive of this question, and also the lit eyes that accompanied it. The shame I used to feel at the need to perform had been largely suppressed by long usage. I got on my hind legs and started to dance.

'Well, all our clients want different things from a library. Some want bare shelves for their own books, some want fake spines to give the room a grander texture. Some people just want a place to hide their safe! But we feel that the library is your best opportunity, as hosts, to create a subtle and lasting impression on your guests. There are three things a guest will look at when left alone in a room. They'll look at your photos, they'll admire the view from the windows, and they'll have a look at the titles of the books you read. Your taste in books says more about you than any other single object in your house. It reflects your interests, your intelligence, your sophistication, your humour, and, depending on budget, they can also be a very successful means of reflecting . . . well, not to be vulgar but – your means.'

I smiled, and Jim smiled too, but in a slightly uneasy fashion that suggested he had not understood the joke. That was a serious misstep; I was not paid to invoke puns beyond the understanding of my clients.

'Look, really I'm no different from the plumber. I'm just here to do what you tell me to do.'

'Can you have a look at the water pressure in the guest ensuite before you go?'

We both had a laugh, and the misstep was forgiven.

'I'm afraid that's a little beyond my competence. But what I can try to do is help you choose a library that goes with the look you've chosen for the room, matches the colour scheme, and most of all helps to reflect you and your wife's image, the way you want the world to see you.'

He blew out his cheeks. 'Well, I can tell you for sure, none of my mates would go for the books. They'd be straight over to the telly and the drinks cabinet.'

We laughed again. We were sitting on the chairs in the newly finished kitchen. The air still held the fumes of the various paints, solvents, varnishes, metals and marbles that had gone into its construction, smells so far from food in my associations that I found the whole effect somewhat disorientating, like entering the bedroom of a beautiful girl and discovering the atmosphere of a petrol station forecourt. I wondered particularly if the air could be healthy for the newly minted Mrs Swanson, who was five months pregnant. Her pregnancy had been the catalyst for the couple's move from their penthouse in Old Street to this terraced townhouse in Vincent Square, a move which, in the light of the summer's events, would later come to seem somewhat premature. The house was being remodelled in two stages, the first of which was now complete. This had consisted of the major structural renovations (the previously poky rooms in the basement were now combined into a generous 'rumpus room' with a lightwell on the street side) and the completion of the decoration to the essential rooms (the kitchen, master bedroom and ensuite, the study and the bathrooms). The Swansons had now moved into the property, and the second stage of furnishing and decorating the library, the basement, the guest bedrooms and the nursery had begun. The front hall and central staircase would be the final areas to get their gloss, left till last to prevent any damage from the tramping of workmen's boots to and from the other sites.

On that summer's afternoon, the atmosphere could not have been more idyllic. The sound of children playing, which I enjoy at a sufficient distance, could be heard in one of the neighbouring gardens at the back. The scent of the garden entered by that same aperture, a large honeysuckle having been coaxed up the terrace outside. Through the front window was the green of Vincent Square itself, on which Englishmen played cricket as if nothing untoward had happened in a hundred years. The whole street had an atmosphere of peace and leafy calm wholly at odds with its position in the centre of London.

There was nothing old in the kitchen, in the sense that there was nothing inherited. There was the centrepiece of the marble worktop, which was a deep relief carving of a lion in white stone purchased by my wife from an estate sale in Somerset (and removed, to my certain knowledge, without the consent of English Heritage). The workmanship was nineteenth-century Georgian, the block of Carrara stone from which the rampant beast emerged would have been mined and imported to England from Italy perhaps a decade before that, and the milky mineral structure metamorphosed from limestone a million or so years before that. But it was newly purchased. The same could be said of everything in the clean, white interior. The silverware, the glassware, the utensils and appliances, all of them new. The Swansons were the perfect clients. They seemed to have been born into their new home as naked as babes. I thought of the myriad objects that Cecilia and I had inherited when we moved into our first home together, a flat in Hackney Wick. There had been gifts from friends, treasured possessions from childhood, items called up from storage in country barns by well-meaning aunts and uncles and grandparents (though nothing from the parents; mine dead, hers disapproving), plates, crockery and an unusual odour from the previous tenant, and of course books. Hundreds and hundreds of books in back-breaking boxes that had to be tramped up four flights of stairs. They reflected every moment of our intellectual development, from favourite children's books we had been unwilling to throw away to student manuals of practical criticism in English (mine) and art history (hers), together with my collection of first editions, then in its larval stage. The Swansons had nothing except the new things they had bought. I rather envied them this freedom of movement. Or perhaps it was their absence of history that appealed.

The man sitting opposite me, my employer, was in my hopes roughly the same age as myself, but in reality probably somewhat younger than my thirty-seven years. He was dressed in a white T-shirt proclaiming its provenance in colourful beading, and jeans. He was short, which was something. He had dark hair and dark eyes and was unremarkable. Cee, as she always did, had given me an account of him before this first interview which had amounted to a retelling of his CV (my wife operates the equivalent of a mini secret service, with agents in drawing rooms, recruitment consultants and prep schools all over London). In brief, he had come from nothing to something via a number of investment banks. He had never been to university, a step I had assumed was indispensable in the modern corporate world, but he was an extremely successful autodidact in matters of economics. He was a day trader, a rising star and earning about one and a half million a year with bonus, a figure that was certain to go up.

The wife was the daughter of a Catholic family, father an English diplomat, mother a fruity translator from somewhere Soviet and grim. Claudia had apparently spent her childhood shuffled up in a deck of foreign embassies and local nannies before a permanent posting to an English boarding school in her late teens. She was several years his junior, and they had met when she secured a work-experience placement in his department. She had been doing a languages degree at Clare College, Cambridge, which for some reason she had abandoned in her final year on returning from Rome. Cecilia had learned this last detail from talking to the youngest brother of one of our friends, who was at Corpus Christi studying engineering. Apparently something of a cloud hung over the reasons for her departure. The young man could tell us no more than that she had left quite suddenly and the exact circumstances were a mystery, giving my wife no little cause for titillation.

I had been surprised that he had known the girl, being in his first year when she was in her second. On seeing her, however, I had understood why a younger undergraduate from a different college might have known who she was, and why her departure would have caused a stir. Claudia Swanson (née McEwen) was unusually beautiful.

I have always thought the quality of advice to be found in the Bible somewhat patchy, but the bit about not coveting your neighbour's wife is spot-on (with one important caveat). I have nothing to say on the morality of the matter, but wanting another man's woman, really wanting her, will drive you mad. This is particularly the case in my own profession, where I so often come across the wives of rich men, and in a context where my success depends on my capacity to abase myself. For it is not desire for the woman that will wreck you in such circumstances, but rather the knowledge that she is possessed by another man. If one falls into this trap, a romantic may characterize it as losing one's heart to a woman; but a realist will tell you it is giving your balls to her husband.

With this in mind, I try to reserve any attraction I may feel for my neighbour's wife until I am certain she wishes to sleep with me. That would be my aforementioned caveat – if you can tup the wife in question, covet away. It is only the jealousy that comes with unrequited attraction which is corrosive. So I reserve my judgement, attaining an indifference which is itself quite a powerful aphrodisiac to a really beautiful woman, until I am certain that a favourable assessment will be reciprocated. It is not a difficult trick, to master the passions in this way – it just requires the exercise of will power to suspend a natural impulse. In the same way that it is only fat people with cheeks crammed full of Mars bars who will mournfully tell you that their affliction is glandular, only the weak will make claims for the primacy of romantic attachment. Whenever a friend has come to me guilt-ridden with some moment of infidelity, I have found myself thinking, cheat, drink and be merry, but do not be so disingenuous, so cowardly as to suggest you could not have done otherwise, or that the moment made off with your self-control.

Over the years, my career has afforded me ample opportunity for practice. Interior decoration has not traditionally been regarded as a seducer's profession. Literature assumes that novelists have all the fun, pop culture looks to sports and music stars, and porn has an odd fixation with repairmen (it's never a burly hunk coming round to assist with the proper hanging of embroidered silk curtains, always a broken showerhead or clogged pool filter that first unites the two or three young lovers). The low profile has been a help rather than a hindrance, as it puts people off their guard. I have found that the macho City boys who make up my clientele often assume that I am gay, something their wives confess a little sheepishly after our first coupling. More than anything else perhaps, it's the stage of life in which a woman finds herself when she calls an interior decorator that charges the job with erotic possibility. My clients are generally at the end of youth and the end of the beginning of marriage, their husbands working long hours, their bank accounts full, their sense of their own desirability beginning to ebb. In those circumstances, a little attention, a fondness for women in general and the odd sincere compliment go a long way.

Even with the benefit of practice and experience, however, I had difficulty in ignoring Claudia, or Mrs Swanson as it would be better to call her. The sound of a muted flush and the loo door opening in the hall announced her imminent return, and when she appeared in the doorway I had to strain to impose my will on my instincts. She was five foot seven in her sandals, as tall as her husband, and would have been taller than him in heels (a trifling thing, you might think, but one that really seems to grate after a few years of marriage). She was possessed of the freshness that leisured youth or television cameras can bestow, and could not have been more than twenty-eight or twenty-nine. Standing in the doorway, she was illuminated by one of those oblong slabs of sunlight that seem only to exist on summer afternoons, when the angle of the long-setting sun passes deep into the shady depths of private rooms.

She had black hair, which was at least in part the work of expensive men. Despite the salon sculpting and the glossy sable undertones, it was escaping from her hairband at the side, a couple of shining filaments in the sunlight, rebelling against restriction in a way that was charming and made her seem younger. Her eyes (brown, though not so you'd notice without checking) had a slight Slavic tilt, this the genetic flourish that elevated her from good looks into beauty. She wore no jewellery except for her engagement and wedding rings (strange indeed for a City wife), though the former bore an ample solitaire diamond. She had bare arms to the shoulder and bare legs from the thigh. Her skin was tanned, though I suspected she would be brown even in the depths of winter. With her dark colouring and the sharp little angles of her face, she had an everywhere look about her. If I had met her in Rome I would have addressed her in Italian, in

Thailand I would have thought her Thai, perhaps with an adventurous European loitering somewhere up the family tree. Although the timings of the move suggested she was at least five months pregnant, she had only just started to show and her figure was excellent; she wore a white cotton dress nipped in at the waist by the broad band of a brown leather belt, a Bohemian look that was a little outdated, not quite on trend.

I comforted myself that the final trimester, when I would be most likely to be in and around the house, might bring on a heftiness that would spoil her beauty, but looking at her I had a suspicion she would be one of those girls in whom pregnancy manifests not in an even spread, but rather like the growth of a butterfly's chrysalis on a sapling.

She was diffident, and remained on the threshold of the room, leaning against the doorjamb with her arms folded. She did not once look at me. Her eyes were all for her husband. He turned to her and smiled.

'We're going to go with the library then, sweetheart.'

There was a breath of air from the garden at exactly the moment she moved away from the door, and it seemed that the floral scent was hers. He rose instinctively as she came further into the room, and pulled out a chair for her from the table. I am used to husbands putting on a display of chivalry for my benefit, but I felt he would have done as much even had I not been there. There was a great intimacy to their formality. I remembered myself and stood up too, but she waved me back into my seat, excluding me from their moment. She sat down, and smiled up at him. He smiled back but did not sit down again, perching instead on the edge of the marble countertop. The position had the effect of amplifying his smallness. He looked like a leprechaun in jeans.

'What is the process, Mr Manches?' she asked.

'It's Mr de Voy,' I said with a smile, 'although, please, Matt.'

'Oh! I'm so sorry, I thought Cecilia was your wife.'

'She is my wife. She keeps her maiden name for business purposes.'

'I admire that,' she said. 'It's stupid to lose a reputation you've built up, just because you get married. I never had that problem with Jim since I never did anything worth remembering.'

Normally a comment like this would have assisted me, in that I don't like it when people denigrate themselves to fish for compliments. It would have been such a blessing to find something not to like about Mrs Swanson, just a crack in the door of her desirability into which I could work my foot. I was about to answer with the required, 'I'm sure that's not the case . . .' when I realized that the observation had been directed entirely at her husband. Not only that, but he said nothing to contradict it. Just smiled again with a mutual understanding. I coughed, and took another sip of my tea, which was cold.

'I'm sorry,' she said, looking at me once again, 'you were going to tell me what happens next.'

'Well, the first thing to do is work out a budget.'

'We've set aside twenty thousand for the library. That's right, isn't it, darling, twenty thousand?'

'Give or take.'

'It seems like such a lot of money.' She said this almost apologetically, as if asking me not to judge her profligacy too harshly.

'That's a good figure. That will allow me to get you a well-bound backbone of new volumes that will look really well on the shelves, and a couple of good pieces to form the basis of a collection, if that's what you would like.'

'That sounds lovely.'

'Now, I understand that the colour scheme is to be primarily cream for the walls and carpets. If I could recommend a majority of red-moroccan leather-bound books with gold lettering, at least for the shelves immediately facing the door . . .'

'You mean you choose books based on what colour they are?' she said, her eyebrows rising in surprise.

'Well . . . yes, my guiding principle is generally the visual effect.'

'Never judge a book by its cover,' Jim said, and winked at me.

'Ah-ha, yes. But as I say, it's mostly a matter of the colour scheme.'

She continued to look at me, and her unaffected surprise made me feel slightly ashamed. I had the feeling one gets when a child catches you out in an adult hypocrisy by asking 'Why?' until you run out of plausible answers and shout 'Because!' I understood her reaction completely. It had taken me many years to get used to the fact that my clients did not really want to discuss the content of the novels, guides and reference books I placed on their shelves, but rather the appearance or, at most, the value and provenance if they wished to start a collection. Now that I had become used to it, I simply assumed that that was what people wished for. Looking at me in that dumbfounded way, she recalled me to my former self, to the young man who regarded library consultancy as a temporary occupation, and who reviled the shallow materialism of his clients. It had been a pleasurable sensation in the early stages, as I promised myself vengeance in satire. Only later had I realized I could never hope to make them as ridiculous on the page as they made themselves in their drawing rooms.

There was, however, a great difference between the emotion expressed by her look and the feeling it recalled in me, for in her there was no judgement. She didn't look scornful, or appalled, merely saddened and surprised.

'That's a shame,' she said. 'I was rather hoping I might have your help in choosing some good books. I used to read a great deal . . .'

'You've been run off your feet recently though, my love, with the move and the works and everything.'

Jim hopped off the counter and put his hand on her shoulder, which she took in her own long fingers lightly and without looking.

'Yes, that's true . . . but maybe now . . .'

'Now you'll have a bit more free time.'

His voice became surprisingly gentle when he addressed himself solely to her.

'I can certainly help you build an excellent reading library, in addition to the visual element,' I said.

'All the works of major writers who were originally published in burgundy dust jackets?' she asked earnestly.

'Oh, we could have them rebound . . .' I said, and then to my utter embarrassment realized she was joking. She gave a solemn little smile, not mean but friendly, offering me the chance to laugh at myself. Jim looked ecstatically pleased with his wife's gambit, and was on the point of interjecting, no doubt something witty about not wanting anything redder than I was, when she leaned forward in her chair.

'So you would be able to give a little more guidance as to content,' she said, generously intersecting my confusion.

'What sort of things are you interested in?'

'Oh, anything really. English and American novels, Indian, African literature.'

'Anything factual? Biography, travel writing, history?'

'I think I'd prefer fiction. But you might like some books on economics, no, darling?'

'I guess that would be pretty cool. If you could find something original by Keynes or Galbraith or Adam Smith or something. How much would one of those cost?'

'I'm afraid I think a first edition of *The Wealth of Nations* might exceed our total budget. But I'm sure I could find a nice earlyish printing for under two thousand. Or I could find you a first edition of *Liar's Poker*.'

Every banker I have ever met thinks they are a character in *Liar's Poker*. It is a rule as invariable as their ability to quote (approvingly) from Gordon Gekko. They are possibly the only social group in history which takes every attempt at literary or cinematographic satire, however vicious, as a back-handed compliment.

'That would be wicked.'

'You studied Italian, didn't you?' I said, turning back to Mrs Swanson. I produced the detail with a flourish, keen to impress after having been caught out by her. 'Perhaps I could find some modern Italian novels, or English books set in Italy . . .'

'No, thank you,' she said, and it was the first time the goodness went out of her voice, which took on the hard edge I associated with City wives. 'I don't want anything like that.'

It was a strange reaction. Immediately I thought of the cloud of intrigue, that impenetrable penumbra hanging around the abandoned town of her degree. The notion that I had transgressed upon some hidden taboo was reinforced by the fact that I noticed a tiny twitch in the tendons of Jim's fingers, indicating the exertion of pressure on his wife's hand. I recognized this movement from my marriage – one would never encounter it in the course of an affair, or if one did its import would be quite different, coming under the table and not above it. I was unwilling to allow the interview to conclude on this note, but Jim came round the table with his hand extended to meet mine. He was playing his wife's protector, casting me as the source of disturbance to be removed from the room.

'So you'll get a list together, and then we can talk it over, see what's what?'

So I was not to be left alone with her.

'Darling, I know the sorts of things you want. I'll see Mr de Voy next week and I'll make sure we get plenty of dusty books with old men talking money.'

'You sure? And lots of new ones with men talking cars?'

'Yes, it'll be fine, and I don't mind. It will give me something to do.'

Jim looked at her, reading the familiar language of her face.

'OK, cool. Guess I'll just pay the bill then.'

'That's my baby.'

He laughed, happy.

She rose too. With both of us standing, I availed myself of a quick peek down her top. What I saw there made me draw in my breath. There was the line of a livid, raised scar sitting plump and pink on her sternum, vanishing swiftly under the cup like a snake escaping under her bra. I wanted to reach straight down her little white dress and grab the tail of that scar and haul it back out of her clothes.

She gave me her hand. It was as cool as water in the hot afternoon. Jim showed me to the door and we shook hands, and I felt relieved when the door closed behind me.

I walked down a short flight of steps from their door into the front garden and out through the gate. The skinny pavement outside their house lay in a pool of shadow extended by a neighbouring tree. The cricket match in the centre of the green appeared to have concluded, and men in whites met their women in light dresses over by the pavilion, where the grass was a patchwork of tartan rugs and striped deckchairs. I have not played or watched cricket since I was eleven years old, but I feel a tingling sometimes at the truncated stub of the memory, signals from a phantom limb of my Englishness.

Actually I'm grateful to have cut the thing off. My one enduring memory of cricket was in my first summer term at my Catholic prep school. My mum and dad had come down to watch me play the Dragon in the third eleven, which was a faux pas in itself; every other parent seemed to know that to attend your kid's sporting events if they were below the second team was sort of cruel, it deprived them of the ability to pretend they didn't care about being crap. My parents were pretty much the only ones there. I was tenth man, and I walked all the way out there to bat with my mum clapping and cheering my name. The other boys picked up on it too, our school and theirs, and they started singing 'Mat-*thew*'. Mum didn't care; she never cared what people thought. She just shouted louder. Now of course I know she was trying to help me not care, to help me be myself, but all I felt then was the humiliation. My scalp was burning and tingling, the little buckles on my pads jingling with each step. The walk from the pavilion to the crease in the hot sun felt like crossing a desert. When I finally got there I was all on my own in the middle of the field, holding this absurd lump of wood. I went for a duck on the third ball. When I trudged back my mum was on the boundary, waiting to give me a hug. I changed direction, walked the other way to where the games master had the pads and gloves in a trunk under a tree. Before my parents left they came over to say goodbye, and Mum said she was sorry, she didn't mean to embarrass me. I felt so ashamed for having been cross with her. The memory still makes me ashamed. It's funny, isn't it, how the conscience can be a bit like an oyster. One little grain of a moment like that gets into the soft naked folds of your brain, and then you do the work, rolling it around and around in your thoughts, making it bigger and more luminous as the years pass with layers of shining significance. And you can't ever spit it out. Though I suppose someone can crack you open and take it.

Out on Vincent Square, the scoreboard indicated that the home side had won by three wickets. I stood for a moment between the black wrought-iron railings at the front of the garden and what I guessed might be the Swansons' car (the sedate-looking Volvos and Range Rovers, many of them smattered with the mud of rural weekend homes, seemed less likely candidates than the canary-yellow Cayenne with the number plate 'MR F1XIT'), and wondered what it was about the two of them that had unsettled me. I lingered a little longer on the pavement, watching the sun set over the Georgian terrace on the west side of the square, and dissected the interview. The birds sang, and the voices of the sportsmen, raised now to a jolly murmur, reached me across the long flat distance of the green. Then I realized what it was. The two of them together reminded me of myself and Cecilia in the first years of our courtship. The parallels were undeniable; she, beautiful, of good family, looking up to her husband and playfully mocking. He, doting, infatuated, protective without jealousy, a young man who had achieved something, but of whom much more was expected. And both deeply in love. Though of course, in our case, I had been considerably taller.

The light of subsequent events (coming as it does from an oblique angle) may throw behind these ruminations some grotesque and elongated shadows, bearing as little relation to reality as the towering columns of shade lying upon the playground at sunset may bear to the three little boys in shorts who cast them. The possible seduction of the wife, the added bonus of humiliating the husband. Of these innocent pigments was the entire palette of my intent composed. If anything more sinister did cross my thoughts, it did so only in the wholly unserious fashion with which any man or woman might entertain such notions – the kidnap of an overbearing employer, for example, or the decapitation of his family by a low-hanging tree branch in some kind of traffic accident. Violence, much less mortal violence, was completely absent from my thoughts.

## 2

IN ORDER TO RESTORE MY SENSE OF ORDER, AND TO GIVE myself time to think, I resolved to make the journey that I always made in such moods, to the bookshops on Charing Cross Road via the depths of Soho. I don't know when I first came to that street, but I know when I first saw its private face. Every street in London has a public and a private face, the smile it gives to a passing policeman and the wink it gives its neighbour just as he goes by. The Charing Cross Road first winked at me in December 1985, a few weeks after my twelfth birthday, and I winked back.

My dad was tidying up our home after the death of my mother, a process which had been going on for some weeks. He had decided to sell part of their library in preparation for the move to digs on campus, a two-bedroom apartment near Goodge Street lent him by the LSE. The move was the beginning of his retreat into the hermetic world of academia, the life of the mind and donnish feuding at the expense of romance, family or politics. He had entrusted one of my mother's old books to me. He impressed its value upon me when he delivered it into my hands. I was so happy to be able to offer him help of any kind, as he had withdrawn from me in his grief. The feeling of practical uselessness in the face of bereavement accentuated the simple fact of my mother's absence, and being tasked with the delivery of the book was a great relief. I was to take it to a dealer friend of his, Lucius Watson, whose shop was stationed just north of Leicester Square.

Back in the early eighties, the London Underground had a character more suited to an Italian opera singer than a mass transport system – if it caught cold, or got too hot, or endured the slightest smattering of rain, it would simply clam up and refuse to perform, no matter how many tickets had been sold. That night, it was snow on the line that caused the hysterics, locking me underground in the tunnels for three hours. After wandering up and down the darkening street, jostled by bus queues and with the tumbleweed of newspapers blowing around my feet, I found the shop wedged between another bookseller and a corner store selling teddy bears wearing beefeater hats. I pulled the bell, which was one of those antiquated affairs that stimulate a tinkle in some interior passageway, and waited, to no response. The street was freezing and dark. I could see my breath in the air, and the temperature stung my cheeks into life.

The sign on the shop door was turned to *Closed*, but my father had told me that the shop was attended practically all night. I pushed on the door and it opened. I closed it behind me, and was immediately enveloped in the blessing of warm air. The shop was empty of patrons, and the lights on the displays, bronze arms holding long bronze shades, were extinguished. There was, however, the glow of light and the sound of laughter and old jazz from behind one of the stacks at the back. For some reason I did not call out. I felt instantly at home, safe and entitled to take such liberties as I pleased. I think it was the smell of the air, which was musty and thick, and charged with an underlying masculinity. It was just like the air in my father's study, and it made me feel I already knew the men in the room, whoever they were, intimately. I crept forward, and staying silent and out of sight behind the stack I peeped around to look at them.

There were four men in a pool of light which came from the shaded bulb in the ceiling overhead. There was whisky on the table, and crystal tumblers of ochre liquid, and the smell of that was part of what I had taken for the smell of my father. I recognized from my father's description Lucius Watson, the owner of the shop, and Carlos Rael, his lieutenant. They were playing poker. Beside each man was a stack of books, some hardbacks, some pamphlets, some letters in cellophane which shone in the warm glow of the yellow bulb. They talked and laughed as they played, and the first words I could distinguish were from Lucius.

'Damned if I will. They'll keep on pushing the old offside trap until every man jack of them is sitting in the bloody opposing goal having their half an orange thirty seconds after kick-off. Now a manager ought to do all that may become a man, but he that dares do more is none.'

'Star striker, hide your fires . . .'

'Oh very good, very bloody good, but I've got thirty on City not because I like 'em, and certainly not because I bloody think they're going to win, but because of the principle of the thing. The principle!' and here he hit the table with his fist, making the tumblers jump. The shock of the sound had a similar effect on me, and I started, bumping into the wooden shelf with my shoulder.

'Who's there? Who's there, I say? Carlos, you bloody dago, did you forget to lock the bloody door again? They'll be after my sumptuous Austens. Who's there? Show yourself!'

I came out from behind the rack gingerly, and held forward the book in my hand by way of introduction.

'What have you got your hands on there, eh? I expect it's one of my sumptuous Austens.'

He snatched the book out of my hands with great delicacy and held it up to the light, swaying almost imperceptibly as he towered over me. He read the title out loud, as if to confirm it to himself. '*The Man of Mode*, by . . . Why, you little scoundrel, I've only just managed to find a copy of this, and already you're trying to steal it from me.'

'No, Mr Watson, I think there's been a mistake.'

'You're bloody right there, me old mucker. Big mistake to fool around with Lucius Watson. Big mistake indeed. Carlos, phone the police. Now, don't struggle, I intend to restrain you.'

'No, no, Mr Watson, my dad sent me to give you the book.'

Lucius, who had been rolling up his sleeves in preparation for the act of restraint, stopped and looked down on me, focusing with the same dubious precision he had mustered when interrogating the title of the book.

'You're Dr de Voy's boy?'

'Yes, Mr Watson.'

'Well, what the bloody hell are you doing crawling around on the floor in the middle of the night? Come in, boy, come in. You can have a snifter. Do you have any money?'

They let me watch the game until my father arrived to pick me up. They played dealer's choice, and, in addition to money, they gambled with their books. I returned many times after that to watch them play, whenever my father would let me in the school holidays, and though the players often changed, the beginning of each session was the same. Everyone got their books out on the table, and each of them would appraise the others' offerings and come to an agreed valuation. They'd trade a bit and buy and sell, and then the books that were left on the table for that night's game would have a fixed price as gambling chips. That was largely how I learned to value books, watching the men picking them up and turning them over, sniffing and peering and listening to the sound of the binding.

Those men became my second family. Lucius Watson would be drunk by ten in the morning, but no more or less drunk by ten in the evening, and he had read every book in the world. Carlos tried to restrict his drinking in the mornings, so Lucius kept whisky mixed with water hidden in a vase on the counter which was stocked with fake silk flowers. The skin around his eyes was composed of a series of tender pink folds, and the eyeballs themselves were shot through with blood, and protruded through the lids as if under tremendous pressure from the brain behind, forced out by the volume of his erudition. The whole effect was fascinating and repulsive, and I found each eye individually reminiscent of the view I had once had of our cat giving birth. Carlos was a Spaniard, and I never discovered the full story of how he had come to work there. I got the idea that he had been a tourist who had stopped by to ask for directions on the way to Leicester Square, and had been unable to find his way back out through the jumbled stacks to rejoin his tour group. In the end he had hung up his camera and his backpack in the stockroom and reconciled himself to his new environment, but he had never become quite used to the idea of working there, so that whenever you asked him a question he took on a startled look of double ignorance, first as to the answer to your query, and secondly as to why you had put it to him at all. Whether they were lovers, or lifelong companions, or whether they simply shared the flat above the shop in an effort to conserve rent I did not know, and it did not seem to matter. Certainly they bickered with the friendly outrage of long familiarity, and whenever Carlos won a hand, Lucius would throw his cards in the air and accuse him of being a dirty, cheating dago, at which Carlos would look hurt and utterly confused, until Lucius came over to him as the next round was being dealt and hugged him, and told him he was as good as any Englishman, particularly a drunken old sod who had seen his best days at Oxford, whereupon Carlos would look confused and touched.

I had been working on and off in there since I was fourteen, delivering books and wrapping dust jackets in clear cellophane, stocktaking and taking inventory. Just before my A-levels, Lucius told me that a friend of his, Sharon, a woman I had already met at one of their poker nights, was taking over a second-hand bookstore on Berwick Street. I started working down there in the summer holidays just after my seventeenth birthday. The running of the shop was entirely at Sharon's discretion. She was an ex-librarian from Manchester University, who had been fired for slapping a student she caught underlining bits of *Das Kapital* in biro. She had cropped peroxide-blonde hair with black roots, and took to me from my first day on the job, entering my name in the duties roster as 'posh twatter'.

The shop stood between the Endurance pub and a haberdashers next door, with Ingestre Court on one side and Peter Street on the other. Opposite was the open maw of a brothel, breathing sweet fumes into the street, with a handwritten sign saying 'Models, 1st and 2nd Floor' tacked up in the entrance hall. It was a good place to develop addictions. Thomas de Quincey had purchased his first wrap of opium from an apothecary up on the corner of D'Arblay Street, and four hundred years later there was still a young Nigerian man there, shifting from foot to foot in all weathers and asking you if you wanted tickets to the party, real good tickets, almost free for you, my friend, keeping London's cultural heritage alive. A fruit and veg stall stood on the cobbles just outside every day except Sunday, and the smell of rotting fruit in the gutter made the air sweet and fly-blown in summer. A few steps to the left stood Walkers Court with the triple-x bookstore Harmony and the Raymond Revue Bar. This last great house of cabaret and striptease owned the tiny closed bridge that ran across the top of the court, and on the one occasion I went inside I was amazed to see that the interior was fashioned to resemble the prow of a ship, with dubious lovelies in sailor outfits lolling amidst the pillows. When you stooped down to look through the windows you had the impression of sailing over Berwick Street, which gleamed in a recent wash of rain like water in moonlight, a black cobbled sea spotted with luminescence, brakelights and neon signs and prostitutes and revellers like strange fish.

Inside the shop the stacks ran along two walls on the top floor, with an open barrow down the centre for back issues of comics and periodicals. The space between the barrow and the shelves was just wide enough for two people to pass abreast. The air was damp and warm and yeasty. The books were supposed to be organized by genre and then alphabetically within their allotted stacks, but the process of classification inspired endless arguments. Sharon insisted that *Naked Lunch* should go in 'cult', whilst Françoise, the young assistant with the pierced nipples that were always quite prominent beneath her tight vest top, and with whom I was wildly in love on account of her habit of typing short stories on an old-fashioned Remington typewriter, was equally adamant that the book should appear face out in 'classic texts' between Bunyan and Byron. She was studying post-colonial literary theory, and she insisted that the 'cult' designation was all part of the mainstream media's fascist agenda to discredit Burroughs by a process of cultural marginalization. I could tell which one of them had been on the shift before me because they always moved the book. The basement, accessed via a small winding staircase at the back, was twice the size of the shop above, and down there the fig leaf of indexing was whipped away to reveal complete disorder. There were books on the shelves and books on the floor, there were books in columns supporting tables and expensive books behind glass doors, there were books fallen behind furniture where no one could reach to free them and books positioned on the tops of cupboards where no one could see them (these my special province due to my magnificent height).

The customers who came to us were not the discerning professionals who sought out Watson Second-Hand and Antiquarian Books in search of collectibles, nor the casual browsers who made their way to Foyles on the Charing Cross Road. They were the mad flotsam of Soho who needed something to read between the pub and the brothel. The authors were the most incompetent thieves, and we almost always caught them. The students were proficient, and the prostitutes were the best; even when they came in only briefly in the winter to warm themselves before getting back out on the street, wearing almost nothing and with tiny handbags, they would somehow manage to secrete something expensive about their person. Even the customers who actually made it to the till usually wanted to pay for the books half in cash and half in swaps. In a kind of Karmic merry-go-round, often I would arrive to unlock in the morning and find a box of good books on the doorstep, the remnants of a dead relative's library or an ex-lover's belongings from someone who had mistaken us for a charity shop.

Somehow in the midst of this weird trade enough money came in to pay the electricity bills by the time they turned red, and to give me and Sharon our meagre wages. But the books weren't really stock. They were valuable not in themselves but for the ideas they contained. Mad people and bad people and brilliant people came in and out and borrowed and stole and donated, and all these ideas moved again and again. The books were just a means to keep their stories moving. We handled them with respect, the same way you handle a lover with respect, not because you intend to sell them but because they are cherished for themselves and for the pleasure they bring.

Sharon used to work behind the bar in G.A.Y. on weekdays after hours, and I often went out to see her there, or to go clubbing in one of the private members' clubs in the magical alleys, Air Street and Half Moon Street, where basements pulsing with riches and beauty waited beyond the velvet rope. I would spend three days' wages on one round of drinks, and see if I could attach myself to a rich Arab's table, where the girls might think my cheap clothes ironic. On such nights the both of us would sleep in the underground warmth of the shop's cellar, nesting like rats among the magazines. Sharon knew many jobbing actors and actresses and directors in Soho, there to make contacts and work and to abuse and be abused, and we held readings and performances in the basement after hours. To supplement our income we served beer from a crate behind the counter, playing music on the shop's dilapidated stereo.

The first time I ever made love, it was on the floor down there, and the smell of dust on old pages filled my lungs and my nose, mixing with the smell of her cheap lipstick, and the taste of chewing gum and cigarettes on her breath. When she came, she stretched her hands back involuntarily, making the stack behind her fall over, and the burst of pride at having made her come (so much more vivid in my memory than my own orgasm) was inexorably linked to the distinctive clap of hardback books connecting with the concrete floor. Afterwards I lay there with her for hours with my head on a stack of old copies of *Private Eye*, and her head on my shoulder, and a blanket over both of us, breathing in the dusty smell of the fan heater.

There was another first in those heady Soho days, and though I haven't thought about it in years I suspect it's germane to the events of this summer. It was a hot night just like this one, heat sitting on the city like a school bully on the chest. I've never told anyone before, not even Cee. I should preface it by saying I do not like men who hit women. There is a moral element to this. I don't like to see the weak picked on by the strong (a probable result of several years of having water poured over my sheets and shit put in my bed at school, for the crimes, if memory serves, of being a book-loving spaz, and having a common mother in the first degree). For all my faults, I am not a bully, and children and dogs are safer in my company than parents and owners. Over the years as the number of tearful women who have faced me across the restaurant table has grown, I have taken comfort from this simple fact. As I sit there with wine dripping down my face or pasta cooling in my lap, with the eyes of the other diners upon me and a list of some of my more colourful personal failings still ringing in their ears, I can think to myself, at least I'm the kind of man who can't stand to see a woman hit.

On this particular evening I had managed to sneak into one of the up-market nightclubs, and my efforts to ingratiate myself had not gone well. At midnight I had found myself sprawled on a bar stool, watching a group of young Italian bankers with their models. Their table was on a slightly raised dais just above the dance floor. At one point they ordered a magnum of champagne, which was carried out aloft by several waitresses in a cooler festooned with sparklers. When the little tableau emerged from behind the bar, the DJ stopped playing and the club was filled with the triumphant swell of a horn section, during which time the magnum on its palanquin of young hands processed around the dance floor like a statue of the Virgin around the streets of some small Mediterranean village, borne aloft by the most beautiful unmarried women. As the procession reached the table of purchasers, I realized that the music the DJ was playing was Copland's 'Fanfare for the Common Man', about which the composer had once said he was all for honouring the common man at income tax time. Magnums went for just under a thousand pounds.

I wondered who was making the joke and at whose expense – was it the DJ at the expense of the club owner? The club owner at the expense of the purchasers? The purchasers at the expense of the other patrons? Then looking at the faces, bored and satisfied and hungry and mean, in the ring of firelight cast by the sparklers I became suddenly afraid that there was no joke, that I was the only person in the club who even recognized the music.

Everyone was looking at the dais as a waiter in a tight

T-shirt that clung to his muscled torso lifted the bottle to pour the first glass. One of the girls, an extraordinary beauty who could not have been more than eighteen, raised her glass, her eyes dazzled by the sparklers, her other hand held up to catch her giggles. The man raised his own flute at the same time. The waiter went to serve her first. The man struck her outstretched arm, knocking her glass to the ground. Then he smacked her hard in the face with an open palm, but without breaking the wrist on impact. This happened so fast that the waiter tipped a small sparkling libation on to the ground before he could right the unwieldy bottle. The girl sat down on the banquette, holding her cheek, collapsing in on herself under the weight of her humiliation. The waiter poured the man his drink, his face a professional blank. The man took it and with the utmost chivalry handed it to the crumpled girl, who thanked him and took it and cradled it on her knee, and the fanfare ended and the club began to dance again.

This was back in the days when you could still smoke inside, and I was lucky that he chose to step out for a cigarette, luckier still that the press of bodies around the velvet rope and the cars trying to nose their way past in the alley and the shoving of photographers caused him to move away from the door. It was a night almost as hot as this one, and the breeze cooled my sweat as I watched him. After he had finished his cigarette he didn't go straight back to the club, but lit another and walked off into the alley that ran along the side of the building to take a piss. When a car squeezed past him he slapped the bonnet with his hand and swore. He went right behind one of the big wheelie bins filled with bottles for recycling, where the stench of urine and beer dregs was strong in the heat. Watching him go I felt suddenly . . . important. Like an instrument of fate, just for a moment. I followed him. I grabbed the back of his head and slammed it into the wall. He had the cigarette between his lips, and when I pulled his head back again with blood starting from his nose and the fag stubbed out between the brick and his chin, he looked like a silent movie stooge who had just lit an exploding cigar. His flies were still open when he fell on the ground, and I kicked him and kicked him, winding him so he couldn't cry out. Then I stepped back out of the alley into the road, with its laughter and drunkenness and bright lights, like stepping back through the wardrobe door and out of Narnia.

I walked off through the hot night feeling happier than I ever had in my life before. It was not the violence that had cleansed me, I am a gentle man at heart. It was the sense of righteousness. I understood then what it was to be a Knight Templar, a UN peacekeeper, the Allies marching through Paris, a Spanish inquisitor – to combine force with the intractable sense of rectitude. But it didn't last. Even the next day, I found the experience distant from myself, something that existed in a different world and time. Most of my memories from that time are so personal, but this one feels more like something I read in a book. I could look you in the eye and tell you it never happened.

The shop went bust some time during my first year at university. It was not exactly a surprise, given the way the business had been run, but it was a shock nonetheless. It was careless of me to leave my happy memories somewhere so vulnerable. I had come down to London after my second term with Cee in tow. She was posh and beautiful and I was in love and desperate to impress her. She used to love the stories I told her about the place. I sensed that what she wanted more than anything was a sniff of my muck. I think she liked to picture me as poorer than I was to heighten the piquancy of our romance, and though my father had been to Harrow and I myself had been a scholarship boy at Westminster, I obliged with stories of Bohemian academic penury. Of all these stories, the tales of the bookshop were by far the most effective, since they were the most squalid and fashionable. Her beautiful eyes would shine in the darkness as I fashioned myself for her. Two months into our affair I allowed her to accompany me all the way down to Berwick Street on a Saturday morning, and I could see her warming her aristocratic cockles at the sight of the molls, the strip clubs open at 11am, and the drunks and the crazy tat on the market stalls. I was excited to show her off to Sharon, and to parade her in front of Françoise, who had never had the decency to reciprocate my infatuation.

Soho has a way of shuffling its landmarks when you aren't looking, and we had to walk up and down the street several times before I could convince myself it was really gone. Cee was disappointed at first, but in the end it added to the mystery of the place for her, and over the next term she appropriated many of my stories and told them as if she had known me back then, as if the bookshop and its inhabitants had been intimately known to her.

Then Watson Second-Hand and Antiquarian Books shut, and 94 Charing Cross Road shut, and the Book Traders shut, and a giant franchise bookshop opened three floors by Cambridge Circus, and Lucius called to tell me that Sharon had been killed in a motorbike accident, and I called Lucius to invite him to my father's funeral and Carlos answered and told me that Lucius had died of a heart attack, and he sounded more lost and confused and sad than ever, and he finally rejoined his tour group and went back to Valencia, and that was the end of it all really.

I set out from Pimlico station and headed for the West End. I got off the tube at Oxford Circus and waded through the tourists, heading east. I cut down Berwick Street, which was resting before the night in the afternoon sunshine. A dreadlocked man in handcuffs sat on the pavement between two policemen, one of whom held a cigarette up to his prisoner's lips as the three of them talked about the war in Afghanistan and waited for the van. I passed the spot where the shop used to stand, which is now a couple of inviting windows filled with inexpensive jewellery. As I always did, I cursed myself for the books I could have bought there but passed up, not then thinking about what they would later be worth. I checked in the remaining second-hand bookshops down by Leicester Square, but they had no good new stock, and I did not harvest my usual pleasure from the racks. At least in my mild irritation at the wasted journey, and in the backward-looking mood that the walk always inspired in me, I managed to forget my interview with the Swansons. As the sun set, and the West End dragged itself before the mirror to get ready for the night, I got on the number 22 at the corner of Piccadilly opposite the statue of Eros and headed back to Chelsea.

# 3

LOOKING AT MY HOUSE, IT WAS UNDENIABLE THAT I HAD come up in the world. My house was certainly larger and more expensive than the Swansons', though I had done far less to deserve it. Or at least to afford it. It was a fully detached Georgian townhouse on Old Church Street, a venerable thoroughfare that links South Kensington to the banks of the Thames. The neighbourhood is situated in the matronly bosom of the Royal Borough. It is the game reserve of rich England. The Russians may have taken Belgravia, the Arabs have Mayfair, the French own Gloucester Road, but here in Chelsea the good and ancient families of the English aristocracy endure, some of them with their men working in finance or art, others like ticks that have lately fallen from the back of an animal, not now sucking, but engorged with such a surfeit of property profit that they will be able to lie in the long grass for a generation simply digesting before another hapless beast ambles past. The calm and leafy streets, the ordered shops, the roadworks instantly accomplished without a sweaty arse-crack in sight, the groups of schoolgirls on half-term giggling in the cafés without fear of molestation, the nods to known neighbours on a weekend morning; all of it creates an impression of humanity as one great and slightly fusty civic triumph. There at the centre of all that is English lay my castle. Although of course it was not really my castle. Not legally. And not in character. And not in name. It was Cee's.

The house itself is cordoned off from the pavement by nothing more proprietorial than a black chain strung between conical grey stones at shin height. The front garden contains a willow tree which blubs on passers-by and an off-street space large enough for two cars to park side by side. The interior of the dining room is clearly visible through the bottom-floor window at the front of the house, though as it is a room we seldom use we have no real need of privacy. The kitchen is situated behind the wall at the back, looking out on to the garden, and it is there I know I am likely to find my wife.

Most successful marriages (and it is strange how 'success' in these matters is achieved simply by the process of avoiding divorce, so that one may labour on in miserable union to a premature death and still have avoided 'failure') are reducible to either a friendship or a contract. My marriage to Cee, after the verger had swept up the confetti and the bedsprings had ceased their happy mewling, had turned out to be contractual. The exact terms were supplemented and varied over the passing of the years, as in any fruitful commercial relationship of long standing, but certain terms were what lawyers would describe as 'of the essence'. Chief among these was the stipulation that I was never, ever, to do anything more to embarrass her. I say 'more' as there was little doubt in my mind that I had failed my wife, and I suspected even less in hers.

She had sacrificed a good deal to be with me. We had been together since the first year of Cambridge. Her parents were not enamoured of me, but did not protest too strongly at first. They found me charming, exotic, cultured and altogether a suitable stopping-off point for their daughter on the way to a proper marriage. I was an anecdote-in-waiting, to be fondly mentioned at dinner parties many years hence as 'That writer chap – you were quite fond of him, whatever became of him?' In the same way that upper-class parents may be tolerantly amused if their child falls in love with India on a gap year and spends twelve months living in an ashram outside Delhi, but less so if they miss the start of the Michaelmas term. For the first year I was given a hearty welcome, the second saw me more frostily received, and for the year of our finals I was never invited to the family seat. Cee's parents were undramatic, there was no great schism, just the drip-drip of a developing understanding. It should have made me love Cee more fiercely, the knowledge that she bucked parental pressure to be with me, only I always suspected that the bucking might be part of the point. There was in her a streak of frustrated rebellion, rebellious because she did not like the boring men her mother would have chosen for her, frustrated because she liked their money and horses and cars and houses. So did I, for that matter.

Cambridge is a terrible place to begin a romance of this sort, since it allows for the temporary suspension of material concerns and the corresponding elevation of the importance of character. It is supremely easy to sit with a rich and beautiful girl in a spacious thirteenth-century room on a medieval cloister, with the many bells of the city ringing out in the afternoon and a black-tie party to attend in the evening, to take her by the hands and to confess that you have no money, that you are not likely to have any money, at least not at first, and that therefore you can only offer her a life of relative privation. It is equally easy for her, looking at an honest and handsome boy in the golden light of the afternoon that penetrates the ancient stained glass of the lead-latticed windows, to believe the best of herself, to look him in the eye and to say in pure hope and truth that the privations will be as nothing so long as they face them together, before the two of them embrace, make love and head off to a heavily subsidized ball. This insulation from financial circumstance amplifies the hopefulness of youth to the point of distortion. It allows a woman to believe she has paid the price for her beloved, whilst really he is the great lie of our age, an article purchased on credit.

Even when we arrived in Hackney, there was a jaunty novelty to the squalor, a frisson to the danger, and we were young enough to enjoy living above a kebab shop. We thought the ubiquitous graffiti the honest art of the streets, the mad drunks characterful, the various ethnic groups sequestered in unending blood feuds cosmopolitan (we never read novels by the white British). It was during that period, those first six months after coming down from university, that our contract went into its first draft. Cee would be beautiful, would never complain, would charm those she met, and would wander through the desolate warehouse reaches of the Kingsland Road like a snow leopard through the suburbs. I would write, and veil our circumstances beneath a sheen of Bohemian glamour. And at first it worked. My first novel came out eighteen months after we came down from Cambridge. Cee would come with me to the interviews I gave in pubs and clubs and sit at the bar with heavy kohl eyes reading Kafka. The publication process shed the fairy dust of significance over the lowliest utensil in our studio apartment, so that even the broken egg-whisk seemed like a writer's broken egg-whisk, ready at any moment to leap from the mundane into art.

It rained. The heating broke. The second novel began

to drag. Cee was mugged on her way down Old Street. The kid punched her in the face and broke her nose in a way that for a while threatened to disfigure her, and left me feeling so guilty about having let her go out for milk (whilst I claimed to write but in fact played solitaire on my computer) that I could barely look at her. She thought this a result of her injuries, and was terrified I would stop loving her. It also put a stop to the modelling that had partly funded the rent. The advance from the first publication was largely spent before the book was even completed, and I was tutoring and doing bar work to supplement our income. The event did serve to reconcile Cee to her parents, who in a fit of remorse purchased us both a flat in Parsons Green, and found Cee work in an interior design firm run by one of their friends. She was so brave about the whole thing, and my residual guilt so enduring that any reservations I might otherwise have had at the sudden acceleration of the union were silenced. In truth I think I had always regarded the estrangement from her parents as a kind of firebreak between ourselves and the ultimate commitment, and was unprepared when it was whipped away with so little ceremony. We were married the year after, and I began to assist the firm (which also helped to develop collections of manuscripts and antiques) with writing up catalogues for its libraries. But though parts of the contract were rewritten or fell away, that one stipulation applied, *mutatis mutandis* – Cee had sacrificed the country landowner or gentleman financier she might have married on the altar of my talent. She had risked losing her parents (so the story went) and even placed herself in physical danger for that dream, and I was to deliver on my part of the deal and make her the muse of a great work.

I remember vividly the night that it became apparent

to me the game was up. It was in the seventh year of our marriage, when Cee was preparing to leave her old company (taking many of its best clients with her) to start up Manches Interior Design. I was of course coming with her, and our preparations together, though happy, were made with the unspoken subtext that I was engaging in yet another professional endeavour that would take me away from writing.

The two of us had been invited to a dinner party by one of our old college friends, the idea of which was to see in the 2005 election, to sit up through the night as the results came in. It was a large group, twenty or so in total, held in a palatial flat at the top of an office block in Victoria, and our host announced when we were all seated that the evening was to be enlivened by a sort of ironic parlour game. Before the returning officer climbed the podium glowing on the plasma screen, every person in the room would have to call the result, and those who got it wrong would be expected to down a shot of tequila. My political knowledge not being all that it should be, I was alarmed at the prospect of drinking 650 shots of José Cuervo, but our host reassured us that no one would be called on to honour their debts beyond the bounds of consciousness.

Cee was sat next to a tall, dull Trinity man with red hair. His name was Hugo something, of the Yorkshire somethings. He had been a talking point during Finals as he had leveraged his student loan to purchase a house on the outskirts of Cambridge when he first arrived, and had then rented it out to students before doing it up and selling it on for a brutal profit in his final year. My understanding was that he had continued this lucrative pattern after graduation, purchasing houses at depressed prices from those who could no longer afford to pay their mortgages, renting to them for a while and then forcing them out when they inevitably defaulted on the rent. He sounded to me like some kind of demented micro-colonialist, expunging laid-off northerners from their ancestral lands before carving them up into flats, but the scheme had been quoted with approval over dinner. Every time he spoke I wanted to look to my wife for that return glance which seems to me almost the whole purpose of prolonging a relationship beyond the stage of mutual ease; the ironic cast of the eye which affirms that you are not alone in thinking what you think. Yet somehow that evening she was continually distracted by news of such-and-such's marriage, or what so-and-so thought of the markets, and the moment of communion evaded me.

After the second course the table began to fray around the edges, some departing to smoke, others to assist with plates or relieve themselves, and I noticed Cee was no longer in her seat. I rose myself, eager to find her and to forge a little conspiracy or two to replenish my sense of righteousness before pudding.

I searched the kitchen and the small queue for the bathroom, and finally headed upstairs to where the smokers were dispersed among the bedrooms. I heard Cee's voice, coming indistinctly from an open door. When I rounded the corner, it was to discover her and Hugo seated by an open window, looking out over Buckingham Palace. The room was filled with the music of cars from the street, and as both of them were facing into the wind they did not notice my approach. Cee protected her health by only smoking the cigarettes of others, so I knew that he must have invited her to this tête-à-ginger-tête and she must have acquiesced.

'I know what you do these days,' he was saying. 'Magda wanted to call you actually, to bend your ear about this work we're having done to the drawing room. But what's your husband up to?'

Cee cocked her head. 'What's his name?'

'Who?'

'My husband.'

'Ah, well, it's, ah, you know . . .'

She looked at him for a moment, and they both laughed.

'Oh come on,' he said, 'it's been almost ten years.'

'Matthew. He works with me.'

'Matthew! Ah, that must be quite something! Living and working together.'

'Oh, it's all right really.'

'Magda sometimes tells me I'm married to my job, but at least my job is a refuge from my marriage.'

'No, it's good.' She laughed. 'We're surprisingly happy, actually.'

Listening to their laughter, I felt an almost overpowering urge to run into the room and push him out of the window. I could picture the look on his face as he plummeted, the self-satisfied chuckle turning to outrage as he went past the floors, maybe a cry of 'Now, look here!' just before he connected with the pavement. To avoid this I walked back down the flights of stairs to the toilet, now mercifully unoccupied. I gazed into the unforgiving mirror, designed to illuminate all the crags and contours of the face to facilitate shaving. There was nowhere for the signs of age to hide themselves, small as they were. It was not the intimacy of the tableau that had upset me, though as I had come seeking the exact same thing it was unpleasant to find her sharing it with the object of my distaste.

She had not mentioned my writing. Once she would have offered it as a kind of reproach, a proof to a man like Hugo that it was not that her husband was less successful

51

than him, but rather that he had chosen a more honourable path through life.

But she had not. She had simply stated that I worked with her in interior design. I felt she had betrayed me to this boring man's condescension. And yet I realized I could not blame her omission. What would she have said? That I had been working on the same book for eight years? That people did not ask me any more how the second book was going, not out of tact or embarrassment but simply because they had forgotten about the first? How long can one keep calling oneself a writer if one is not being paid to write? And how would I convey to her my sense of betrayal? By saying that the business into which she had poured all her energies, and which in truth funded our very pleasant existence, was somehow not a worthy employer of my talents? As I looked into the mirror, I saw that I was not better than everyone else. I did not wear my profession as a secret talisman, holding me aloof from all conversations and all people, so that my talent might scavenge for material from an ironic distance. I was the same as all these other people, only worse, for I had clung on to teenage ambitions like a former pupil constantly turning up at school to cheer the old team, and pat the back of the star fly half, never seeing how the boys laugh at him.

When I returned I called Glasgow East, Hammersmith and Fulham and Brent East wrong in quick succession, and downed the requisite three tequila shots. For Brent East I snorted the salt and ate the lemon, rind and all. Cee was eyeing me a little warily. It took me half an hour to work my thoughts to a sufficient velocity that they might escape the gravitational pull of social convention, but when they had I cornered Hugo where he stood behind one of the sofas.

'Look, old man, I've been meaning to bend your ear about something,' I began.

'Oh yes? Consider it bent.'

'I will! That's very kind of you! Yes, look, it's a bit awkward, but the truth is, well, Cee and I have been having a bit of, well, you know, financial difficulty recently.'

'I'm sorry to hear that. She didn't mention anything before . . .'

'Oh no, she wouldn't, you see, not to you. Proud woman, my wife is, proud woman, and she admires your dynamism, you know.'

'Well, that's very . . .'

'Your business acumen. Your genius. The service you provide to the community.'

He laughed uneasily.

'Anyway, so what I was going to say was, we've been having a bit of trouble paying the mortgage recently. So we were wondering if you could, you know . . .'

'What?'

'Buy our house.'

'What?'

'Come on. Buy our house. You buy everyone else's houses. And I just know you'll give us a good deal. Buy our house and we can be your tenants.'

The volume of a social gathering modulates itself with all the unconscious elegance of a flock of swallows turning in flight. The awkwardness of my own conversation had spread first to the clusters standing immediately around me, then further into the body of the group.

'I'm not sure that would really be appropriate . . .'

'Why not? You provide a service. We need a service. Just market forces and all that. Buy our house.'

'Look, you've obviously had a drink . . .'

'Come on. We can be serfs and grow you bushels of

wheat in the window box, until you evict us. Buy our house.'

'No.'

'Buy our house. Is our house not good enough for you? What, you'll take on financially illiterate unemployed families with no connections, but not someone your friends might know? Come on, buy our house.'

He turned away from me, and walked towards the kitchen. As I saw him go, I noticed a slight tremor in his shoulder. He was actually shaking with rage.

'Go on!' I called out. 'Everything must go!'

The majority of the party had fallen silent. Some were looking at me with naked contempt. Those who were still talking to one another did so with an air of trying to save the evening from utter disaster. Cee was sat on the sofa in front of the television, looking at me with a rage I had never before seen in all the years of our relationship. Good, I thought, it serves her right for sneaking off alone with him and not with me. The TV called Birmingham South for the Lib Dems. I downed the shot in my hand.

We left the party at three in the morning, resigned to another five years of hard Labour. Cee was no longer speaking to me. Tony Blair had won Sedgefield against the bereaved father of one of his dead soldiers, and delivered some heartfelt bullshit about how he totally got how everyone was so totally fed up with him for lying about Iraq and making us go to war in all these places and kill all these people, and he was totally going to listen from now on and not take us for granted any more because it was, like, wrong to lie. As a citizen I felt like a wife listening to the excuses of a husband who has recently been caught balls deep in his secretary, but has been allowed back into the house for the sake of the children. It made me so angry I almost resolved that at the next general election

I would vote. My anger also provided a useful insulation against the creeping sense that I had behaved appallingly at the party, that Cee would be incredibly angry with me, and that the whole thing would have to be repaired with endless emails and phone calls and reciprocal invitations. In this I was not deceived (unfortunately I was to have ample opportunity to apologize as Hugo began to refer to us business redecorating his more upscale acquisitions).

The day after the dinner party, with a searing hangover, I telephoned my agent and asked him how we could go about repaying my advance on the second book. After I had reminded him a few times who I was he expressed sorrow but understanding, and promised to contact the publishers direct. Although of course in addition to the money I had received, I would also have to make up the difference in respect of his 15 per cent . . . I told Cee later that week when she resumed talking to me, and afterwards she never again referred to me as a writer. She became acutely uncomfortable if anyone mentioned the old book, even (or especially) with lavish praise. It was as if we had had a wonderful child who had died, and were forced to continually explain this loss to a range of new acquaintances.

I had had a few extra-marital dalliances before all this, viewing them as just compensation for one who had been cursed to fall in love young, but guilt had been a kind of anti-Viagra which had kept them in check. I had also confined myself almost exclusively to actresses, artists and poets, with one eye on my autobiography. Shortly after the dinner party, however, guilt seemed to ease off the brakes. At the same time the creative criterion I applied to potential bedfellows was relaxed, the autobiography being well provided in bedroom incident and increasingly thin on incidents taking place anywhere else. My growing taste for infidelity led to much repeat business for Manches Interior Design, as the women with whom I was sleeping discovered they wanted their bathroom and their bedroom and the children's bedrooms done as well, and they would all need books for the shelves. It also caused me to involve myself more fully in the business, acquainting myself with colour schemes and fabric samples, as there is a finite amount of time one can realistically be involved in the compilation of a library, particularly for a woman one's wife has met and who does not at first glance give the impression of being a heavy reader. It was only when Cee praised me for my new-found professional acumen that the feather of guilt tickled my nose in sleep.

That was the story of how I had failed my wife. She had expected no more from me than I had expected from myself, but had perhaps taken disappointment a little harder. She did not marry the man I was, but rather the man I expected to become. But I was barren of books. All booked out. A gentleman would probably have withdrawn when it became apparent that it was not to be, but by that time her parents had upgraded us both from the Parsons Green flat to the house on Old Church Street right opposite the Chelsea Arts Club, which is excellent for lunch, and divorce involves endless forms. Besides, even one's own conscience eventually forgets to give credit for self-sacrifice, and whilst the benefits are generally fleeting the consequences tend to endure. A martyr may or may not be remembered for ever, but he will certainly be forever dead, so no thanks, says I. I stayed put.

So, the contract stated that she was never to be embarrassed again. Her part consisted of the provision of an elegant life, and to be fair to her she had embraced the role of provider with steely aplomb.

As I unlocked the door in the surprising cool of the

evening, the hall carpet was spotless and thick underfoot, the air smelt of a candle that had been made to smell of some kind of flower, and warm light bounced from every surface. From the kitchen there came the sound of the Ting Tings playing on the Bose speaker system hidden in the ceiling. Cee had an uncontrived passion for new music that allowed her to make small talk not only with her clients but also with their rebellious teenage sons.

'Darling?' a voice called out from the kitchen.

I was three things to my wife, Sweetheart, Darling and Matthew. I had not often been a sweetheart in the last few months, but when I was it was a sure precursor to the parting of the clouds of marriage, beneath which the great sun of my wife's soul waited to bestow the warmth of its love. As a darling I was on neutral ground. A Matthew knew to fear for his life.

'Hello, my love,' I said as I came in, and kissed the top of her head. She was sitting over a book of fabric swatches, wearing her glasses, with her hair marshalled into a pony-tail so tight at the back it amounted almost to a facelift.

'Where have you been?'

'First con with the Swansons.'

'How did it go?'

'They said twenty thousand pounds.'

'Well, that's more than they were planning on spending. You must have made a good impression.'

'As if I could ever make anything else.'

'So what did you think of her?' Cee asked, flicking through the samples.

'Who? The wife?'

'Yes, of course the wife. And Claudia, Claudia is her name, there's no need to pretend you've forgotten.'

'Claudia. Well, actually I had forgotten.'

'All right. Well, what did you think of her?'

'She was . . .' Cee left off the swatches and looked at me over her glasses. I retreated to the sink to fill the kettle, though it was already half full. 'Pretty, I thought, in a kind of conventional way.'

Cee did not look back down. 'So you didn't think she was beautiful?'

'No.'

'Just conventionally pretty?'

'Hey, what can I say? I'm an unconventional guy.'

'Any clues to the mysterious disappearing act?'

'What?'

'You know, the failed degree.'

'Ah yes, of course. Your endless thirst for gossip. Nope, couldn't see anything. No corpses in the garden or Nazi paraphernalia in the hall.'

'I think it might have been an affair with a fellow.'

'What? Why?'

'I don't know. Just a hunch. Something about her, something . . .' She looked up, her brow knitted in a familiar pattern that made me feel a surge of affection, and then gave up and returned to her fabrics. 'I don't know.'

'I know a way to find out.'

'How?'

'We invite Don Joan down for dinner.'

'Are you making fun?'

'No! A little. But I think it's lovely you're so interested in *people*.'

She looked at me, her head cocked. Don Joan was an academic friend of my parents, given a kind of surrogate godmother role by my father on my mother's death. She was ageing and a little deaf, but she kept her hearing aid affixed to the earth. Still, it was not entirely appropriate to drag her down to London purely to try to extract information.

'Well then, good thinking, batman. We can have her over with Magda and Hugo. She'll like them and we still owe them for that thing they did last month.'

'OK,' I said, 'that would be absolutely great. Absolutely.'

She made a face at me, mock anger as a foretaste of real anger if I didn't watch myself. Part of the reparations that had been exacted from me in exchange for the declaration of lasting peace after the election-night dinner party was the promise never to vocalize my feelings towards Hugo. It was a curious situation, for if I had met her alone as planned that evening to share with her a private moment of mockery at his expense, I had no doubt she would have come to despise him as I did. As it was, when the battle lines were drawn between the two of us he had happened to end up stranded on her side. In order to take maximum advantage from the rudeness which had embarrassed her, she had been forced to rootle around in Hugo's character for something that might make that rudeness seem less reasonable, as you cannot be too angry with someone once you've admitted they're telling the truth. She had searched and searched for his positive qualities, and had at length found some, and had ultimately taken the whole process to the extreme of declaring him a mutual friend of ours.

The kettle boiled, and I went over to make myself a cup of tea.

'Do you want one?'

'Yes please.'

'Builder's tea or lesbian?'

'Lesbian.'

There was a brief pause as I found the chamomile tea-bags at the back of the cupboard. Cee closed the book of samples, turning her attention to the open Mac with its spreadsheet of accounts, and it was the numbers on the screen that inspired her next comment.

'I'm trying to encourage them to pay up front for the rest of the works. And I wouldn't get too many books on credit for them either.'

'Why? I thought this guy was rich as Croesus?'

'He is, now. But they've got no money behind them, these bankers. Plenty of money beside them, and lots in front, but none behind.'

'But isn't Jimmy the Trader their star turn?'

'Oh, he's all right. But apparently his bank has got itself into a lot of trouble. Knee deep in credit default swaps.'

With her authoritative tones, her glasses, her beauty and her straight back, a stranger would have assumed that she knew what she was talking about.

'Credit default swaps, eh? Is it a nasty case?'

She smiled, pleased to be known well enough to be found out. She stood to receive her tea.

'Terrible. Possibly fatal.'

'Where do you pick this stuff up?'

She looked at the modernist painting above the fireplace and smiled as if distracted.

'You haven't been educating yourself again, have you?' I asked.

'Only a bit.'

'A bit?'

'All right, fine. Whilst you snore on Saturday mornings I sneak downstairs and roll around naked in the pages of the *Financial Times*.'

'Like an erotic tramp?'

'Exactly like that.'

'Well, all right. I won't so much as lend them a postage stamp without getting the money up front.'

She released the painting from the grip of her appraisal and snuggled into me, clasping her tea between her hands for warmth so that it formed a hot ceramic core to our embrace.

'Anyway, I hope for her sake there isn't a hiccup in the cashflow,' she said from the midst of my chest. 'I wouldn't want to see what would become of that woman without the hairdresser and the personal trainer. She has the most appalling taste in clothes.'

She sipped. I kissed her head and parted from her, and went back to my tea on the sideboard. It was at that moment, I think, that I resolved myself definitely to seduce Mrs Swanson. Cee was quite secure in her own attractiveness, and not given to casual criticism. I honour my wife's opinion in matters of aesthetics before all others, and if she felt the need to denigrate a client to this extent, it was a confirmation that she thought her genuinely and unnervingly beautiful.

# 4

IF THERE WAS AN OMEN ABOUT THAT SUMMER, A DARK patch in the sifted entrails that would have caused the soothsayer to start and stumble backwards from the carcass, it came the following weekend. On Friday evening, Cee and I prepared to answer the call of a stiffie stuck into the corner of the hall mirror, enjoining us to party like it was 1929 in celebration of our friend Marcus's thirty-eighth birthday. Dress – depression chic. The party was to be held at his apartment, which Cee had decorated, and the Facebook group attached maps and photographs of suggested outfits, ranging from men wearing pickle barrels to ravaged traders in stained shirtsleeves.

Cee looked lovely in a torn gown, and I caught the doorman looking at her bare back. He looked down in embarrassment, and I wanted to go over to him and tell him it was all right, but by then we were in the lift. We pushed and shoved each other in the elevator on the way up to the penthouse. In Marcus's hall, there was a piano with a fine coating of dust on the black lid. Above the piano hung a photograph of Marcus enveloped in spray on the deck of a sailing boat, and a black-and-white shot of his model girlfriend, clothed in nothing but the artistic aspirations of the photographer.

As soon as we came out on to the mezzanine level that

constituted the bulk of the apartment, Cee's hand left mine, as the bond between us dissolved in a lukewarm bath of acquaintance. There were thirty or forty guests already present, and I was gratified to see that the majority had observed the dress code and were clothed as the Wall Street barons and dispossessed farmers of a bygone age. The giant plasma screen that faced the view was playing a black-and-white movie, and the walls were decorated with poster-sized photographs taken under the auspices of the Works Project Administration, featuring abandoned Kansas towns and impoverished families. Indeed, those who had come in modern clothes stood out from the crowd, and it was in the guise of party-pooper that I registered Jim Swanson. He was wearing a dark modern suit. It was no great surprise to find him there, as Marcus worked at the same bank. My first thought on seeing him was to look for Claudia, but she was not in the room. I went out on the balcony in search of her. The balcony was deserted but for a tubby young man sitting in the jacuzzi, dressed in a broker's white-collared shirt and little else, drinking from a bottle of champagne. I remember thinking him indecently drunk, for such an early stage of the evening. He sat chin to chest, commiserating with the bubbles.

Back in the living room, the waitresses were moving about with platters of brightly coloured cocktails, and the volume of laughter and conversation was beginning the long ascent towards cacophony. Marcus was now standing with Jim Swanson. The latter in his work suit had the stern, slightly embarrassed look of teacher at the school disco, and Marcus was doing the talking. I had known Marcus at Cambridge – he had been a physicist, and thus an oddity at the wilder parties organized by the students of humanities who mostly ran the social scene. He was known for seducing women with drink–addled speculation about string theory and dark matter, his dreamy passion for these subjects being a rarefied aphrodisiac on fire escapes beneath summer stars. As a youth he had the wild bearing of a man destined to look into the face of god, but Hutchings Bank had snapped him up in the milk round to help develop investment algorithms, and he was now extremely rich. He still drank and took coke and had a prodigious beard, though his dreams of understanding the universe had rather taken a back seat.

'All right, bookworm?'

'Hello, Marcus. How's the soul doing?'

'Better for seeing old friends. Do you know Jim?'

'We do know each other actually. He has very kindly asked me and Cee to decorate his new house.'

Marcus drew in breath. 'Well, watch out for this one, Jim. Check your bills, that's all I'm going to say.'

'I always go over every invoice.'

'Yeah. Well, I'm only joking. I love what you guys did to this place, you know that. So you're not suffering too much, from people cutting back?'

'It seems a very shallow kind of depression. Nobody seems to be spending less. I mean, how much did this evening set you back?'

Marcus laughed.

'It's like . . . OK, did you ever see those Road Runner films when you were a kid?'

'You mean the cartoons?'

'Cartoons. And Road Runner's chasing the bird, that fucking bird.'

'Road Runner was the eponymous bird. I believe you're referring to his predatory nemesis, Wile E. Coyote.'

'Oh, yeah, yeah, that fucking wolf. So it's like the bit where the bird tricks the wolf into running out over the edge of a cliff, right, only he doesn't fall down. He only falls down when he realizes there's nothing under his feet. So long as he doesn't look down, he doesn't realize and he just keeps on going. Well, that's where we are now. We're running with our feet in the air, like the wolf, and nobody's looking down.'

Marcus lost the thread of the conversation, and his eyes went with a woman to the external balcony.

'So what happens next?' I said.

'What?'

'When people look down?'

'What? Oh, fuck knows. Maybe if you run in the air long enough, you actually hit solid ground on the other side. Maybe you can keep going for ever and just never look down. Fuck knows. I'll catch up with you in a sec.'

'Sure.'

Marcus broke away from us abruptly, and lavished an extravagant greeting on an older gentleman with a young black woman who had come up the stairs behind us. Left alone, Jim and I each took an involuntary mouthful of our drinks.

'I see you opted for modern dress,' I said at last.

'I came straight from work."

'Isn't it Saturday?'

'Yes.'

'Ah.'

'But if I'd gone home I would have come out in jeans anyway.'

'What, a hardy cowboy eking out a frontier pittance in the dustbowl?'

'No, just jeans.'

'Why?'

'I think it's not right.'

'What, tasteless? Yes, the thought had occurred to me

on the way over. Although I think the tastelessness is the point . . .'

'No, not tasteless, not right, as in wrong. I lost two guys from my team last month who've got kids in school.'

Jim glanced down at my stevedore's suspenders and the ripped white workman's shirt with the ornamental patches sewn on by Cee in the hour before our departure. I thought I saw a little sneer of superiority when his eyes bobbed back up.

'Why are you here then, if it offends your sensibilities?'

'Claudia wanted to get out,' he said, and took a quick mouthful of his beer. I felt as if he regretted this disclosure the moment it was made, and wanted to gulp it back down.

'And you're more a stay-at-home bod? Very sensible, once your beautiful new house is complete. Unfortunately Cee and I rarely manage a night in, socializing is pretty much part of the job.'

He looked over my shoulder, quite deliberately.

'Besides, you're probably too tired for any kind of fun when you get home. The hours you chaps work . . .'

'What do you mean?' he asked.

'Oh, I just know that City hours can be rather unsociable.'

A man walked past us, and Jim caught his arm. I was left alone with my drink, wondering why I had felt the urge to needle him. It was a stupid thing to have done, motivated by a wish to demonstrate that I found his insecurities transparent. It was the same effect I sometimes experienced when speaking French or Italian as a young man, driven to make foolish disclosures by nothing more than a desire to prove how well I spoke the language. It would make both the job and his wife more difficult to manage, and I clicked my fingers.

I went back out on to the balcony, which was now quite full. The jacuzzi was empty, the premature drunkard nowhere to be seen. Two men stood beside it, threatening to throw a girl in a flapper dress into the water. Her flirtatious shrieks of horror echoed from the surrounding buildings. London continued its distant and implacable life in the streets below, with cheers, football songs, car horns, screaming and the sounds of sirens. I caught the waft of cut grass coming up from the Bunhill Row graveyard, where the old gravestones lay in the shadows of the trees. The smell made me feel calm, just for a moment.

I first became aware of Claudia by the effect she had on the crowd. I did not see her coming, but heads twitched lightly at something moving through the bodies, like the tips of long grass betraying the movement of something powerful and silent underneath. Women moved imperceptibly closer to their men, a hand going around a waist. She appeared directly in front of me, and I was surprised to see that she had ignored the dress code, Jim's dour abstention, and indeed any sense of decorum. Most beautiful women past the age of twenty know enough to moderate their looks somewhat in the presence of those with whom they may be expected to make friends and generally 'get on', especially if the women are wives, especially if the wives are a touch older. There is a thin line between making the best of one's gifts, and making the less fortunate feel their deficiencies. Claudia either didn't know or didn't care, and she was wearing an indecently short print dress and high-rise heels. Through the fabric, her skin and the swell of her body were just discernible. It was less a fuck-me dress than a fuck-you dress, and I reflected that wise husbands (myself included) would join their partners in its disparagement. It delighted me, less by the sight of it than in its implicit disdain for the sorts of people with whom she socialized and, by extension, for myself.

When she saw me she smiled, and with a forward gesture of her wrists offered herself gratefully to my company. From her readiness to engage with me I inferred that she had spent most of the evening negotiating the arch company of new women and the over-eager company of new men, and that she regarded me, if not as a friend, then at least as a temporary safe harbour.

'Lovely to see you, Claudia.'

'Lovely to see you too. I like your braces.'

'Thank you. You look stunning.'

'I was so embarrassed when I came in. Jim completely neglected to tell me there was a dress code. That sort of thing doesn't even register with him.'

She took the lap of material below her midriff and gave it an ineffectual downward tug. I saw in an instant that she had simply misjudged the evening. Her embarrassment came across as hauteur. It occurred to me then that there was a part of her missing – there was no way that a girl with such a sardonic streak could possibly have run the gamut of her own beauty through her teens and early twenties without picking up a little more experience along the way. Had she been raised in a nunnery? It was a fascinating absence.

'It just doesn't register.'

'I suppose he has his mind on higher things,' I said, extending a feeler.

To my dismay, she nodded earnestly. 'Oh I know he does, I know, I shouldn't complain and I'm not really cross. I just wish I didn't feel like a prostitute on an oligarch's yacht.'

'But a very high-class prostitute. If it's any consolation, these braces are starting to chafe my nipples.'

She laughed and reached forward, and pinged one of the elasticated braces against my chest. Having done so she swallowed, and took a step back.

'I've just had the most lovely conversation with your wife.'

'Oh yes?'

'She's the only woman I've met so far who's been really nice to me. Except the lady collecting coats downstairs. She's from Košice . . . My mother taught me Slovak: she wanted me to have some connection to her family. I never expected it to be any use, and now I know the dry-cleaner and the plumber and all the waiters at the delicatessen . . . Anyway, sorry, I'm monopolizing you, I should find Jim.'

And with that she moved off to resume her awkward prowl, gone from me but not forgotten.

It was late in the evening, after the sun had passed below the jagged crenellations of the London horizon, when the front-door bell announced more guests. The party had been billed on Facebook as an all-night event, starting at 7 p.m. and ending at 4 a.m. the next morning, and revellers had been leaving and arriving all evening. I was waiting for the downstairs loo to be vacated by a couple, listening to the tell-tale tap of a credit card on the toilet top.

It was not Marcus who opened the front door but one of his friends from the bank, a man sufficiently familiar with him and with the majority of the other invitees to provide an official welcome to whoever might have arrived. He cheered as he swung open the door, and the bravado froze in the headlights of the scene that greeted him. Two large policemen, each in their summer uniform of short-sleeve white shirt and black stab-proof vest, stood on the other side with grim faces. I was amused to see the young banker turn back to look at the closed loo door with its intimate symphony of snorts, and was myself grateful that the evening had not yet reached that stage of intoxication at which drugs would be laid out in plain sight on the black ceramic dinner plates on the kitchen table.

'What can I do for you, officers?'

The two policemen exchanged uneasy glances. Their silence amplified the man's discomfort.

'Is it a noise thing? It's a noise thing, isn't it, I bet it's a noise thing.'

'The noise is fine, sir.'

'No, no, you're far too sweet, it's very loud.'

'Did you not call us?'

'Well, no, I didn't. I don't know if anyone else here did.' Unconsciously he looked back into the empty hall to see if anyone's attitude betrayed a recent call to the police, but he could see no one and hear only the party, rolling its merry way towards riot as the music played and peals of laughter mingled with cigarette smoke in the dregs of daylight. The police peered past him at the closed doors, and exchanged meaningful glances.

'May we come in, sir?'

'Well, I don't want to – I mean, look, it's not my place, I'm just a guest. Is there some kind of problem?'

The two policemen stared at him, completely non-plussed by the question. Seeing it was their turn to be shocked, the man regained some of the authority of which their appearance had relieved him.

'Look, I don't know what you want, officer, and I don't want to be rude, but this is a private party and I think this might be some kind of mistake. Now, if we promise to turn the music down . . .'

'Sir, I really think it's best if we come in. I'm afraid there's been an accident.'

'What?' He looked up the stairs again, towards the laughter and the music. 'No there hasn't. As I say, I think there's been some mistake . . .'

'Sir, I really think we should come in. I'm sorry to have to tell you that someone has fallen off the balcony.'

'Oh my God . . . what? No, no they haven't.'

'I'm afraid they have, sir. Now, I think we really should come inside.'

Firmly but resolutely, the first policeman pushed past him into the interior of the flat. A girl had skipped down the stairs on her way to one of the ground-floor bedrooms, and she screamed in amusement and tried to take the hat from his head. He grabbed at it in alarm. She looked sufficiently attractive to be unused to such defiance, and it made her frown and put her tongue out at him. Abandoning my post by the loo, I followed the three of them up the stairs into the party proper. As one of the men stood at the top of the staircase readjusting his hat, his colleague walked over to the stereo and turned it off. The instant the air was stripped of music, everybody turned to the machine, a general cry of disapprobation taking up where the house beat had left off. When the assembled revellers saw the policeman standing there, the voices frayed variously into shrieks of amusement and alarm, cries of abuse, protestations of innocence and one loud shout from some wag that the strippers had arrived at last. The policeman put out his hands for silence, but the noise showed no signs of abatement. Eventually the first officer who had entered put his fingers in his mouth and unleashed a whistle of such devastating volume that the whole rabble were stunned into silence.

'I'm sorry to have to inform you there's been an accident,' he began.

'What accident?' Marcus said, pushing his way to the centre of his living room.

'Is this your property, sir?'

'It's my flat.'

'I'll tell you everything in due course if we could just begin by—'

The young man who had first let them in, and who whilst the music was being dealt with had gone over to the railings of the roof terrace to check the policeman's hypothesis, at this point, white-faced, stepped back across the threshold of the sliding doors. 'Chirag! Chirag's jumped off the balcony! His guts are all over the fucking pavement,' and having delivered this, he proceeded to vomit into the plastic sculpture nearest the door.

I ran to the balcony along with several other guests. I looked over, and saw below in the street the body. It was the man who had been sitting in the jacuzzi at the start of the evening, I recognized him by his pink shirt and by the fact he was wearing no trousers. He had fallen down from the penthouse into the poverty below, and broken himself on the surface of the street. His head was cradled in the gutter, his legs splayed under him in a confusion of his anatomy, as if a child drawing him had got him completely wrong. His fixed eyes looked accusingly up at his colleagues looking down on him from the balcony, and around his soaked pink shirt and his pale legs his lifeblood slowly spread its silent wings. The ambulance had already arrived – it was slewed across the street – and the men in fluorescent jackets ran around him. They had affixed a respirator to his face, and they trod his blood back and forth between the body and the open doors of the ambulance. A stretcher lay empty on the ground beside him. The blue lights on the ambulance turned with mute urgency. Police at either end of the alley were holding back growing numbers of onlookers. In a trick of physics that seemed to me vaguely obscene, the champagne bottle from which he had swigged in the rooftop jacuzzi (or its distant successor) had made the journey with him over the railings and into the air, clasped in his hand, and his body had cushioned its fall. It had rolled into the gutter, released from twitching fingers, and was perfectly intact. Around this scene, the street made no concessions. There was the bus stop, the parked cars, two lovers sitting on a bench in the Bunhill graveyard quite unaware of what was unfolding in the street only thirty metres away, and overhead a blimp made its stately progress through the purple sky advertising Sky Sports. The birds sang. The men and women in their costumes stared down with their hands on the railings. They were quiet, their expressions reminiscent of an audience watching a comedian die on stage; part embarrassment, part pity, part resentfulness at the price of their tickets.

After a few moments one of the girls began to moan, and the police intervened to guide people away from the railing and into the body of the apartment. I turned back, looking for Cee, and saw instead Claudia and Jim Swanson standing in the empty interior. They alone of all the guests had not come out to see the accident. Claudia had her arms around her husband and clung to him in a way that their difference in height would have rendered comic, but for the expression visible over Jim's shoulder. She looked crazed with fear, the way a wild animal looks when you hold it in your hands and it waits to see whether it will be murdered or released. I found Cee, and together we went inside where notebooks emerged from pockets and names and numbers were taken. All through this process, the bell sounded to announce the arrival of new partygoers who were full of excited gossip about what they took to be a traffic accident in the street below, and it was some time before someone thought to tell the doorman to deny fresh admissions.

An hour later, Jim invited me and Cee to share a cab with him and his wife. None of us knew the dead man or had seen anything that would be of use, and the police were content to let us go. Jim had to return to the office to deal with the kind of weekend crisis that makes City workers feel that what they do is important, and the bank had sent a car. He intended to go home, take a shower and change his clothes, and he had generously proposed to Cee and me that we should take the cab on from Vincent Square back to Chelsea. I felt some misgivings at the idea of touching knees (or worse, hips) with Jim Swanson on a hot summer's evening. I also sensed the self-assertion in this act of largesse. I knew, however, the net of shocked revellers cast out from Marcus's apartment would snag all the free cabs coming from every direction, and I felt desperately tired.

In the back of the taxi, Claudia seemed calmer. Whatever crisis it was had passed. She held her husband's hand in the reel of streetlight that passed frame by frame across the back seat. I held Cee's hand too.

When we reached Vincent Square they disembarked, and Jim requested his receipt. The driver handed him a piece of paper from the dashboard.

'What's this?'

'It's your expenses form, sir.'

'It's blank.'

'Yeah,' said the driver, misinterpreting this statement, 'so you can put whatever you like in there. Better than a receipt.'

'Fill it out,' Jim said. He squared his feet to the window.

His wife stood behind him on the pavement, and as the driver scrabbled about on the dash for a pen, she folded her arms and glanced quickly back to the main road. In the orange cone of the streetlamp I saw a look of resignation pass swiftly across her features. It had for me a hint of intrigue, like the sweep of headlights across a bedroom ceiling. We waited with the idling motor as the driver completed the receipt, and when we finally pulled away from the kerb Jim slapped the roof of the car with an ill-judged farewell that made Cee grimace. As we pulled out on to the Vauxhall Bridge Road, she began to cry. I suffered the guilty realization that I had been thinking more about Claudia's reaction than her own.

'Shh, shh, it's OK, it's all right, my love.'

'I'm sorry, I'm being silly, I didn't even know him.'

'You're not being silly. It was completely shocking.'

'I just can't bear the thought that we were all dancing, all still drinking and laughing and he was already lying dead in the street.'

'He couldn't have been down there for more than fifteen minutes, my love. The paramedics had only just got to him.'

'It's just tragic. I hope they find out whether or not he meant to do it. I mean, I don't know if it's worse to slip by accident or to mean to do it, but I think the worst thing of all would be if nobody ever knew for certain one way or the other.'

I kissed the top of her head. When we reached Old Church Street I walked her to the door and let her in, before going back to pay the cabbie for our half of the trip.

'What was all that business with the receipt?' I asked.

'Oh, that was nothing, nothing to worry about.'

'The guy looked pretty annoyed.'

Reassured by my reference to Jim as 'the guy', the driver leaned back in his seat and held out both hands.

'Well, I only offered him a blank one, only so's I could get the two of you home quicker with less on the meter. I mean, I can see the lady's upset, he can fill the bloody thing out himself. He knows how much he's paid, and he acts like I'm offering him a stolen telly!'

I laughed, and shook my head. The driver laughed too. I gave him a three-pound tip, and he said, 'Oh, thanks very much, sir, that's very kind of you.'

'I don't need a receipt, thanks. Have a good evening,' I said, and he laughed and replied with something friendly and inaudible as he drove away.

That night, I dreamed of men falling from tall buildings.

# 5

TWO AND A HALF WEEKS LATER, THE MORNING OF THE Wednesday that was fixed for my second official meeting with Mrs Swanson, Cee rose early as was her wont to attend to the paperwork, and left me in bed to think. We had had a small fight the night before, and though my status had not dropped quite to the level of a Matthew there was definitely still frost on the ground at dawn. It occurred to me that, knowing my own amorous intentions, I might have engineered the fight in preparation. One cannot go out a-seducing on a breakfast of marital bliss.

I used to sequester myself in my study in the mornings and write, and though the purpose had dried up, if for any reason there was discord between us it had left behind a useful little ritual of separation in which we could both pretend to believe. So I lay in bed masturbating and thinking about Mrs Swanson. I have often found that, when I am afflicted with a touch of excessive attraction, masturbation with the object in mind is an effective emetic. So first Mrs Swanson joined me in a hotel room, then my attention turned to two Mrs Swansons, then Mrs Swanson with Cee, and then briefly and incongruously to a production of Dvořák's *Rusalka* which I had recently seen at Glyndebourne, then back to Mrs Swanson and Cee, then as my climax announced its imminence with the silent fanfare of my curling toes, to teach Cee a lesson I kicked her out of my fantasy and turned all my attentions to Claudia. Just as I had ushered my wife's rosy buttocks from the doors of my imagination, I turned back and found that far from being grateful for this display of preference, Mrs Swanson had betrayed me and turned into the tenor who played the Prince, a portly man I had thought at the time ill-suited to the role of Dvořák's romantic hero. I orgasmed rather despairingly, conscious in the convulsive moment of the absence of any tissues from the bedside table. My failure to persuade even the Mrs Swanson I had conjured from memory to participate fully in sexual activity did not bode well for my real-world attempts, and I was struck down by post-masturbatory regret of the type I usually associate with particularly outré pornography as I limboed my way to the toilet.

Brisk ablutions imparted some of their briskness, and I took comfort from the enthusiasm that the imaginary Mrs Swanson had shown in the early stages of the enterprise. Showered, shaved and dressed in new clothes early on a summer's day, I took the steps down to the hall three at a time.

Cee was in the kitchen. She had a study on the first-floor landing, and in the months immediately after we moved into the house she made extensive use of it. Her decamping to the kitchen table was explained to me at the time as an effort to get closer to the kettle and tea-making facilities, though I had always harboured the suspicion that she wished to make herself more prominent in order to reproach me with her labour.

'Who are you going to see today?' she asked, cocking her head in amusement and observing me above the tortoiseshell rim of her reading glasses as I sprang through the door. In one hand she held an unpaid invoice tremulous with fear in the air before her. On the table the Mac purred smugly.

'I thought I'd go to Pordes first and see if my Hamilton had come in.'

'They always call you when your books come in.'

'Yes, but I thought I'd see anyway. Then I have a meeting with the Al Badrs at eleven o'clock to discuss the price of that Sufi text I told you about. I think they're very close to buying, you know, they just keep wavering on the price. Then Claudia Swanson at twelve thirty, then lunch with Peter and Mr and Mrs McAdam in the afternoon. They want the whole room done, by the way, floor-to-ceiling shelves, so it should be another good commission.'

'I see,' she said, the same amused smile playing on her lips. Only there was something a little querulous in it now, and she paused long enough to constitute a demand that I continue the conversation.

'What do you see, darling? Pop me on your shoulders so I can see what you see.'

'You're going to see Claudia?'

'Mrs Swanson? Yes, at eleven thirty.'

'Twelve thirty.'

'Yes, twelve thirty.'

'So you do think she's beautiful,' she said, and only then did she return her attention to the invoice.

'I told you, I thought she was perfectly pleasant to look at. Not a patch on the perfect peachy denim-clad buttocks of my beautiful wife. Why do you say that?'

'Because you're wearing that blue shirt.'

'This? It's just my shirt.'

'It's not just your shirt. You think you look sexy in it.'

'I do not. Anyway, I look sexy in everything.'

'You think it brings out your eyes.'

She stapled the invoice to a receipt, and set the two

of them down in the 'done' pile at the edge of the table. She looked triumphant at being right, although she would have preferred to be wrong. And she was right, of course, and so was I: the shirt did bring out my eyes. Had this been my conscious intention I would have enjoyed sparring with her, and would not have let her carry the victory, but as it was my choice of garment had taken me by surprise. My train of thought that morning had been running smoothly through the lush countryside of erotic daydreams, and I had simply picked up the clothes that came to hand as I stared out the window. The mind can be an over-helpful servant, throwing out priceless artefacts as junk and posting letters that were never meant for sending. Cee was now focused very deliberately on the remaining pile of paperwork, engrossed in the stack of bills with a scholarly disdain for distraction. I made myself a loud cup of coffee, banging the 'World's Best Husband' mug down on the countertop and ringing the stirring spoon from side to side like a tiny bell clapper.

'Do you have to make such a racket, darling?'

'Well, my love, you could always retire to your study. We have so many beautifully decorated rooms in this house, it seems such a shame to use so few.'

I smiled at her innocently over the rim of my cup.

The day outside did not promise to be generous to a man bent on an errand of love; even at nine in the morning the air was humid, the exhaust from the buses on the King's Road did not disperse but rather clung to the ground and insinuated itself into the fabric of trousers, and I had no doubt that the evening's freesheets would bear pictures of London taken from Primrose Hill, showing the whole city labouring to breathe under a glowing pall of smog. The Al Badrs, who lived in Mayfair, had an apartment clad in a rather oppressive Arabic style which accentuated the heat of the day. Their drawing room was awash with golden ornaments and heavy swathes of fabric, thick Persian rugs and a beaten-bronze coffee table surrounded by pouffes, so that the whole effect reminded one of a Bedouin tent, with an internal temperature appropriate to the desert. My desire to escape this atmosphere before the enchanting effects of my blue shirt were spoiled by excessive sweating was such that Mr Al Badr negotiated several thousand pounds off the price of his manuscript as his beautiful wife looked on, smiling.

After we had shaken hands I emerged, flapping and gasping for air, on to the pavement. It occurred to me suddenly that so far that morning Mrs Swanson had already cost me one lost battle with Cee (the price of which would doubtless be exacted in the fullness of time) and five grand at the hands of a man who kept horses and a private aeroplane. This, I thought, was the sort of misfortune likely to befall one who covets, and I was almost ready to write off the whole enterprise. I stumbled off past the gleaming hulks of the luxury cars sitting in their showrooms, and the multiple lanes of traffic honking between Hyde Park Corner and Marble Arch. After ten minutes walking in the cloying but mercifully open air, and a bottle of water purchased at great expense from the lobby of the Grosvenor Hotel, I regained my composure and reassured myself that I was not coveting, but seducing; that the exercise of a little effort in attainment would sweeten the achievement of pleasure; and that my vague desire for vengeance on the Swansons could only benefit from their further interference with the smooth countenance of my existence. I rejoined Piccadilly and took a bus to the Hatchards bookshop past the gaudy colonnade of the Ritz. I knew what my first gambit would be. I intended to purchase Mrs Swanson an erotic book.

The role of erotic fiction in a clandestine love affair is far more subtle than most people would credit. The purpose is not bluntly to announce one's intentions, nor is it to stimulate the desire of the other party with wordy fantasies. The function of an erotic novel in these circumstances is rather to begin the subtle process of driving a wedge between husband and wife.

To seduce someone, you must form a conspiracy of two against their partner. The giving of a gift which teeters on the edge of propriety, if combined with its proper receipt, is the first step, the innocent first footfall on the path to hell. I, a library consultant, give to a client a novel filled to the brim with explicit sex, but sheathed within the covers of a Penguin Classic. The unsuspecting wife begins to read the novel, and it is not until she is some way in that it dawns on her that the subject matter is racier than that which she is accustomed to discussing in her bi-monthly book club. Now, there is always the chance, the small chance, that she will be the righteous woman who throws the book down in disgust and calls you up to complain, or the happy and uninhibited woman who mentions it to her husband, so that the two of them can have a laugh at your expense. But the vast majority of women are simply a little embarrassed. They do not want to tell their husbands, or indeed anybody else, because they are halfway into a dirty book. More than that, they dare not risk looking prudish and uncultured by being shocked. What do we think now of the judges who presumed to bring the work of Lawrence within the sphere of their authority? And anyway, it cannot possibly have been the intention of the gift-giver to ensnare them: people are not so calculating! So they read on, congratulating themselves for having broadened their horizons, and they do not tell their husbands about the book.

On a subsequent meeting, scheduled in the perfect innocence of professional relations, you may casually ask
them what they thought. You may casually ask them what
their husband thought, and of course, 'Harry? Oh, I don't
think he'd go in for that sort of thing, not at all . . .' and
then you have a laugh together at how unsophisticated is
Harry's taste in literature, and how he would never be able
to talk about . . . 'well, about sex like that, like a grown-
up', and before you know it you can see for yourself what
kind of books Harry keeps on the table on his side of the
bed. It's usually Dick Francis.

I pushed into Hatchards and performed a kind of
double inventory, once over the orderly shelves in front of
me and once through the capacious but somewhat chaotic
library of my own recall. I considered the *Story of O*, but
rejected it for fear that it might not so much telegraph an
intended seduction as a desire to subject her to forcible
buggery. *Venus in Furs* stood out from my thoughts, but
I replaced it on the mental shelf for fear it might suggest
a desire on my part to be forcibly buggered. *The Sexual
Life of Catherine M* was on display in Hatchards' biography
section, but the cover featured a photograph that looked
like a still from a seventies porn film, which completely
undermined the subtlety of intent. I was about to despair,
both of my own reading and of the selection on offer,
when I saw Anaïs Nin winking from the bookshelf.

Anaïs Nin wrote pornography for a dollar a page when
she lived in Paris with Henry Miller. She published all the
stories together in a collection called the *Delta of Venus*.
I first read the book when I was sixteen, desperate to
find some girl upon whom I could palm off my virginity.
In that cruel burst of acceleration that nature affords to
teenage girls emerging from childhood, all my female
classmates had suddenly evolved into long-limbed aliens,

denizens of the world of adult sexuality to which I could not find the door. When I read Anaïs Nin, I was so grateful to discover that women were capable of writing about sex in a way that betrayed an erotic imagination outstripping even my own obscene cravings. Admittedly it was an imagination directed primarily towards handsome Hungarian barons rather than pimply schoolboys, but both the baron and I were men, and perhaps I could make myself more like him. So I did press-ups and learned French and washed my face daily, and slowly I emerged from my unwanted purity to the glorious embrace on the floor of the Berwick Street bookshop. I had not thought about the book in years, but rather than simply purchasing it and heading on my way as I would normally have done, I found myself leafing through the first few pages.

Anaïs Nin did more for me than merely reassuring me that at some point a woman might deign to sleep with me. She told me something of the difficulties the English language has in encountering the sexual act. In her diaries she described sex as an act for which 'man's language was inadequate. The language of sex has yet to be invented.' Though she framed the problem as one of gender, I thought it more of a flaw with the English language itself. It is not the writers' fault; the words simply are not there. English, a language with such a superabundance of vocabulary that one can talk all day and never say the same word twice, is sadly under-endowed in the bedroom department. On the most basic level, what can you call it? Cock? Obscene, the word is scratched on the bathroom wall, shouted by builders! Penis? Clinical, my po-faced biology teacher brandishing a banana wrapped in a condom. Member? Comic, would the honourable member please be upstanding. Strong sword of love? Absurd, poetry a teenager would burn. Purple-headed womb ferret? I like that one best, but my few attempts to bring it into common parlance have met with hostility.

I read the first story, which had become for me an erotic palimpsest, the impressions gleaned by the horny teen of yore still visible beneath the bright ink of present desire. I found myself becoming slightly aroused. Flushed with this organic testament to my virility I slapped the book shut, and went decisively over to the counter. This was the book for Mrs Swanson.

Vincent Square was cooking in the same humid pot as the rest of the city, though the openness of the grass made it rather more tolerable. The canary-yellow tank that had looked such an affront to the local gentility was absent, marking Jim Swanson as one of the few men in London who still drove to work. As I approached the Swansons' front door, I found myself experiencing a familiar excitement. It is an important sign, the second appointment, as the woman will have been expecting you and will have dressed accordingly. The moment my client opens the door, I get a peek over her shoulder at her cards. From the first glance at what she has chosen to wear, and how she presents herself, I can make a good guess at the likely pace of the affair. If I don't get some kind of favourable indication, it can be fatal; there are only so many times a library consultant can believably drop in on a client on official business.

I think of it as one of those hunter's techniques that comes with experience, like the ability to gauge the proximity of a quarry by assessing the heat of its droppings with a judicious finger. I once had a second consultation with a slightly older lady so heavily adorned that I made the mistake of asking her where she was going after our meeting, a question occasioning such confusion on her part that we were on the sofa together almost before I had removed my coat. As I heard footsteps in the hall, I was perhaps aware of a slightly heightened sense of tension. Mrs Swanson's choice of clothes seemed ever-so-slightly more significant than that of the average client. She opened the door in a tracksuit.

'Oh, hello, Mr Manches. Mr de Voy!' she corrected herself indistinctly. Not only was she wearing a tracksuit but her mouth appeared to be full.

'Matt. Good morning, Claudia.' I leaned in to kiss her on her smooth and food-filled cheek, and at the same time she put out her hand for mine, forcing me to abort my kiss in mid-incline and convert it into an odd sort of peer into her hallway.

'Oh, they haven't started on the downstairs rooms yet,' she said in response to this manoeuvre. 'Actually there's no one in the house today but me. I was taking the opportunity to practise some wife stuff. Do you want to try one of my croissants?'

'Uh, that would be . . . I've already had breakfast, actually, but I'm sure that anything prepared by yourself will be so delicious as to—'

'They're a bit burned,' she said over her shoulder, turning round to reveal that she had sat on something covered in flour.

The kitchen, that sterile and faultlessly elegant space born of my wife's sense of style and witnessed by me on our first interview, was a terrible mess. There was a massacre of eggs on the sideboard, their discarded shells, part in and part out of the clear mixing bowl beside them, telling a tale of a doomed attempt to separate out the yolks. I could discern at least three cookbooks lingering among the debris, with three different celebrity chefs mugging on their glossy pages. Smoke and an infernal heat emanated from the open oven, from which the cremated remains of a selection of breakfast pastries had been but recently disinterred, and the heat had burnished Claudia's cheeks to a happy glow. As the wafts dissipated from its open maw, I was able to distinguish a meat pie still lying inside, indicating that she had cooked both this and the pastries at the same temperature, and that the pains au chocolat were likely to be impregnated with meat juice. There was flour in abundance, on Claudia's tracksuit as well as on every conceivable surface. Her buttock prints were visible on one of the high stools by the breakfast bar. The whole scene of devastation had Tina Turner for a soundtrack, playing not on the integrated speaker system installed at great expense by our engineers, but rather on a small CD deck jostling for space on the countertop with the myriad other appliances that had contributed to the mess. Mrs Swanson was clearly the last woman in the United Kingdom not to have been issued an iPod. Somehow all her efforts had succeeded in dispelling that disorientating smell of newness I had experienced on my first visit, as if the chemical tang had been coaxed from the air by her enthusiasm.

The thing that made the greatest impression, however, was Mrs Swanson herself. There was not a trace of the fragility she had displayed at the end of Marcus's party, and looking at her contented face it was impossible to imagine her features accommodating the look of horror I had seen when she clung to her husband. So powerful was this feeling, I found myself doubting my own recall.

'Oh God, sorry, how embarrassing.' She smiled as she turned the stereo system so far down that it was inaudible, and then unplugged it from the wall. 'I love Tina Turner. I know I'm not supposed to . . .'

'I think she's making a comeback, actually. She's becoming quite stylish again.'

'Really?' she said, brightening at the news. 'That's great. It seems like if you keep liking anything for long enough it eventually comes back into fashion.'

'It would sound even better, you know, on the Bose speakers.'

She blushed. 'Oh, yeah, sorry. I can't figure out the blipper. Jim tried to show me three times but every time I think I've got it I push some button and the drawbridge retracts or we cancel our milk order or something.'

'It's considered poor form to have your drawbridge up after ten anyway.'

She smiled, more in gratitude for having her joke picked up than as a result of my own wit.

'I'm sorry for all the mess. I've been trying to teach myself to cook. I want to be like this giant cow when I get really pregnant, just waddling backwards and forwards and producing stuff to eat and drink.'

I nodded, unable to think of a charming response to this statement.

'And this way he'll love Tina Turner from the womb.'

She patted her belly mound reflexively and smiled.

'It's a boy then?'

'What? Oh! No, actually I don't know. It's just I hate saying "he or she". It makes me think of people who say "chairperson", like they're being brave.'

She laughed. It came with an ease that was itself pleasing, like something given by nature – like ripe blackberries on a bush by the road. It was an influx of happiness from somewhere else, maybe from the thought of the baby. Not hopeful from a seducer's perspective.

'Anyway, I think if I really practise the whole dutiful wife thing I'll have it down pat before I have to upgrade to ambitious mother. Only I don't think I'm any good in the kitchen. I never ever cooked when we lived in Hoxton.'

'Too busy clubbing every night?' I said, keen to steer the conversation back from the domestic towards something less salubrious.

She smiled, a private smile at some experience hidden from my view. 'Something like that. A regular raver, me. But look, I'm being incredibly rude, do you want a tea or something? I reckon I can manage that. You can have it with a croissant.'

'Aren't you supposed to have coffee with croissants?'

'I don't drink coffee,' she said, smiling brightly. 'We don't have it in the house.'

'Well, I'd love a cup of tea.'

She made tea and together we agreed to try one of the croissants. It became apparent when we attempted to break it in half that the thing was hopelessly dry. It put up a starchy resistance to fingers and then exploded in a shower of umber flakes. We were both laughing with anticipation by the time we got it up to our lips, and when I took a bite the overwhelming taste of meat from the oven made me inhale in shock, sending a flurry of burnt flakes into my windpipe. I bent over in a coughing fit whilst she administered apologies and flat-palm percussion to the area between my shoulder blades.

When I had eventually regained my breath sufficiently to speak, I looked up at her with watering eyes, and she said to me with a look of absolute sincerity, 'So, what do you think?'

'I . . . ah . . .' Again there was that tiny time lag, closing now but still there, between her speaking in her ingenuous voice and my detecting the twinkle in her eye. This time it made me burst out laughing, and she smiled, pleased at having made me laugh.

'OK, it was absolutely horrible. What possessed you to put them in with steak and kidney pie?'

'Well, I thought, you know, they both needed the same temperature, only for different times, and I wanted to get everything right at once, or at least to try it all at once. And it's not like I put the pie above the pastries. I put them underneath with a solid tray in between.'

'You have egg yolk in your hair.'

'Uh-huh. It's coming back in.' By that comment, and the fact that she looked me in the eye when she said it, she let me know she thought I was pretentious for my earlier comment on the fashionable status of Tina Turner. It was a pledge of growing intimacy, to bring me in with her on a joke at the expense of my earlier self. I had a sudden urge to grab her and tickle her, so strong and instant that I actually put my hands flat on the surface of the counter.

'Look, we have a wonderful cook, Marcel, who does dinner parties and things for clients. If you want to know how to cook a croissant without necessitating a weekly refurbishment of your kitchen, I know that Cee would be only too happy to put you in touch with him. But I thought we could discuss what books you might like for the library. I've drawn up a shortlist myself, and some provisional prices.'

'Oh, that's wonderful,' she said, and ran her hands under the tap, 'only I made a list for you too.'

'Did you think of some things you might like to have?'

'I did. There are a few names at the bottom I've read about or heard about, you know. But mostly they're books and authors I don't want.'

'Books you *don't* want?'

'Yes. I mean, no. I've read them. I didn't like them. I don't want them in the house.'

She said this in such a matter-of-fact way, and so simply, that for a moment I thought I had again missed that hint of irony that indicated a joke was on the loose. But there was nothing, no twinkle. She removed the list from her trouser pocket with her freshly cleaned hand. Well, at least she had not forgotten our appointment, I thought, even if she had not dressed up for it – why else have the list on her person?

'Why don't we go through your choices and I can tell you if I especially like the look of anything. And we can cross off anyone who appears on the banned list,' she said.

As we went through my list of suggested titles, and the visual and thematic schemes I had mapped out for the new library, part of my mind turned the banned list over in fascination. What was this, her anti-library? Was there some kind of fanatic lurking beneath the easygoing surface? I tried to use the banned books as reference points for the triangulation of some identifiable prejudice, but there was none that I could find. They were not, for example, anti-Christian or anti-gay, there was nothing in them that would have specifically offended a committed communist or a vegan. Mindful of my little gift I wondered if they might have fallen foul of some censorious spinster lurking in the attic of her taste, but there was nothing in there that seemed especially graphic. I remembered a sex scene in *Nineteen Eighty-Four*, and *Last Exit to Brooklyn* appeared on the list as well, so just to be certain I suggested to her some D. H. Lawrence. She said she had never read him but she knew there was sex in an outhouse, which had to be a good thing. This scuppered any notions about her moral delicacy having shaped the list.

As we spoke, I became aware of something else unusual in Mrs Swanson. She actually listened to what was being said to her. Conversation with her was a slightly unnerving experience, as you got the impression that the next thought to come out of her mouth was not a fixed and unalterable quantity, but rather some living and breathing thing whose life would be influenced by your own views. Generally I find conversation with strangers an untroubling affair, since it consists of no more than unpacking for one another a lifetime of pre-existing prejudice and then having a look at each other's goods, like two vendors setting up shop next door to one another at a car boot sale. Claudia Swanson appeared to be just browsing. She had nothing of her own to push, just that warm, disinterested, acutely perceptive humour with which to inspect the goods already on offer. It was a kind of flattery to the speaker, to have such a beautiful woman listen so closely. It made me forget the time, and speak for longer than I should have done, and I found myself on one or two occasions going dangerously off-message. Nodding at the wheel of my conversation, veering away from the smooth surface of my professional patter towards the steep embankment of honesty.

Towards the end of our conversation, we discussed what she had read as a child, and what books she would read to the baby in her belly. A particular feature of having been deprived of a parent at an early age is that it risks making any discussion of one's childhood a kind of confession, a highly personal statement of loss occasioning apologies from one's interlocutor. For this reason I avoid any mention of pre-pubescence like the plague, but still I found myself describing a maternal reading of the *Songs of Innocence*.

'My mum used to read to me when I was little. Only she was from Barnsley, and she had this really thick northern accent. It was a good deal thicker than it would have been if she'd actually stayed in Barnsley.'

'Where did she meet your dad?'

'At Cambridge. This was in the days when someone still paid for you to go if you were smart enough. Anyway, she used to read to me, and I don't remember a lot of what she read, only I do remember *Songs of Innocence and Experience*. When I was at prep school I had to read "The Tyger" out in class, and I pronounced it just like she did:

'What the hammer? what the chain?
In what furnace was thy brain?
What the anvil? what dread grasp
Dare its deadly terrors clasp?

'And all the kids in the class started laughing, and the teacher, who was this large gentleman who liked the popular kids to think he was cool, said, "In civilized society, we pronounce 'grasp' to rhyme with 'arse', young man."'

'What did you say?'

'I told him that wasn't a rhyme, that was assonance.'

She smiled.

'He was so cross he made me stand in front of the class every day for the rest of term at the beginning of each lesson, and repeat, "I will not grasp my arse in class."'

The image made her giggle, and I had presented it as an anecdote, but the actual memory was rather painful. Every time I had pronounced the sentence 'correctly' at the teacher's insistence I had felt as if I was betraying my common mum, with her short flat a's. I was annoyed at myself for offering up this private humiliation for Claudia's amusement. It was this realization which pulled me up short, and made me clap my knees and stand up from my chair.

'I've taken up far too much of your time.'

'Yes, I've got the whole of world cuisine to brutalize before this evening and so far I've barely crossed the Channel.'

There was a sense of very mild offence in the air. The conversation had taken quite an intimate turn, and my breaking out had been perhaps too abrupt.

She showed me through to the hallway, and any tension dissipated. I took my man-bag from its place beside the radiator, and was confronted with the sight of the Hatchards plastic bag poking from under the Italian leather flap. The *Delta of Venus* was still sealed in my satchel. I had almost omitted the purpose of my mission. It crossed my mind not to mention it to her, a strange urge given the care that had gone into its selection. It was the impulse to leave it in there without giving it to her which decided me to do the opposite, and I plunged my hand into the bag.

'I got you something, by the way. A start to your collection, if you like. It's one of my favourite books and I saw it when I was browsing this morning and I just thought . . .'

'Oh! Oh, that's so good of you,' she said, her face lighting with pleasure. She made to unfurl the plastic bag, and to forestall the moment when she saw the title I stuck out my hand to say goodbye. She laughed, but left off opening the bag to receive it. She moved it slowly up and down, looking at me with grave eyes and her head on one side. Then she leaned in lightly and kissed me on the cheek. Just for a moment, the proximity of her flesh and mine allowed my senses to penetrate beyond the miasma of burning and egg yolk and flour and floral shampoo, and to smell the scent of her skin. It smelt natural.

'Well, goodbye then. We can discuss it next time I see you, I hope, and maybe we can talk about some of the other books too. If you come back after tasting my croissants, you'll never have to prove your bravery to me in any other way.'

'Oh, no, they were good, really . . .'

She waved happily and closed the door.

I went on to my lunch appointment and to various other meetings and stopped off at Peter Harrington to pick up their new catalogue. I felt oddly elated despite the sticky heat. All through the afternoon, she played on my thoughts like a catchy song. The only thing about the meeting which troubled me was the fact that neither of us had mentioned the events of Marcus's party. The omission did not even occur to me until after I had left, and when it did, I knew instinctively that the reason for avoiding the evening was that themes of death and dissatisfaction were inappropriate for superficial discourse. In an ideal world, Mrs Swanson and I would have been comfortable discussing such transgressive subjects right from the off. I found the heat bothered me even more than it had that morning. The space between my skin and the fabric of my clothes appeared to have been lined with damp prickles.

Looking back, I suppose it is easy to recognize the early symptoms of a serious condition, but I wonder if anyone in the history of man has ever set out upon an addiction in the full consciousness of how it will later exert its grip. Has there ever been a heroin addict who did not tell himself, even as the neuroreceptors in his cortex stretched out their needy fingers for the second hit, that he is embarking on an adventure within his control, and that he will never be like the ruined men he has seen on the platforms of stations? Any addiction presents itself at first beneath the false face of a new and minor pleasure, one to adorn a life already replete with others of its own kind, and by the time the illusion of friendship shatters, it is far too late for warnings.

My last appointment of the afternoon was in a room I had booked at the Met, and for which I intended to pay cash.

I had been seeing Laura Rees for about four months. She was twenty-nine. This is the most fecund sexual period in a beautiful woman's life, when she first becomes aware of the imminent failure of her own powers. I always imagine there must be some particular incident which sets it off. Perhaps it is something as mundane as the discovery of a grey hair during morning toilette. The twitches of the dead writer in me envisage something more subtle and dramatic – the waiter or the shop assistant for the very first time according priority to some other patron, even though the two customers arrived at the same moment; the husband (for whom she is the second wife) giving an appraising look, quite without intent, to the buttocks of a passing teenager; a smile unreciprocated by a handsome stranger in a hotel bar, where she is accompanying her man on a business trip.

It should be said that not all women reach this particular stage of instability, not even all beautiful women. Rather it manifests as nemesis. In order for the charm to take effect, the woman in question should ideally since early adolescence have indexed her place in the world solely against her beauty. The further her sense of self-worth has been dissipated upon such trifles as intellectual advancement, professional achievement, the fostering of lasting connections with friends and family, or the pursuit of almost any kind of ambition external to her own vanity, the less likely she is to be stranded by the receding waters of her beauty. Indeed, if these affectations are allowed to rage unchecked, she may actually become more confident as life progresses past the flush of youth, and therefore less likely to succumb. Cee was such a woman, and though at thirty-six the most glorious days of her freshness were probably behind her, the pleasure with which she inhabited her life continued its increase. This pleasure in turn served to tauten the slack and smooth out the wrinkles (though she had even less of both than I did), giving her a kind of grace and physical presence which would sustain her allure long into the reaches of middle age. As a lover, I wouldn't have stood a chance. It was only by virtue of my position as her husband that I had the opportunity of sleeping with her at all.

Laura Rees had arrived at Manches Interior Design by way of a husband fifteen years her senior and a hostessing job at a nightclub in South Kensington. She was sweet and sad and pleasantly dumb, and I was presumptuous enough to hope that our sessions served to cheer her up.

'You look very beautiful,' I said upon entering the suite.

'Thanks,' she replied, standing.

'How long have you got?'

'I have the whole afternoon. In fact I have the whole evening. Geoff has a work drinks thing . . .'

'Ah. I have to be back home in about an hour unfortunately. We have some people coming round.'

'OK.' She looked at her hands.

'How are the new blinds working out?'

'What? Oh, they're really great, thank you. They do that thing, that thing you said, they . . .'

'Enhance the presence of natural light without compromising the privacy of the home?'

'Yeah. How are you?'

'Good, good. Busy,' I said, unbuttoning my shirt.

'That's good. Well, shall we . . .'

While she was undressing, I went to peel back the bedclothes. I found she had placed a pair of pyjamas under the pillow on her side, which made me briefly concerned for her.

It is a strange lie that generosity of spirit makes for a good lover. It is precisely my egotism which has helped me hone what skills I have between the sheets. I got down between Mrs Rees's gym-pressed thighs and coaxed her into relinquishing her orgasm. I pursued it with the dogged empiricism of a Victorian chemist, listening out for sighs and muttered imprecations, tracking minute adjustments of the hips and stomach, rewarded at last with a rapturous eureka that made me swell with confirmation of a job well done. I emerged from beneath the duvet, panting and triumphant, to find her head lying stunned in the deep white cradle of the pillow. I turned her over and saw to her from behind (which, I am ashamed to say, led to the imposition of Claudia's image on to her well-turned features), then placed her on top, fixing my eyes on hers, not only to heighten passion and to prevent my attention wandering to other women, but also to exercise a gentlemanly discretion in the matter of the small scars on the underside of each breast, which it would have been bad form to notice.

My fatal mistake was to place her beneath me in act five, as it gave to her hands a broad purview which my favourite positions generally restrict. Just as I reached the point of orgasm, she proved the wisdom of my usual policy by shoving the pointed spade of her index nail up my rectum with all the force of a workman digging his shovel into the rock salt stashed in the council gritter. Unable to bear the pain, but unwilling entirely to forfeit the pleasure of my orgasm, with a great shout I thrust into her harder in a spasm of effort to escape the merciless digit. Either Laura misinterpreted this shout as an expression of pleasure or some impulse for revenge swam upwards in the murky fishbowl of her mind, for she greatly and suddenly increased the pressure.

Immediately she became conscious she was hurting me and the little goldfish of vengeance (if vengeance it was) took fright and darted back into the dank waters. She tried to withdraw her finger quite suddenly, a process at least as painful as its insertion, and I had to reach around behind my back to catch her wrist, causing me to collapse on her breast. After a measured extraction I rolled off, and lay panting in recovery from my injury.

'What the fuck did you do that for?'

'I thought you'd like it,' she said, taking a wet wipe from her handbag on the bedside table and cleansing her compromised finger.

'Why the hell would you think that?'

'You're always doing it to me,' she said, and got up to use the bathroom.

Splayed on the mattress, my chest heaving, I turned my head to check the time. Her bag was toppled on the bedside table, and I saw that she had inside it a half-eaten apple, with dark flecks of make-up and tobacco now trapped in the browning flesh where she had taken chunks with her neat white teeth. There seemed something curiously pathetic about this; why hadn't she just thrown it out? Did she intend to eat the rest later? There was a blister pack of pills in there as well, some of the little foil buds already opened. Antidepressants? Sedatives? Contraceptives? This glimpse into the leather folds of her handbag was infinitely more intimate than my recent foray between her legs, and it made me feel guilty enough to get up. I opened the door of our seventh-floor balcony, breaking the air-conditioned seal of the room. The heat was waiting out there for me, loitering on the balcony itself like a sleazy paparazzo, and further on, beyond the fuming strip of Park Lane, out in the hazy reaches of Hyde Park, where the trees crisped for want of rain. There was a nasty madness in the weight of it. She stayed in the bathroom for more than ten minutes, and when she re-emerged I was fully dressed. She was wearing a large white towelling robe, and when she saw that I was no longer naked she put her hands in the pockets and closed it around herself, as if cold.

'Don't you want to use the shower?' she asked.

'I'll take one at the gym before I go home.'

'Do you want a glass of water or a sandwich or something before you go? We could get something sent up.'

'No, thank you.'

'When will I see you again?'

'I'll give you a call next week.'

'It's half-term next week. We'll have Daniel and Miranda. It's Geoff's turn.'

'Do you like them? Geoff's kids?'

'Yes, I like them. But they're not mine.'

'OK. The week after, then.'

'OK.'

'I'll settle up downstairs. I'll leave a hundred or so over in case you want anything else. Please do order food if you want, or stay and relax. The checkout isn't until tomorrow.'

She nodded and smiled, and we kissed on the cheek. When I left she was sitting on the bed, leafing through a glossy magazine. Usually in these encounters she persuaded me to stay, and her zoned passivity was a new feature. I descended seven floors in the lift, but even after the deceleration announced we were coming to the lobby something in my stomach kept on going down. I was not satisfied. I did not feel proud of myself, and the frenetic coupling had not replenished my stock of ego in the way to which I had become accustomed. Part of this was concern for Laura (hypocritical, but no less sincere for that), part my injury. I was compelled to walk in the manner of a man who has had an accident in his trousers, and the very worst thing of all was that, in some mad way, I thought I rather deserved it. As I strode with my cowboy swagger out of the lobby and into the sweat, I had the uneasy sense that the ultimate source of my discomfort was not Laura's finger, but Claudia's smile.

# 6

I ARRIVED HOME AROUND SIX, AND WAS SURPRISED TO SEE two cars I did not recognize parked in the drive outside our house. My first thought was that I had forgotten some dinner engagement or party, and I grasped my phone in a panic, expecting to see a dozen missed calls reproaching me from the smug little screen. But there was nothing. I peered through the back of the car nearest the door. It was some kind of environmentally wonderful family saloon. The back contained a baby seat, minus the infant, and the footwell had the corresponding accumulation of brightly coloured 'learning toys' and an empty pot on which I could make out the word 'organic'. Mothers with money and social consciences. It was book club night.

I let myself in as quietly as I could, but the house was like an extension of Cee. Although I took off my shoes in the hall, I never stood a chance of making it past the second-floor landing without her sensing my presence. Had we been in a state of amity, I would have been allowed to continue my ascent of the staircase without molestation. Indeed, had we been in a state of amity Cee might have warned me about the evening and given me the opportunity to make myself scarce entirely. As it was she had evidently not forgotten the morning's battle, for her summons rang out from behind the drawing-room door as I tried to sneak past.

'Matthew, is that you?'

I had become a Matthew. I steeled myself.

'Yes, my love.'

'Would you come in here a moment? You can help us settle an argument.'

My heart sank with dread. I entered upon the room to find my wife and five identical women in varying shades, two of whom (not including my wife) had once shared my bed (or at least my champagne-coloured sofa), all of them looking up at me with slightly flushed faces. A bottle of Sancerre was open on the coffee table in front of them, and three empty bottles lurked rather ominously beside it. A chorus of welcomes, some arch and some less so, emanated from the circle. The room had the cloying smugness of shared opinion.

'Hello, ladies,' I said, trying not to sound too much like a daytime TV host.

'You used to write books, didn't you, Matt?' said one of the ones I had fucked.

'Yes. Yes, I did. Well, I wrote a book.'

'Ah, then you can't really help,' said the other one I had fucked. 'You see, we were discussing whether or not a second novel can ever be as good as the first if the first one is successful.'

'You know, whether or not it's an impossible psycho-logical burden,' said one I hadn't, trying to be nice.

'Performance anxiety,' said the one I had.

'Drooping quill,' said the other.

Cackling.

'Only you'd have to have written two books, really.'

'And the first one would have to have been successful,' said Cee, looking up at me from her upholstered throne.

More laughter, and then Cee told me that she was only joking, darling, and why didn't I come and join them as I'd read the book. There was an empty glass and a space on the sofa for me. A Greek chorus of further invitations, but I said I'd had a long day and I was tired, and wished the ladies goodnight with a deep and ironic bow.

'Oh, and Matthew darling,' Cee said, as my hand found the doorknob, 'you will remember to bring the Swansons' billing up to date, won't you?'

I did not blame the book club for their choice of material. I did not, as some commentators did, view their endeavours as a puzzled furrow in the middle brow, whose pretensions kept them from Barbara Cartland even as their tastes rebelled against Chekhov. I was happy to see anybody reading any book, *any* book, even one I thought was crap. But for some reason, their presence in the house was even less tolerable than usual that night. Their voices pursued me through the floor, so that even when they were resting at the distant cusp of my hearing my annoyance was not diminished, like the barely audible buzz of someone's headphones.

Cee did not come to bed until after midnight. She snored rather during the night. The next morning she offered me tea when I came into the kitchen. Offering tea was in the order of an apology. Dehydration had damped the lustre of her skin, and it seemed as if the retreating waters of Sancerre had left behind them a residue of remorse. It is a strange thing how often the physical effects of alcoholic overindulgence become mixed up in the metaphysical stuff of guilt. I accepted the tea and sat at the kitchen table looking brave.

To my amazement, I was able to eke this out for several days. Perhaps because we were busy and did not see each other much the status quo was slower to re-establish itself, but I was surprised that Cee's contrition should have sweetened almost the entire week. As kind as she was to me, following my afternoon in the hotel I felt there was something clinging to my skin which I could not wash off. She remarked one day (more with surprise than suspicion) that I was taking a great many showers, and it was true, I was showering three times a day.

She was so solicitous that when the occasion of my next visit to the Swansons came around, she greeted the news with the wish that I should have a good day. I had offered to take some of the further work relating to the Vincent Square property off her hands, for as the process of assembling the library was becoming more involved it seemed to make sense to deal with some of the outstanding building works as well. After all, there was no point in us both traipsing over there at regular intervals. She accepted this proposal meekly, and almost with gratitude, for though it may have been founded on a modicum of self-interest, it was also actually necessary. Cee had been receiving more and more work from Hugo, and was having difficulty in giving proper attention to existing clients. In fact, she informed me, she had been asked to assist him and his business partner in the conversion of a stately home in Buckinghamshire into the kind of place to which successful lawyers could take their secretaries for the weekend. It was a big job and she intended to be away for a few weeks, a prospect which seemed to increase her guilt even as it swelled my heart with joy.

On the occasion of our next meeting I hopped off the tube at Pimlico, and as I crossed the Vauxhall Bridge Road I was acutely nervous. I had confirmed the appointment with Claudia by email, and the email I had received in return had not been notable for its warmth. My hatred for emoticons knows no bounds, but at the moment her stiff reply pinged into my inbox I would almost have been grateful for a smiley face. I even caught myself worrying that she might have discovered my visit to Laura Rees in the wake of our last appointment. To my utter shame, I actually found myself on the corner of the square in a state of some distress. My palms were sweating, my breathing heavy. I took a moment to collect myself. To distract myself, I spent some time gently fondling the new acquisition I had collected that morning, a near fine copy of the first UK edition of *Hangover Square*, piping hot from the dealer.

The day was bright and fresh, with a clear blue sky over London. There was a pleasant breeze in the street, enough to turn the pages of a magazine without blowing it off the table. I ran up the stairs to the Swansons' front door, but before I could knock there was the sound of a disturbance in the hall. Claudia opened the door, and an extraordinary thing happened. Her face, as it came blinking into the daylight, bore an expression of tremendous joy emerging from sorrow, as if the universe had taken her on its lap in the midst of her tears and kissed her forehead and told her that everything was going to be all right. She had been crying, and her big eyes shone with the slick of tears. She appeared to be slightly stooped, as if suffering from indigestion. The sun was behind me, and the hallway stood in daytime shadows, so that I suppose for a moment she could not make out who I was. The tiny delay in recognition kept that beatific expression suspended on her face for a fraction of a second, an expression as beautiful as a vase filled with fresh flowers somewhere between the mantelpiece and the ground, falling. I did not instantly surmise that she had mistaken me for someone else, and in that accursed lacuna I thought that she had fallen in love with me. Her expression chimed in complete harmony with a desire in myself that had hitherto been hidden. The thought, quite unlooked for and wholly unwelcome, made me suddenly ecstatic with joy. Then in a fraction of a second her eyes adjusted to the disparity in the light, and she saw it was me, and the vase was broken. She looked shocked and embarrassed, and I was left to ponder the horrible significance of that moment of elation I had had at our mutual misunderstanding.

'It is eleven thirty?'

'What?'

'I mean, I'm not early, am I? Only, you looked like you were expecting someone else.'

'Oh! Oh yes, I was. I had forgotten completely. Do you want to come in?'

She said it in such a way as to strongly suggest that I would not want to come in, that what I would want most in the world if I really thought about it was to immediately vacate her front step and allow her to close the door and await the man whose arrival would trigger a legitimate bout of rapture. In fact she looked as if she had grasped at the stock phrase to steady herself in the wake of her disappointment, and had not had time to consider its practical implications. But I was still smarting from my humiliation, cross with her and cross with myself.

'Yes, I thought we could discuss the shelves, if you're not busy.'

As I said this I was making my way past her, and at the same instant wondering to myself what the hell I was doing. It was clear she did not want me in the house, and that she was expecting someone else. The shelves were not a bountiful topic for discussion; without co-operation from her and a desire on her part that I should stay, there was nothing to keep me in the house for more than the minute it would take to get out my tape measure.

'No, not busy, though Jim will be here to pick me up in a minute.'

Her husband! A look like that for the midget! I felt a sudden rage towards him. I recognized it, it was kin to the joy that had doorstepped me. Let one emotion in, and you will find yourself hosting the whole bloody family!

'It shouldn't take long at all. I can just measure the shelves and then I'll be out of your hair.' I walked on blindly, but her words, combined with the familiar sensation of being alone with a strange woman in her home in the middle of the morning, stirred a well-honed instinct. 'Isn't . . . shouldn't Jim be at work? I mean, doesn't he have work during the day?'

'Yes, he works,' she said, and sat down on the stairs. She did so in the manner of one resuming a customary position, and it explained the speed with which she had answered my knock. Waiting for the midget like a dog in the hall! It was too much to bear. The thought should have plunged her in my estimation like a Spartan baby tossed from the cliff for its webbed feet and cleft palate, but instead it made me flinch with envy for the man she awaited. Once she was seated, she wound one hand through the banister and drew her knees up to her chest. She had a cashmere jumper around her shoulders, and she held one of the empty cuffs in her hand. Her face appeared to me in a quarter profile, one eye and the corner of her lips visible from behind. As I watched, her cheek twitched briefly with pain.

'Are you all right?'

'Yes, I'm fine, thank you,' she said. 'Actually no, no I'm not. Do you mind if we do this next week? Or tomorrow or any other time really.'

She did not look at me when she spoke, but continued to stare at the door. For a moment she really did seem like an animal, with an animal's singular purpose. When I had come in I had stepped on letters which were lying unattended on the doormat. I looked back down the hall, and noticed for the first time that there was a tea towel dropped on the carpet, covering a mound of spilt pasta sauce. It was a good thing that the hall was to be recarpeted, as a stain like that would not take eviction lying down. It crossed my mind that she was insane, or that her husband kept her imprisoned on the ground floor, spooning her Spaghetti hoops through the downstairs letter box.

My desire may be an excitable companion, a man who cannot be relied upon when the going gets tough, but my ego is a level-headed friend. Having been silent throughout these proceedings, though with clouds darkening on his fine brows, he now leaned forward in his high-backed chair and declared, 'Enough!' I had come with the intention of being welcomed like a lover, and here I was being treated without even the courtesy that might have been afforded a common tradesman. To hell with her beauty, her being-unlike-others, her unreliable loveliness. I resolved to leave and not to return, but before I did I would relieve myself in her loo, peeing audibly into the amphitheatre of the bowl so that she might hear of my defiance in the hall. I was already congratulating myself on having come to my senses.

'Of course I don't mind. In fact we can have one of the workmen send me the measurements and I will email you through the list for your consideration. Might I just use the loo before I go?'

I stepped over the jumper on the hallway floor, and made my way to the bathroom by the turn in the stairs to the basement. I opened the door and closed it behind me. Most of the loos I experience in the homes of my friends and contemporaries are filled with books, a tacit admission of the biological functions which are to be performed and which may require the visitor to sit for a few moments without entertainment. They are a kind of extension of the duties of the host. The Swansons' toilet was still unfinished but already contained a stack of magazines on the window sill, including several back issues of *The Economist* and, hilariously, one surreptitious copy of a periodical for model train collectors protruding halfway down the pile. I lifted the lid and the seat and was about to render my song of defiance when I noticed that the water in the bowl was a peculiar pink colour, like rosewater. There was a smear of blood, almost gore, a long lateral handprint on the wall by the toilet that suggested it had been made by someone seated on the bowl. When I turned in the confined space, I saw there were further smears of blood around the sink on the enamel taps, and the soap in its dish had a little lather of wet pink bubbles, one of which burst as I watched. I thought suddenly of the pasta spillage partially covered in the hall, and of the unusually vibrant red of the flecks of sauce on the carpet. I zipped myself back up without having peed, flushed the loo and walked back out into the hall.

'Excuse me, ah, Mrs Swanson, are you all right?'

'Yes, I'm fine.'

'Only there's some blood in the toilet.'

'I've had a miscarriage.'

'That's . . . that's awful. When?' I said.

There is a scene in *Macbeth*, just after the death of Duncan, where the Princes run from their bedchambers in the castle to hear the news that their royal father is murdered. Stumbling from the warmth of sleep into the cold morning of sounding alarms and screaming, Prince Malcolm's first reaction on hearing of the recent regicide is to say, 'Oh! By whom?' I had to deliver the line once to a group of schoolchildren at a matinee production of *Macbeth* in the Cambridge Arts Theatre, and it made them all burst out laughing. As I clanked offstage in a pair of studded leather trousers rented from the RSC, I saw the stage hands tittering, and cursed the bard for an inadequate fool. Standing in the Swansons' still-to-be-renovated hallway, waiting politely for news of the precise timing of my employer's miscarriage, I reflected how wise he was to know that tragic events do not invariably promote one's speech to the tragic register.

'Uh, I started to get pains about three-quarters of an hour ago. I thought it was nothing so I just kind of went on. Then I noticed this spot of blood on the floor in the kitchen, and when I went to mop it up it was wet, and then I saw it was coming . . . it was coming from me. So I tried to get to the loo and I fell over just there and then everything got worse.'

I sat down beside her on the step, but did not touch her. I disowned my original intentions, and decided clumsily to try to help.

'Have you called an ambulance?'

'I don't like ambulances. They make me feel panicked, they make everything seem worse than it is. Jim will take me. I'll be fine when Jim gets here.'

I understood then her single-mindedness in waiting by the door. She was maintaining her composure by fixing her attention absolutely on the return of her husband. By focusing on that moment to the exclusion of all else, the grief and pain and fear that might otherwise have overwhelmed her were locked outside her door, exiled beyond the boundary of that one certain event. Beyond that event, no future occurrence existed. Her husband would come home to take care of her, and she had only to hold herself together until that safe house on the horizon, growing closer with each passing second, was reached. I felt myself awestruck that one person could invest so heavily in another as to be certain that their arrival would make everything all right. Particularly given that the other was Jim Swanson.

At that moment I noticed the copy of *Delta of Venus* I had given her, which was lying on top of the radiator cover that lined the hall. It had taken up position among car keys and house keys and a ceramic urn containing rubber bands and several different pens, objects that saw a great deal of use and would be instantly apparent to anyone entering or exiting the house. It was not a vantage point which one would use to conceal something of dubious significance. Its place there was enough for me to surmise that my attempt to get the thin end of my wedge between her and Jim had failed, and I felt a selfish disappointment mixed in with my sympathy and shock. I looked at the book for a moment too long, and she caught the direction of my gaze.

'That book.'

'You . . . you didn't enjoy it?'

'I read it when I was at school. It used to get passed around the dorm, and everyone said you'd get suspended if they caught you reading it. Why on earth of all the books in the world would you give me that?'

She winced again. I squirmed. I had presumed to shock her from the grip of her conservative connubial cocoon with a book she had read and digested as a teenager. How badly I had underestimated her.

'I'm so sorry if I embarrassed you.'

'You didn't embarrass me. You embarrassed yourself. In fact I was going to ask you today not to come again, and to complete the library without coming back to our house.'

'You weren't going to fire me?'

'I would have. But I like Cecilia. She's been nice to me, and I wouldn't have wanted you to have to explain.'

She did not elaborate on what it was I would have had to explain, but it was instantly clear to me that her understanding penetrated to the very depths of my intentions. At the same time she was clearly in great pain and distress, yet they did not seem to cloud her analysis, only perhaps to have opened up a dialogue that propriety might otherwise have prohibited. I am used to having my intentions to myself, though Cee sometimes joins me there, more by instinct than perspicacity. The sensation of going to that quiet place of my hidden motive, and finding there waiting for me the object of my scheme, was disorientating. The effect was heightened by the fact that throughout this exchange, beyond the fraction of a second it took her to detect my noticing the book, her eyes and the better part of her attention remained fixed upon the door. I felt not only discovered, but also impotent, powerless to alleviate her suffering.

'That was . . . very kind of you. And better than I deserve.'

'People never get what they deserve.'

'I apologize. I won't trouble you again. Any questions of taste we can settle over email.'

'Oh, look, I think we're a little past that now. Apology accepted. Really I was disappointed, I wanted to talk about writing with someone. Just no more dirty books.'

From this response, I inferred that her pain was easing. She spoke for longer, and even darted her eyes at me near the end.

'Are you sure I can't call you an ambulance?'

'No, thank you, really. The bleeding stopped before you arrived. And it hurts less now.'

'And you don't want . . . I don't know, a mug of sweet tea or a pint of whisky or something?'

It was intended as a joke, but immediately after I had said it I had a horrible feeling there was some kind of connection between the drinking of large quantities of whisky and the inducement of premature labour – or was that gin? The entourage of general knowledge that usually attended me in conversation, fawning upon my every whim and scattering references before my feet, had peeled away.

'Ice in the whisky,' she said.

After a few minutes of silence I opened my mouth again.

'They're really common, you know . . . I mean, miscarriages. They happen to many women who go on to have lots of . . . Cee's sister had three, and she has two boys and a girl.'

Listening to myself speaking, I had the sensation of quiet horror one must get watching one's parked car begin to roll down the incline of a busy high street, gathering speed towards the Sunday shoppers, the elderly women with their tartan trolleys and the young mothers with their strollers. I was aware that it was my own fault for having left the brakes off my tongue, but its progress into disaster seemed now completely beyond my control. Thankfully she did not feel the need to respond to this crass commentary, and simply kept looking at the door. I lapsed into a grateful silence. All the time, the shroud of the tea towel lay behind us in the hall.

Five minutes later, we heard a car pull up outside, the loud slam when the driver's door is shut at speed, and footsteps taking the porch stairs three at a time. Claudia looked up at the sound of the car, and when the steps in the garden put the matter beyond doubt she launched herself off the step so that Jim arrived at the front door to find it flung open and replaced with his wife's passionate embrace.

'Are you all right, babe? What happened?'

He broke away from her, and held her by the shoulders. He asked the question in the manner of one trying to establish the facts of the situation in the shortest possible time, so that the best possible remedy may be instantly deployed. His masterfulness made him seem less short. Claudia described what had happened, starting to cry now, her reserves of self-possession having lasted her exactly as long as it had taken for him to effect this rescue. I stayed sitting on the bottom step in the hallway, unnoticed by him and forgotten by her, until he came into the house to grab her coat.

'Oh . . . what the fuck?'

'Uh, oh, sorry, Mr Swanson. I, ah, I came round to see your Claudia, wife, Mrs Swanson, and to talk about the library, and then I thought I would wait with her until you got back.'

'OK, thank you. Can you get out now, please. I'm taking her to the hospital.'

I got up off the step and put out my hand to shake his, but thankfully he was rummaging through the pockets of the coats on hooks by the door and did not see me. I was utterly enraged with him for interrupting my communion with Mrs Swanson, the most intense and honest interaction I had enjoyed with another human being in years, and for showing me up with his competence. I whipped my hand away and walked out into the sunlight, and it really was blinding after the gloom of the hall. Mrs Swanson was leaning against the car, crying quietly now, though clearly relieved that her vigil had been thus concluded. I saw she had put the jumper that had been wrapped around her shoulders down over the passenger seat. I felt sorrow for her loss. I was struck by the desperate desire to do something for her, anything, both to try to put myself in some kind of standing in relation to the miniature hero in the house and to try to make amends for my behaviour and for her suffering.

'Look, please, take this.' I thrust the first edition of *Hangover Square* into her hands. 'You can read it in the waiting room or whatever. It's not a bad book, I promise, it's a wonderful book.'

With that I turned away from her, and made my way briskly and in the wrong direction east along Vincent Square, heading for Embankment. I heard the front door slam behind me with the jangle of the brass letter-box flap, and then the corresponding slamming of the car door, and then the screech of tyres (an oddly desperate sound in a suburban street) as Jim, a man of action, reversed the wrong way down the one-way alley leading into the square, and spirited his wife towards the latex hands of the Chelsea and Westminster.

As I walked back to the embankment for a cab, Claudia's words kept rising above the general hubbub of impressions. Most women would have said, 'I've lost my baby,' but she said, 'I've had a miscarriage.' She had talked about herself the way one talks about someone else, distancing herself from the emotion, trying not to evince a self-conscious pathos. Why had she done that? Had it been shock? An attempt to maintain self-control through denial? Or was it pure strength of character? English is the language with the greatest in-built sense of responsibility on earth. Most foreign tongues are partly reflexive. The Japanese say, 'A shower happened.' The language is geared to acknowledge the inherent randomness of the universe, the extent to which even the smallest actions are partially beyond our control. The Spanish in their tardiness will never acknowledge 'I am late' but instead offer 'It has become late for me,' subtly shifting the blame on to a hostile world of circumstance. But Englishmen and Americans do things to things. They do not have things done to them. They take showers. Sometimes they even grab them. They run late, and even mortality is no excuse for a delayed appearance; on death, they become late for ever. It's heroic, this linguistic attitude, and full of hubris, because it attempts to take responsibility for the world and overstates the power of man to change it. If Claudia had said she had lost her baby, she would have been casting herself as the victim, a role she was more than entitled to assume. But to have a miscarriage is to do something, to actively possess suffering.

I had been walking for almost ten minutes when I realized I was shaking, and I had given her a £2,000 book to take with her to the hospital.

The strange thing about collecting books is that the more I have collected, the less I have read. It's not just that, though. It is the physical condition of the books. Much of the value of a first edition, aesthetic and financial, lies in its physical condition, particularly the dust jacket; indeed, in older books the dust jacket can represent as much as 80 per cent of the value of a book, so that a copy of Evelyn Waugh's *Vile Bodies* (1930, Chapman and Hall) will set you back £300 for the book, and £7,000 for the book in its wrapper. The most common injuries suffered by any hardback volume are price clipping (where someone removes the price from the inside corner of the jacket) and owner inscriptions. When I was younger and handling second-hand books on Berwick Street, I used to love these indelible little signs of the past; price clipping meant the book had been bought as a present for someone else, and the book would hold the generous residue of a gift. An inscription meant someone had owned it and loved it, and the little ink statements on the flyleaf always struck me with the poignancy of old photographs. As I grew older and became a more serious collector, however, they offended my sense of ownership. The books were mine, and any evidence to the contrary was an affront to the covetous instinct.

There is also a great deal of incidental damage with which to contend. Some characteristic injuries reveal the history of a book – prison libraries, for example, often do not allow hardbacks because of the potential for concealment presented by the cloth boards, and the books are converted into paperbacks by the running of a Stanley knife down the interior sides of the cover, after which the pages go into the library, whilst the dead bird of the cloth boards is discarded. I have always thought that this rather misses the point – the most dangerous things concealed in books are ideas, though to be fair I suppose you can't shank a nonce with Swift's satire.

Even if it escapes all such traumas, the condition of a first edition will inevitably deteriorate over time. Books may become rolled from being too tightly packed on the shelf, losing their pleasing square shape, or faded in the dust jacket from exposure to the sun. The spine may become cracked, the endpapers torn, the cloth boards bumped. The pages of a book, like the flesh, are sown with the seeds of their own destruction – metallic impurities and acid used to treat the wood pulp react with the air over time to create characteristic circular stains called 'foxing', from the fanciful notion that they look like the footprints of a fox. When a publisher or bookbinder used cheap wood pulp for the pages, the economy reveals itself over the years. Every time one opens a book, or removes it from the shelf, or touches the pages with one's fingers, tiny increments of damage accumulate. The hinges weaken. The dust jacket gets bumped. Grease from the fingertips infuses the page. In short, a collectible book is not intended to be read. Indeed, a book dealer's euphemism for a sub-standard book is a 'good reading copy'. So I did not read the books I collected. As I walked away from Vincent Square, I realized I could not recall the last time I had read a book for any reason other than paid reviewing. I had wanted the copy of the Patrick Hamilton so desperately because it was a book I had loved when I was younger. Claudia made me want to read it again, and I resolved to buy a paperback copy on the way home.

As I set out for home, I was struck by a difficult problem: how best to approach the matter of the miscarriage with Cee. My first instinct was not to tell her. I felt protective over Claudia's suffering. The experience seemed a tender spot, a hole in the armour of her honest charm, and I did not want my wife or her friends to poke in there with their neat little nails. But unfortunately the strategy was too high-risk. It was likely that either Jim or Claudia would mention the incident to Cee, if only because they would assume I had myself, and it would be difficult to explain why I had concealed it.

When I got home I told her the whole story, with the small omissions and glossings one might expect. I did not, for example, mention the first edition of *Hangover Square*, as I was not sure how I would explain the impulse I had had to give the thing to Claudia. Cee knew that I had been trying to get hold of a copy for some time, and it was impossible to account for the sudden unimportance of something that had seemed so dear to me. She questioned me on various points of detail. I had feared that she might be inclined to sift the incident for gossip, but I quickly saw I had done her an injustice. She was genuinely concerned for Mrs Swanson's health, and for the fate of her unborn child. Cee, a mercifully unmaternal woman when it came to her own household, had a deep and abiding love for other people's children, and although she had been happy to disparage Claudia to me she liked the Swansons really.

'Don't you think we should do something for her? You know, give her something?' I said, when the story had been told and Cee had lapsed into rueful digestion.

'I think that's a lovely idea,' she said, brightening at the thought of some practical assistance that could be given through the medium of expert gift-wrapping. 'Of course we should.'

'We could take her round something . . . flowers or fruit or something.'

'Oh, I don't think we need take anything round. I think it would be better to send it. She won't want her decorators tramping round her sickroom.'

I nodded, but kept my own counsel on this point.

'I'll have a look for something in the shops tomorrow.'

'That would be really sweet of you, darling,' Cee said, and came under my arm, driven there by the cold of another's misfortune. 'You will remember to put me on the card, won't you?'

And there the matter was allowed to drop.

# 7

WHEN I HAD FIRST MOOTED INVITING DON JOAN TO DINNER with the intention of pumping her for information on Claudia's university days, it had been a kind of joke, teasing Cee for her desire to get the all-smelling nose into everyone's business. Cee had taken it in good humour, and began to discuss the practical arrangements with me as a continuation of the game, but with a half-seriousness that made it all the more fun. It was my own growing interest in Claudia that caused me to dare Cee actually to go ahead, which I accomplished by upping the ante every time it was discussed; first, to prod her into fixing dates and then making invitations. By the appointed day my anticipation was far greater than hers, though I did all I could to conceal it.

The day of the dinner party was as hot as any other, and was spent in preparation. I was irritable in the morning as Laura Rees had called me on my mobile, in direct contravention of our agreed modus operandi (which involved a hotmail account accessible through my iPhone), and had attempted to engage me in a conversation about herself. I was in Marks & Spencer trying to find cumin, and was able to leave the handset in the basket while she talked, picking it up every minute or so to agree with whatever she happened to be saying, but the experience was nonetheless a grave irritation. I had also caught the words 'lonely', 'children, he knew that' and 'nose-job' during the intervals when the receiver had been against my ear, which alerted me to the fact that it was perhaps time to bring our liaison to a close. It took me almost twenty minutes to untangle myself from the conversation, and I was in a foul mood when I returned to Old Church Street.

The cooking process favoured by my wife is carefully and expertly designed to give the impression of spontaneity. Gossip is exchanged over the woodpecker sound of an expertly handled knife on the chopping board as fine young people cross their legs and perch on the countertops, the men with their ties loose and collars open or, if they are in the arts, their ironic sunglasses on and pastel cigarettes ablaze. Cee never allowed anyone to smoke in the house unless they were artistic, in which case it would be bourgeois pudeur to deny them. Particularly if they had recently placed a work in the home of one of our clients. It was a good index of an artist's career, whether or not he was allowed to smoke in our house. On one occasion I had seen Cee ask a young journalist to take his cigarette outside at the same time as a rather better-known photographer was exhaling smoke and opinions on the window seat. When the boy of letters pointed out the inconsistency, Cee informed him that the photographer smoked Parisian black tobacco, a scent she found tolerable and even pleasant, in contrast to his own Marlboro Lites. I had a suspicion that I myself might have been permitted the odd puff in my novelistic heyday, but in present circumstances was more likely to be asked to sit out on the step.

The guestlist was a carefully managed affair. Cee tended towards a kind of A- and B-list policy in which the guests in whose honour the event was to be thrown were supplemented with a hand-picked supporting cast from the range of our social acquaintance, chosen for their ability to complement the central characters rather than for any particular qualities of their own. She was never short of guests. As the colouring she picked to trim cushions matched the walls, as the spices she chose to flavour meat enhanced its inherent juices, so the guests she selected always worked harmoniously together, and if some were the dish and others the garnish, they were nonetheless blended to a universally pleasurable effect.

On this occasion the guests of honour were to be Hugo and Magda. My understanding was that our little business had not escaped unscathed from the collapse of the financial markets. Hugo, who relied on the oil of distress to power the engine of his business model, was increasingly the client from whom we derived the greatest part of our work.

Don Joan constituted an exception to the usual rule. She was not quite a top-billing personage herself, but nor would she be expected to please Hugo and Magda (what's more, I privately thought that she would have little success in doing so, a situation greatly to her credit). Had my father believed in God, Don Joan would have been my godmother. After my mother died, he decided that to prevent the coarsening of my soul I should be mollified by some regular female influence. He may also have been balancing this decision against the certainty that he would never salvage his own romantic appetite from the wreckage of his bereavement. To this end he chose the kindliest, most worldly and least prepossessing woman in his extensive acquaintance, and made sure that she was present at family gatherings and bi-weekly dinners. Don Joan had no children of her own. I got the impression she had cheerfully written off sexual attachment in her youth the way a short boy very fond of his books may write off a career in basketball. But she was one of those academics who seek the company of the young without ever pretending to be one of them. She was happy, I think, to be granted a more proprietorial role in the matter of a timid and bookish young boy, and I, for my part, loved her. I had had tea with her once a week without fail in her digs in Cambridge during my time there, and she had watched over the whole of my courtship with Cee. Don Joan then was an exception partly in being one of the family, and partly because a different kind of office was expected of her: that she would unravel for us the Great Mystery of Claudia's Unfinished Languages Degree.

The final two were a couple, Gerald and Lisa. Lisa was one of Cee's nieces and worked at a photographic studio in Battersea, thus fulfilling the artistic portion of the guestlist without which no Manches Interior dinner party was complete, but it was Gerald who really constituted the prize invitee. He was a captain in the Household Cavalry, and had lately returned from Afghanistan with a Military Cross. He had apparently been caught in an explosion which, whilst it had left no outward scar, had damaged his eardrums and left him incapable of sustaining loud noise, and Lisa had called Cee to request that no music be played at dinner. There was a shimmer of glamour to this esoteric disability. He was also black, which served obscurely to protect Cee's Bohemian credentials against any accusations of hypocrisy in inviting one of Her Majesty's young officers into our hotbed of radicalism.

Lisa and Gerald were first to arrive. Their eagerness not to get things wrong was evident in their clothes and the wine they had bought, both of which were a touch too smart and expensive for the occasion. I had to confess that I was curious about Gerald myself. I looked him over on the doorstep for latent signs of heroism, but there was nothing overt to distinguish him from other men. He was so neat in his chinos and his collared shirt (fastened, I noticed, with gold regimental cufflinks) that his trousers looked like they had been pressed with him inside them. His shoes had received a stiff talking-to. His curly black hair was cropped close to the skull, which gave his ears a slightly awkward prominence. It occurred to me that I was looking at a man who had probably killed somebody. He had normal hands, normal eyes, a normal neck and shoulders. I marvelled at the alchemy of training that took a young man from the rugby fields of Durham University and had him slit the throat of a foreign stranger, and then slipped him back into a dinner party as if nothing had happened.

Lisa, by contrast, offset a youthful evening dress with a pair of feathered earrings and a set of neon gloves. Against the intense sun of the Chelsea night she carried a black lace parasol. This she handled with some self-consciousness, indicating perhaps that what had seemed hot in the Notting Hill dressing room had cooled rather in the back of the taxi. Had it not been for Gerald's handsome young face, he might have passed for a father delivering his wayward teenage step-daughter to the party, with strict instructions to be home by one. As it was, however, they made a beautiful couple.

Don Joan was the next to arrive. She had a flat in Hampstead, and she had come down from Cambridge by train for the night. She had always had a peculiar aversion to the doorbell, and the rat-a-tat of her ivory-handled stick on the front door was a sound as welcome and familiar as ice-cream chimes. Cee opened the door for her, and the two women greeted each other warmly. Had anyone else hammered away at the gloss finish of the paintwork of our home they would have been given short shrift. The sight of their embrace made me uncomfortable. Somehow I forgot every time, but Don Joan was very fond of Cee. Something about the fact that this old woman cared for Cee made me feel guilty about every bad thing I had ever said or done to my wife. Every unpleasant notion that had ever come into my head was made to writhe by the clear and bright light of those kindly old eyes.

Cee began her preparations, and I had to admit it was a jolly way to begin the evening, sitting around sipping wine and talking, with the sounds and smells of what was to come being conjured along with the appetite. Still I could not forget how much trouble had gone into setting it all out, and how hollow was the immediacy. Gerald did not know quite how to handle the informality, and stood rigidly in the centre of things with his glass of beer, somehow managing to be constantly in the way. 'I'm so sorry we've come early. Only, you see, it's become almost impossible to judge the journey from Ladbroke Grove. Do you know, they've shut off the whole of Ken Church Street for roadworks . . .' He was the kind of man who enters a party with a description of his journey – not a bore, but uncomfortable with words when without something specific to communicate. At one point Cee crushed two cloves of garlic on the chopping board with the flat of a blade, using her fist as a hammer, and I saw him wince at the loud bang.

Hugo and Magda arrived three-quarters of an hour late. The flurry of the cooking was done, and things were simmering. The other guests had established a happy equilibrium, and were a little miffed at the infusion of fresh blood. Hugo strode through the door with extravagant apologies, the fluency of which suggested he had never for a moment thought we might actually start without him. Magda followed on behind, and her quiet embarrassment expressed far more remorse. I took her coat and kissed her cheek. She looked grateful. I often had the impression with Hugo that his success had allowed him to obtain for himself over the years a gradual but steady parade of nicer things – nicer cars, nicer holidays, nicer houses – and I had no doubt that at some point he would treat himself to a nicer wife. Nicer in the sense of younger at any rate, as Magda was as friendly and intelligent as one could wish.

As we took our seats I opened the window to let in the breeze, closing the shutters to obscure the view from the street. The first course was produced, and those who had sat through the entirety of the cooking process awaiting the arrival of Hugo and Magda fell to it in appreciative silence. Cee asked Don Joan a few innocuous questions about university life, before brushing my foot beneath the table to get my attention.

'Talking of the old days,' she said, 'we've invited you here partly under false pretences. Actually that's rubbish, we don't have to make any pretence of our desire to see you, but what I mean is we have an ulterior motive as well.'

'Oh yes?' Don Joan said good-humouredly. Gerald with impeccable manners poured her a glass of wine and she held up her hand at the half-mark and thanked him.

'Yes – you see, we've got this client at the moment, and she was a student at Clare . . .'

'What did she study?'

'Italian, I think.'

'And what has this poor *ragazza* done to inspire these inquisitorial attentions? Has she skipped town without paying or something?'

I was silently impressed by the accuracy with which Don Joan divined Cee's desire for dirt.

'God, no, nothing like that. We'd be asking Gerald if it was something like that, to see if any of his friends had gone into bounty hunting.'

Gerald smiled and his skin flushed dark. I wondered if the casual flippancy of the Chelsea dinner table would sit quite well in an ear so recently used to gunfire.

'Well then, spit it out.'

'We were hoping you could help clear up a little mystery actually. I've met her a few times and she doesn't seem like the type to just quit on something, or indeed to fail. But we heard from someone who used to know her that she abandoned her degree halfway through. We were hoping you might know why.'

'What's her name?'

'Claudia Swanson. She would have been Claudia McEwen at Cambridge.'

At the mention of the name, Don Joan's features clouded for a moment. Then she folded her brow and took up her glass of wine. 'Claudia McEwen . . . No, I'm sorry, I don't think I knew her.'

She was clearly lying. Don Joan was not good at lying, keeping an almost exclusive company with truth and silence.

'Oh no!' Cee said, and threw up her hands in mock despair. 'Don Joan, you do disappoint us, you know everyone and everything! You must have heard something?'

'Really, I'm sorry, my dear, I've simply never heard the name.' She put her cutlery together on the plate, indicating she was done with the course, and indeed the conversation.

'Oh well . . . this is too much for me,' said Cee, laughing.

'Now Don Joan is being mysterious. I'm just going to have to ask Claudia myself. I can't take this any more.'

'I'm not being mysterious.' Don Joan looked alarmed at this prospect. 'I just don't know who you mean. Honestly, Cee, you always were the most appalling gossip. It is most fortunate you are such an excellent cook or I shouldn't be able to grace your table at all. That was absolutely delicious. Now, shall I clear plates?'

'Oh, please, allow me!' Gerald said. He stood up too quickly and upset his glass of red over the table. The malevolent wave of liquid was headed for Cee's dress and the cream carpet beneath, but Don Joan trapped it with her napkin. Cee had begun telling Gerald that he wasn't to worry even before the first apology had left his lips.

Cee told him that the only thing he could do to make amends was to remain in his seat and relax. It was patently obvious that asking Gerald to relax whilst his hostess cleaned up his mess was like inviting him to keep his fingers wrapped around the handle of a burning-hot frying pan, but he gamely remained sitting. Hugo, quite recovered from his late entrance, leaned over the table to engage him.

'Cee mentioned you were in the Royal Dragoon Guards.'

'Oh, it's the Household Cavalry, I'm afraid.'

'I was going to ask if you knew a friend of mine from school, Toby Darbyshire. He's in the Royal Dragoon Guards. But you're in the Household Cavalry.'

'I'm afraid so.'

'So you don't know him then?'

'I'm terribly sorry but I don't think so, no.'

Hugo leaned back in his seat.

'So, what was it really like in Afghanistan? We get so

much information over here through the papers, but you wonder, you know, what it's really like.'

'Oh, I'm sure if you've seen it on television and things then you've seen what it's like,' Gerald said, and smiled at the table. I liked him. There is always modesty in disclaiming specialist knowledge of a subject in which others are interested.

'Oh yes, yes, but come on, there must be an inside story. What's it really like on the ground, out there among Terry?'

'Terry?'

'Terry Taliban!'

'Oh. Oh it's, it's very cold. In Helmand, I mean. I know it looks hot sometimes because it looks dusty on the television, but it's really very cold.'

'And what are they actually like? The Afghans, I mean.'

The question seemed to animate him, to wake him for a moment from his civilian slumber.

'They're good men. Bloody good men. And tough. But they don't really want the same things as us. Elections and women's rights and things. They just want to be allowed to have music and dance at their weddings. And that makes it a bit tricky. But they're bloody good men. Excuse my French,' he said to Don Joan, remembering himself.

'It's quite all right, dear. I've been teaching French for forty years.'

Lisa laughed, and put her hand on her fiancé's arm.

'Does anyone mind if I spark up a fag?' Hugo asked the table.

People waved their consent. Don Joan looked annoyed but did not positively protest. He removed the packet from his blazer pocket and tilted it towards my wife, who was setting warm plates on the table. Quite apart from the artists rule, Cee hates smoking in between courses. She thinks, quite rightly, that it leaves an aftertaste in everybody's food. To my surprise she smiled at Hugo, and nodded her acceptance. It was a new pack. Hugo picked at the cellophane tab a couple of times with the nail of his index finger, and caught it. Whilst he made these attempts, Cee stood over the table in the exposed attitude of someone smiling whilst waiting for a photograph to be taken. He pulled off the cellophane, scrunched it and placed the clear plastic ball on his side plate. He removed the silver paper and flicked the bottom of the packet with a practised motion. As with a cheap magician summoning cards, two cigarettes jumped obediently from the packet. He took them both in his mouth and lit them with a Zippo lighter. Then he passed one from his mouth to Cee. Don Joan cleared her throat. Hugo exhaled smoke from his cigarette over my wine, and I felt a momentary but pleasingly intense desire to feed the hot end to his eye.

'This wallpaper is quite beautiful, Cecilia,' Magda said. 'Where did you find it?'

Dinner continued, and the enchantment of Cee's calculation fell over the scene. New friends were being made, and in each of the conversations a pleasant little world was being reconstructed from first principles. Bottles of wine were drained and replaced without ceremony.

I had not really been listening to Hugo, and had been talking to Don Joan. Cee had discussed with him some of the practical arrangements for her imminent business trip to the stately home in Buckinghamshire, but was too good a hostess to allow such a conversation to run on, and had engaged with Lisa and Magda. It so happened that each of us concluded our respective dialogues at the same time, and became aware that Hugo was talking in the declarative fashion that indicates an open discussion. All five of us looked towards him without any collusion. It was one of those strange turns in conversation that leave one man, quite without design, carrying the attention of the entire table. I always feel for someone when this happens, for if a joke falls flat in front of two or three people beneath the cover of other voices and laughter it can be glossed over. A failed anecdote before an entire audience of silent listeners can lead to abject humiliation. Hugo must have noticed the sudden increase in the burden of expectation, but he simply ploughed on with what he was saying, acknowledging the change in circumstances by turning his body away from Gerald and down the length of the room.

'My feeling is – and I don't know if you agree with me, Gerry – but my feeling is that our generation has been shaped by two real conflicts. Now, pretty much everyone from my year at school, they either went into the City or the Army. The chaps in the City had the fall of Lehman Brothers, and the chaps in the Army had the war in Afghanistan. Now, don't get me wrong, I'm not saying that the chaps in the City were dodging bullets, I'm not saying that, you understand! But it did get pretty hairy back here for a while, Gerry, let me tell you . . .'

'Yes, I suppose so.' Gerald smiled with infinite mildness, and looked down at his plate.

'And you know, the stakes in Afghanistan were pretty high, God knows they were, global terrorism and the Taliban and all that . . . but the stakes back here were almost higher, in a way, if you get my line of thinking. I mean after Lehman Brothers fell, there were a good few days where it looked like the end of western capitalism, you know. When Congress refused to approve the TARP, and the losses came out at RBS. Ah, the TARP? Troubled

Asset Relief Plan, there's no reason for you to know. The end of our civilization. And that was something even Osama bin Laden didn't manage. Lehman Brothers used to be in the building next door to the Twin Towers, and you know what they did the day after 9/11? They set up in a hotel just down the road and kept on trading. Hundreds of porters carrying beds down to the street and desks into the lobby, and this with paper and dust from the towers still in the air. Now picture that, all these bankers who couldn't be stopped with an explosion in the building next door, and the Credit Crunch stopped them dead in their tracks! So in a way, you see, the conflict in the markets has been even more serious for this country than the conflict in the Middle East.'

'Afghanistan is in central Asia,' Lisa said. From the angle of the portion of her forearm visible above the table, I guessed that her hand was on her lover's leg. Her eyes beneath their bejewelled false lashes were cold. Gerald himself had not looked up from his plate, but the same utterly mild smile suffused his expression. I wondered what things he had told her in the privacy of their bedroom, where darkness and silence smooth the way for confession, and whether he slept easy. I wondered what her bohemian artist friends made of him, or his officer chums of her. I glanced over at Don Joan, and her eyebrows looked as if they were straining to escape the orbit of her sockets and fling themselves into the white thicket of her hairline. Cee, constrained by the need to be seen to think the best of Hugo, held her wine glass and smiled at him politely.

'Ah, central Asia then. But the point is the real heroes, of course, they're men like you, you know. I mean, I read about what you did in the papers and I know you won't talk about it, but I don't mind telling everybody here it was bloody amazing. He went out under enemy sniper fire and dragged an injured soldier a hundred metres back to cover in the middle of a firefight. Now, I won't have anyone say that's not heroic. I won't have anyone say that men who do those kinds of things shouldn't get medals. And of course there's the business of medical care and pensions and so forth, and you people deserve the very best. But in a way, the people who really kept things going – I mean, the ones who really preserved our way of life – well, they were the people who kept the money flowing back home. I'm told some of these chaps can expect a gong in the New Year's Honours list. And quite right too, you know. Because if it wasn't for men like them we might not be sitting here at all.'

The volume of Hugo's voice had risen during his peroration, and he was leaning over and speaking quite close to Gerald's ear. I saw the young man wince again, and thought about the delicate mechanism of his cochlea.

'Shut up.' Lisa was white with fury.

The words slapped Hugo across the face. She said them quite quietly, but with an intensity of feeling that made the glassware sing. He was one of those men that smile when they have been embarrassed in order to pretend that they have not.

'Excuse me?'

'Shut up. Shut your mouth. You don't know what you're talking about.'

For the first time since Hugo had begun speaking, Gerald raised his eyes from the table and looked at him. Cee's mouth had fallen open. Magda looked down at the table, red with shame.

Hugo laughed. 'Well, actually, young lady, I'm rather afraid that I do. In fact I probably know a damn sight more about the real world than a Goldsmith's graduate working in a trendy gallery.'

This was not the end of the speech, but what more Hugo had to tell us about the real world was lost to posterity, for at that point Gerald brought his fist down on the table. It made the room jump, occupants, cutlery, furniture and all. I would not have been surprised if a painting fell off the wall in our neighbour's drawing room. I watched Gerald's face as he looked at Hugo. He looked . . . magnificent. Lethal. His love and fury had transmuted this polite, slightly bland young man into the warrior of the epics. The promise of violence in defence of his woman made him the hero I had imagined. It filled me with an admiration that rather unbalanced me, for its shadow was a sense of my own inadequacy.

A silence descended on the table, and I wanted to hug Don Joan when she said, 'There is one thing I was hoping a military man could clear up for me, Gerald. Now, I understand that the metal for the Victoria Cross was originally taken from one of two bronze cannons captured at Sevastopol during the Crimean War. What do you think they'll do when the metal runs out?'

The moment was forgotten over the course of dinner, and by the time the cafetière was empty it had become the subject of amusement, as Lisa and Don Joan took turns banging the table. Hugo did not join in directly, but he laughed, and Gerald smiled his shy smile, as happy to deprecate his moment of anger as he was any other part of his persona. As the guests were gathering on the doorstep to say goodbye, Don Joan took me by the arm and looked up into my eyes, and claimed an old lady's right in having me come and help her find her purse, which she seemed to have misplaced. Don Joan had never misplaced anything in her life, and whenever she referred to herself as an old lady it was a sure indication that she was plotting something. I smiled at her and said of course I would help her, and the two of us parted from the scuffle of summer coats and kisses and walked back into the kitchen, where the candles were still burning and the smell of cigarette smoke and open wine hung in the air. She walked over to the seat which had been hers, beside which lay her purse on the table. She picked it up without ceremony, and for a few moments she seemed lost in thought, contemplating the cheese plates and half-empty glasses like a general reviewing a battlefield on which his troops have won, but at great cost.

'I see you found your purse then,' I said, to recall her from her reverie.

'Yes. Yes, thank you. Here it is.'

'I needn't have come at all really.'

She looked up from the table, catching my meaning, and smiled. She looked younger when she smiled, for although age had worried the flesh, the feelings that gave it expression were as sharp as ever.

'No. But you were always such a good boy. I wanted a quick word alone with you before I left.'

'Yes?'

'Are you and Cee getting on all right?'

I was completely taken aback by this question.

'We're fine,' I said. She nodded to indicate that she had understood my answer as meaning both that we were not and that I did not wish to talk about it.

'That's good. I've known the both of you a long time. I was worried watching the two of you tonight that familiarity might have dulled your sense of appreciation. I was going to tell you, if it turned out you did need a bit of perspective, that I still sift every new year of undergraduates looking for a couple as beautiful and lovely as the two of you were together, and I haven't found one yet.'

'That's very . . . that's kind of you to say, Joan.'

'It's no more or less than the truth.'

'You don't think you might be a bit partial?'

'Silly boy. If I am partial, the feelings grew out of observing a beautiful and lovely couple. And if you ever did need to talk to someone . . .'

'I understand.'

We were facing each other in the candlelight. As she looked at me, with her unflinching insight and desire for my happiness, I wanted desperately to shoo her out of the house. I could not stand the imposition of her goodwill, the goading of my emotions into a painful response. I could not stand the thought that soon – maybe not this year or next or even five years after that, but soon – she would die, and because of this cord of love between us the weight of her body falling from the mountain-face would rip me away from the ledge I had found, where neither hand nor foot was obliged to grip, but a cold and sedentary stability might be maintained. Perhaps I was already slipping; holding on had become more difficult every day since I had met the Swansons, and I could not absorb any additional grief. Even in the low light, I could make out the skin of her scalp beneath her fine white hair, spotted like the pages of an old book. The pale pink hearing aid curled inside the shell of her ear. Then I heard Hugo's laughter in the street, and I leaned forward and hugged her gently, feeling the delicacy of her bones.

'Oh! All right, you nancy boy, get off. You'll have me on my arse.'

She made towards the door, and we heard Cee calling the end of a protracted farewell on the doorstep. She turned back to me and said, 'Oh, and look, that girl you were talking about . . .'

'Claudia McEwen?'

'Claudia, yes. As it happens I did hear something at the

time. She was involved in some kind of car accident in Italy. I believe her passenger was killed. She spent several weeks in hospital, though from what I have been told it was her mental health that really kept her from returning to complete her studies. I didn't want to parade her gossip in front of that awful property man. I think he's extremely lucky Gerald didn't take his head off. I'm not telling tales, you understand, I thought it best to tell you, if only to stop Cee steaming in and asking her outright. I trust you will be discreet yourself?'

Cee came back into the room offering to help with the hunt for the purse. Don Joan's taxi was still waiting outside, the engine idling. The faint sound of Bhangra music emanated from the closed windows. We waved her off from the step, and then the two of us went back in to confront the mess, and load the dishwasher before bed.

As we were undressing, she said, with unaccustomed timidity, 'I think Hugo was incredibly rude tonight.'

It was the loveliest thing she could have said, and I wanted to rise to her example. 'Oh no, he wasn't really. I think he genuinely wanted to hear from Gerald, because he looks up to him a bit. And though I completely understand his reaction, Gerald might have been a little bit more forthcoming, rather than just letting him wank on and then scaring the crap out of him.'

Cee's face softened with relief. In the light of the bedside lamp she looked quite beautiful. 'Sweetheart, do you think it was a terrible evening?'

'No! No, it was wonderful. Not without its fraught moments, but you know, I think a little bit of conflict adds spice to an evening. It's so boring when everyone just agrees and gets on and nothing controversial is said or done. We both hate dinner parties like that – that's half the reason why we like throwing our own. Do you remember . . .'

And here the two of us exchanged anecdotes whilst we moved in familiar patterns around our bedroom, folding clothes and closing drawers, applying the creams that stave off age and the pastes that fight decay, affirming a decade and a half's partnership. There was the time the Jewish artist had thrown coffee over the journalist from the BBC for repeatedly referring to Palestine as a country, the time the New Labour parliamentary assistant had accused the energy lobbyist of undermining democracy, the evening when the Marxist professor had taken the knife and fork from the investment analyst and refused to return them until the latter conceded the exploitative nature of profit, causing the analyst to eat a wild boar ragu with his hands. Each story was exaggerated almost to the proportions of an outright lie, but we silently agreed to suspend our disbelief. The recapitulation of our oral history reminded each one of us of the store of love with which we had set out on our lives together. When my wife came to bed, she did not wear the T-shirt and shorts that lately had lain under her pillow, but came softly naked as she used to. We made love, and we were happy, but as I lay with her head on my chest I was conscious also that this was the furthest we could ever now go with our happiness – this friendly harmony. You often hear people talk of the moment they realized a relationship was over, but it always seems to be the worst of times, the level below which they could not allow themselves to sink. What happens when after long absence one reaches again the uppermost level of joy, and finds it suddenly too close to the earth? In the end the night was too hot to lie together. Cee's hair on my chest drew prickly sweat, and we moved to opposite sides of the bed.

After Cee fell asleep I lay awake and thought about what Don Joan had told me. I thought about Gerald, his ears now incapable of the absorption of passionate conversation or music without pain. I wondered if he would ever be able to go to the opera when he developed a taste for such things, and how he would deal with a baby's ear-splitting screams. I felt ashamed at how little his sacrifice had changed my life. Thinking back on Hugo's speech, I realized it had been so insensitive not only because it patronized Gerald and the experiences of his comrades, but because it risked being true. How silly was his heroism, the lives lost in the deserts and all the medals forged from the spoils of nineteenth-century wars, when the real threat to our country's stability came from overweight white thirty-year-olds clicking buttons in Canary Wharf, and was best addressed by clever men in offices. I mourned the loss of that martial significance, and the dawn of the age of grey suits. It was the Hugos and Jim Swansons of the world who had between them seen off romance.

I thought too about the image of Claudia on the step, all her suffering held down inside her. I am not now, nor have I ever been, one of those who is aroused by female pathos. Give me a choice between the picturesque brunette crying tears from her doe-like eyes as she sits alone on the promenade watching the sea, and the drunk blonde in stilettos flashing her breasts to the dance floor from her vantage point on top of the bar, and I'm ordering three more strawberry daiquiris for Michelle and her friends every time. I mistrust the kind of men who are drawn to women they think they can help, because it seems to me a creepy fetishization of female vulnerability. Such men derive self-esteem from playing the role of hero, which leaves the awkward question of how they see the woman after the crisis has passed. My feelings towards Claudia, although they were undoubtedly influenced by this story and by the stoicism which she had displayed in the face of her miscarriage, were not carried along by the mere fact of sympathy at her suffering, or a desire to make her better.

In order to explain what I felt, I'm afraid I'll have to impart a brief (a very brief) lecture, only because if I don't do that, I'm worried I will come across as purely ridiculous. I'm happy for someone to think me ridiculous, but not on the basis of a misunderstanding. When the West first began to think about itself in literary terms, the Greek playwrights formulated a concept of tragedy based on the fate of heroes. Our tragedy as mortals lay in the inevitability of our destiny, and to inspire our fear and pity at the spectacle we were provided with the sight of the very best of us, of Achilles and Hercules and Oedipus, groaning under the yoke of fate as capricious gods cracked the whip.

When the English came to consider the same point, we formulated tragedy not as a divinely imposed destiny, but rather one resulting from character. Psychology was the prime mover from which all the subsequent action flowed, and, as one critic observed, Othello in Hamlet's play, or Hamlet in Othello's, would have had no problems. The Moor would stroll off the battlements in Act 1 Scene 2, go straight to Claudius's chamber, ramble on a bit about how he once stormed a castle and found some other potentate cowering in his pyjamas during a distant campaign, and then smite him, before going on to conquer Norway. The Dane would have run rings round Iago with witty word-play until the arch villain broke down in a blubbering confession, and offered to eat Desdemona's handkerchief by way of apology. But these men were betrayed to circumstance by their particular qualities, and again they were not so much men as paragons of humanity. Like the half-gods Achilles and Hercules, they were heroes, 'the soldier's, scholar's, eye, tongue, sword', the 'full soldier'. Still no room for mortals in these tragedies, we can only observe with fear and pity the fates of our betters.

Come the turn of the century, Ibsen and then Brecht gave us tragedy again, not this time in the guise of destiny, or of character, but of socio-economic position. Your fate is the place you are born in society; your tragedy will be the tale of your struggle to break through the bonds of class expectation. You will inherit from your father and your mother a fatal dose of social position. Even at this relatively late stage in literature, however, we see the tragic figure as heroic, whether it be the allegorical stature of Mother Courage or the indomitable will of Hedda Gabler.

It's not until you get to Joyce that the convention of the tragic hero starts to slip. *Ulysses* was a book based on the premise that to survive even a single day in twentieth-century Dublin was a heroic act. That simply to amble from one pub to the next in search of a bit of lunch without becoming overwhelmed by the conflicting currents of duty and place and time and understanding, ideas and wars and newspapers and adverts, desires and hatreds and confusions and trams and irritable bowels, was to accomplish a heroic journey worthy of its own epic narration. Post-modern writers really took up the baton and ran with it, until eventually all the heroic features of a tragic protagonist were gone; as Roth puts it, 'The tragedy of the man not set up for tragedy – that is every man's tragedy.' The day of the hero was past. The everyman reigned. Tragedy was become a democracy.

I was aware that to view Claudia, an urban housewife

I hardly knew, as a figure capable of overturning the discourse of a half-century of western thought was perhaps to overburden the lover's privilege of reading unlikely virtues into the brow of his beloved. I was equally aware that Claudia was not a character in literature, and that her story was in many respects quite mundane, and, beside the daily diet of genocide available on television, perhaps even trifling. But there was in her nonetheless some enduring . . . seriousness. There was something faintly classical in going away to learn with a passion for your subject and culture, and being driven to madness as the unwitting instrument of death. There was equally a kind of cosmic injustice in surviving this, in restoring to yourself some sense of happiness, only to be struck by the second calamity I had witnessed on the stairs. Most of all, however, in coping with both of these episodes, there was something in her, a transcendent quality of calm endurance that had saved her both from the destructive force of the events themselves, and from the active courting of victimhood which was the worst of modern vices. I felt that, more than Cee, more than our friends, certainly more than myself, more even than Don Joan, here was someone I might take seriously. Take one person seriously, just one, and the world again becomes a serious place. I repeated her name to myself, each iteration like a smooth rosary bead between my fingertips: Claudia, Claudia, Claudia . . .

Some hours later, with the first light of dawn touching the curtains, I started from a nightmare forgotten in the instant of waking, and found a thought delivered to me fully formed, like a black-bordered letter leaning neatly against the teapot on a breakfast tray. If Claudia was indeed a tragic figure, if that was part of the fascination she held for me, how could I attain her register? I could no more kiss her than the Fool could snog Cordelia. Suffering had granted her a reprieve from inauthenticity; she was free to feel and to mean with the power of a vanished age. For myself, I had nothing, no disaster to scrub the film of trivia from my skin. All my feelings were mediated through what I had read and watched on the television; how would I dare present myself to her? The answer was inescapable. I would have to remake myself by some specific deed, to find some action that would elevate me to the same plane of meaning. I would have to engineer my own tragedy.

# 8

THE NEXT DAY I CALLED THE SWANSONS' HOUSE TO SPEAK to Claudia, and to check on her recovery. As I waited for her to pick up, my throat was so dry that I could not swallow. The rings sounded, and I projected myself into their home. Where would she be? Downstairs cooking again, or upstairs in bed? Not upstairs: that was the second ring gone and the bedside phone was on the nightstand. In the kitchen then. Striding forward to take the portable phone from its cradle on the marble countertop. Her cool hand stretching out . . . No, not the kitchen. Three rings and she still had not picked up. Was she in the shower? Downstairs in the basement? The phone rang through to the answering machine, and I hung up before it had a chance to record my silence.

I went to Cee's contact book. We kept lists of all our clients' work and mobile numbers in case of emergency – the burst water-pipe, the broken burglar alarm, the sudden scarcity of high-quality carpets. The contact book was kept in a drawer in her study, and I was aware as I delved into it of a distinct air of trespass. Whether I felt naughty for simply plundering her private space, or whether the naughtiness was heightened by the fact it was Claudia I was calling, I could not tell. When I had found the number I left the book ostentatiously on the glass surface of the desk itself, beside the closed Mac, so there could be no accusations of subterfuge. I did, however, take the trouble to close it, so that the book would not be open to a page bearing the Swansons' name.

I called the number (ignoring the fact that the screen of my mobile harboured several missed calls from Laura Rees), and trembled as I waited for Claudia's voice to appear from the ether. It was a delicious and agonizing suspense. Halfway through the third ring, the pressing of a button cut the tone short and a man's voice said, 'Speak to me.'

'Uh . . . hello?'

'Yes. Who's this?'

'This is . . . this is Matt.'

'Matt who?'

I realized suddenly I was speaking to Jim Swanson, though the identification did nothing to lessen my confusion. Rather it increased the awkwardness of the situation.

'Matt de Voy, Mr Swanson.' At least having figured out who it was I could pretend to have called him on purpose.

'Matt . . . ? Oh, the library guy. Look, Matt, I don't mean to be rude but you've got me at work. Can we speak tonight?'

'Of course. I just wanted to check on Claudia. How she was, I mean.'

'Yeah, well.' Here I heard muffled shouting in the background, as Jim excused himself from his desk. There was a further series of muffled bumps, and then the background noise on the other end of the line appeared to vanish with the closing of a door.

'OK, we can speak now.'

His voice had a slight echo. I guessed at the weird

atmosphere of a forty-floor internal fire escape.

'I really am sorry, I should call back tonight.'

'Cheers for sitting with Claudia when it happened. I owe you one for that.'

'No, no, it's quite all right. I wasn't much use . . .'

'Yeah, but thanks for being there.'

'Oh. No, of course, that's fine. Look, I actually called to check if Mrs Swanson was OK.'

There was a pause on the other end of the line, and the sound of Jim clicking his tongue. It was clear that he was deciding whether or not to tell me something he considered private.

'She's not that great, as it goes. There was some kind of complication. Anyway, she had to stay in for a few days, for observation. She's on the mend now though. Should be out in a day or two.'

I felt a great pang of fear for her at this description.

'So she's out of danger now, yes?'

'Yes.'

'At the Chelsea and Westminster, right?'

'The Lister now.'

'Can she have visitors?' It just slipped out.

There was a pause on the other end of the line.

'Yes. I visit.'

'Oh, fantastic. It's just that Cee, my wife, wanted to take her some flowers or something like that. And maybe run her through some fabric swatches and things if she's up to it. I know it can get pretty dull being in bed all the time . . .'

'Fine.' The background noise of the office suddenly came back on the line. I could visualize the pale face of a junior leaning into the room, the atmosphere of suppressed crisis bleeding in from the trading desks behind him.

'Listen, Matt, I have to go.'

'Of course, I understand. It's my own fault; in my line of work there's a tendency to forget that other people lead rather more grown-up lives . . .' I became aware I was speaking to a dead line. I cursed Jim Swanson.

Two days after the dinner party, I went to visit Mrs Swanson in her room at the Lister Hospital. This private establishment succeeds in giving the impression that anyone with enough money to afford its bright, hygienic attentions is too well-off to be inconvenienced with death. It was mercifully cool after the heat of the day.

I had not rung ahead to inform Claudia of my visit. I felt that the conversation with Jim had been more than enough warning, and that if I was unwelcome I would have been informed. I did not want to risk having this assumption disconfirmed by actually checking for myself whether or not she wanted to see me. This course had seemed eminently sensible in the previous twenty-four hours, when my cowardice made a virtue of this generous unwillingness to disturb her with troublesome phone calls, but as I took direction from the receptionist and made my way up to the third floor it seemed increasingly foolhardy. The last time I had seen her, she had been planning to banish me for ever for my clumsy attempt at seduction. More than that, might seeing me again trigger a flashback to the miscarriage itself? Could my appearance in her doorway cause some kind of relapse, brought on by the stress of the association? I brushed these thoughts aside with the fact that Jim Swanson was not a man to leave his wife unprotected if protection were required, but they still fed into a general uneasiness as I came close to her room.

She was sitting up in bed, propped on a heap of pillows and wearing a surgical gown patterned in the manner of unfashionable wallpaper. The rules of the hospital obviously precluded stylists, as her hair had become rather frizzed. There was a saline drip on a metal stand beside the bed, the stand mounted on wheels to facilitate trips to the toilet (I felt an obscure sense of relief that she did not require the use of a bedpan). Despite all this, she looked quite wonderful, her beauty as resilient as her spirit. The room itself looked like a florists.

She was listening to a portable CD player when I entered, and she did not immediately register my presence. She was obviously listening to a book. I could tell because her lips moved slightly with the words. As I watched her from the doorway, I found myself wishing that I had jacked in English and taken a medical degree, studied and worked for several years against my artistic proclivities, endured the endless jokes and innuendo facing a man choosing to specialize in gynaecology, jettisoned any left-wing notions of public service in order to enter the private sector, and attached myself to the stultifying excellence of the Lister, just so I might have had some hand in making Claudia Swanson better. And indeed have caught a legitimate glimpse under her nightgown. I felt my apprehension intensify with every moment I remained unacknowledged on the threshold of her room. It had mounted almost to an unbearable pitch before she finally looked up, and when her first reaction was a smile a great relief washed through me.

'We bought you a fruit basket to assist with your recovery. I don't know why a pineapple wrapped in clear plastic would be of medical assistance, but one is included just in case.'

'That was very kind of you. And Cee. Will you thank her for me?'

'Of course. Only I feel almost embarrassed, with all

these.' I indicated the profusion of foliage with a sweep of my hand. 'It seems a rather paltry gift.'

'Oh, no, Jim's cornered the market. It's led to artificial gift inflation. Pretty much all these are from him.'

'He loves you very much,' I said, looking at the flowers.

'Yes, he does. There are so many of them the nurses have to put them in a separate room at night. Apparently they breathe themselves, even after the stems have been cut, and they're worried they might take up all the oxygen.'

'Suffocated by your husband's get-well flowers?'

Claudia smiled, leaned her head back on the pillow, poked her tongue out of the corner of her mouth and let her eyes roll back in her head.

'Actually, I think it's me who should be sending you flowers,' she said, resurrecting. 'I wanted to say thank you, for being so good the afternoon it happened.'

'I didn't do anything at all.'

'You stayed calm. That was all I needed, and you stayed and you talked to me until Jim got there. Also, you pissed me off a bit, and that was really helpful. It was a great comfort at that point, to be really annoyed with someone.'

'Well, that is something I am very good at.'

'You'll get a thank you in the post, just as soon as I find a "Thank you for pissing me off during my miscarriage" card.'

It was my turn to smile. It was a strange feeling, but with her I felt I shrugged off the winter coat of social nicety, which always made me sweat indoors. She said what she thought, giving others the freedom to do the same, and seemed completely unaware of how exceptional this quality made her. The majority of people who think themselves plain speakers are in fact afflicted with the winning combination of rudeness and self-delusion. When Claudia was rude, it was the truth and not she that was unpleasant. I found myself wondering whether she was wearing anything under her surgical gown, or whether if she had to be helped to her feet to head to the loos I might get an uninterrupted vision of her naked back. I pictured an alluring network of scars. I dispelled the image with a metaphorical shake of the head, and it was only when Claudia's expression changed that I realized I had made the metaphor literal.

'Are you all right?'

'I . . . yes, I'm sorry, I just . . . twitched.'

'All right. Oh, listen, I read that book you lent me. I wanted to give it back to you.'

'Oh yes?'

'Yes. But, look, this is quite embarrassing, ah, there's a thumbprint. I mean, there's blood. I didn't mean to. Anyway, I'm sorry.'

She retrieved the book from a drawer in her bedside table. I took it in my hands. I waited for the internal wince. I opened it, and turned through the pages looking for the terrible thumbprint, the mark that would make the whole book uncollectible. I found it on the front flyleaf, and felt . . . well, actually, strangely aroused. Her blood was in the page. It was like a little sign meant just for me, an inscription in the book she was giving back to me. It was a hieroglyph as meaningful in its way as any of the printed passages. Pleasing, this evidence that our thoughts had crossed paths within the pages.

'Oh, forget that, please, it's completely irrelevant.'

'But is it not a first edition or a collector's something? I mean I looked and I thought it might be . . .'

151

'No, no, it's just an old copy. I picked it up from a second-hand bookstall as I hadn't read it in a while.'

She observed me with her head cocked on one side. I tried to give a look of complete openness. If there is one thing I have become good at over the years, it is counterfeiting sincerity, but she had a collector's eye for the truth.

I sat down on the chair beside the bed and talked about the book with her. I was pathetically grateful to the gods of chance for actually having reread the thing, though it was she who had inspired me to do so. We talked about moments when we felt ourselves understood by the dead author in a way that no friend or lover had ever understood us. The walls of the hospital disappeared, and the afternoon went with them. It was an effect I had begun to associate with Claudia, this warping of time. When we talked about the book's bloody denouement, she said, 'I liked the way he murdered her in the end.'

'How do you mean?' I asked her.

'Just . . . calmly. The way he drowns her in the bath. And he holds her under with his golfer's hands. I love that. And all the time you have Chamberlain's voice on the radio, telling Britain they are at war with Germany, and the narrator calls it nonsense. It seems so right, that murdering someone you love and hate should be logical, a normal part of life like your grip on a golf club, whilst heading overseas to murder a bunch of strangers because someone you've never met says you ought to is nonsense.'

Her idea struck me then, and was to stay with me for many days.

It was the entrance of a nurse that eventually brought the afternoon back in. She had come to administer some routine check or procedure, and Claudia remarked she couldn't believe it was that time already. The pleasant nurse said she could come back, but I said I had to be going myself. She gave us five minutes to say goodbye.

'Look, I've really enjoyed myself this afternoon. I've been so bored in here, you know. Jim and all my friends work in the day, and he comes round to see me every night, but he's so tired. Plus it's so nice just to talk about books.'

'You can't talk to Jim about books?'

She coloured a little. 'Of course I can. It's just, we talk about other things.'

'I understand.'

'I know this might be a bit weird, but, I mean, can we talk like this again? I'll pay, of course. Well, I'll ask Jim if he'll pay. I don't mean to take advantage of you or take up your professional time or anything. Unless it's like a chef never wanting to eat? I mean, you spend all day handling books for money so the idea of talking about them in your free time . . .'

It was quite impossible that Jim should pay. If Jim paid, the amounts would be credited to the company accounts. I could hardly ask for cash in hand. The company accounts were Cee's domain. It had never required the slightest fraud or effort on my part to convince her that the clients with whom I had affairs required further assistance with interior design, but to convince her that for the first time ever a beautiful young woman wanted to pay me to sit around and talk about books (a subject on which Cee herself had been known to bribe me to shut up) was out of the question. Strange to tell, there was an imperative almost greater than the need for deception – I felt an obscure resentment at the idea that our conversations should be undertaken on the basis that one of us was being paid to be there.

'God no, no. I mean, no, I don't feel like a chef and no, I don't want you to pay. Or Jim, I mean Mr Swanson, to pay. Look, the truth is I enjoyed it too. I never get to talk about books myself. I remember when we had our first consultation, I was embarrassed because I just assumed you'd only be interested in what the books looked like, and how much they cost. But to talk about them again, that would be great. I've had a really wonderful afternoon.'

She looked down, blushing with pleasure, rightly understanding what I had said as the highest (sincere) compliment I had paid anyone in years.

'Oh, I couldn't not pay you . . .'

'I wouldn't take your money.'

'Jim's money.'

'Mr Swanson's money. If you're happy with the idea, why don't I just arrange the money side with Cecilia? We can add a little extra on to your final bill. That way neither one of us has to go through this ridiculous English pantomime.'

She nodded, 'OK, and I'll talk to Jim.'

It was clearly an inflexible point for her that her husband should know about these meetings if they were to take place. I had no intention of informing Cee that we were engaged in anything beyond a general discussion of the library.

'Done. Is there any book in particular you'd like me to bring you?'

'Actually I've got a bit of a request. The ward here has a kind of mini-library, and it's almost completely full of novels with heaving bosoms and tight jodhpurs. The only thing I could find to read after I'd finished your book was *Nineteen Eighty-Four*. Could we talk about that?'

'Of course we could. But wasn't that on the banned list?'

'Yes, it was. I'm impressed you remember. I thought I might try to narrow down the banned list.' She smiled, but moved on quickly before I could comment further. 'Anyway, do you have a copy?'

'No,' I said, 'but I'll pick one up on the way home.' I did have a copy of course, the 1949 Secker and Warburg first edition in red dust jacket (the book was published in two different jackets in its first edition, a red and a green, though the red is slightly less common).

'Well . . . thank you then.'

I raised my hand and turned to go, desperate now that an excuse for a further meeting had been arranged to get away.

'Oh,' she said, 'will you call me to tell me when? Or do I call you? Only I don't think I have your number . . .'

'Please, let me have yours and I'll give you a missed call,' I said, returning to the bedside. She entered her number with careful fingertips. When she did so her tongue poked out of the corner of her mouth, a little pink escapee from the tower of her dignity.

'I should be out of here tomorrow.'

'We can meet then.'

'Will that be enough time for you to finish the book?'

'I read pretty quickly.'

'I'm a bit scared,' she said.

'Why?'

'Well . . . I don't know if I remember how to talk about books. How to analyse them. I'm worried you'll think I'm ignorant.'

I was delighted by her deference.

'Oh no! You talk very well! All you have to remember is that the author is dead. What the writer intended has no significance. Only what you find in the text has meaning. If you see something, and have the evidence to back it up, it's there.'

She smiled, but there was something a little uncertain in it. 'That sounds a bit mad.'

Because of her reclining position, any normal goodbye was made impossible. To shake her hand was ridiculous, to lean down to kiss her cheek in the midst of her bed-clothes seemed too intimate. I gave a cheery and idiotic little wave in the doorway.

Hindsight is a curious thing, because there is in all of us a vault of infinite recall. All the details of our experience are stored there, and it is only the indexing system which lets us down. Schopenhauer said, 'We only remember our own lives about as well as a novel we once read,' and I have always taken that as a comment on the importance of books rather than the frailty of human memory. But the fact remains that the vast majority of the information we take in is simply filed under the wrong letter, and try as we might to bring it up from storage, we cannot know where even to begin to look. So it is with great uncertainty that I mention the unprepossessing figure in the Puffa jacket sitting reading a magazine in the waiting room. Did I see someone there? Did I add someone to the picture in the light of later events? Was the brandless T-shirt and baseball cap sufficiently conspicuous among all those moneyed button-down collars to draw my eye? I can't say.

On the way out of the hospital I ran into Jim Swanson. I stopped on the steps, and he continued to ascend a few steps above me, so that when he turned to shake my hand he was looking down on me. Strangely, he did not seem surprised to see me. I was rather more ruffled by the encounter than he was himself. To my amusement, he was carrying yet another bunch of flowers with which to unconsciously suffocate his wife. He might have noticed the slight sneer with which I regarded it, as he made no attempt to hide his displeasure at seeing me.

'What are you doing here?'

'Oh, well, since you mentioned that your wife could have visitors, I thought I'd bring down the fabric samples we discussed. I must congratulate you on all the flowers.'

'You said your wife was coming.'

Jim Swanson was possessed of an extraordinary bluntness. It was an un-English quality, and I resented it, for it revealed to me how much of my superiority in conversation was based on an expertly tuned judgement of what others would be unwilling to say. It was a critical refinement which allowed me to invite my enemies to collaborate in their own destruction. A good test for a real Englishman is to stand on his foot and wait for an apology – Jim Swanson looked like he would threaten you with a lawsuit. A lack of a proper education had apparently inoculated him against my most potent weapon, in the same manner that the milkmaids of the eighteenth century who stimulated the discovery of vaccination were immune to the smallpox that struck down their betters, having spent their youths rolling in dung.

'I did, I did,' I said, nodding emphatically, 'but unfortunately she was too busy.'

'You're lucky to be so busy. I thought property was shot.'

'Yes, it's bad out there.'

'Can I have a look at these samples, or does the bloke not get a say?' he said, looking at my hands, empty apart from the copy of *Hangover Square*.

As I smiled, and awaited the arrival of the charming and plausible explanation that would bat away this quite reasonable request, an odd thing showed up in its place. It was a complete hatred of Mr Swanson. It was a purified form of the thing that had gripped me in the hall of his house in the aftermath of the miscarriage, and also, I realized, the distant descendant of the distaste I had felt at our very first consultation. It was as if the many City husbands I had met before him slid between us like a magnifying glass between an ant and the sun. The gentle glow of my disdain, which nourished me and allowed my fat-cat clients to stretch and recline in its warm rays of flattery, was focused suddenly into a searing beam of loathing. It was so powerful that the surrounding landscape began to melt and run. The effect reminded me somewhat of the descriptions of hallucinations given by Huxley in *The Doors of Perception*, or of Van Gogh's 'Starry Night'. Everything around us – the trees of the park sighing in the breeze, the broad back of Chelsea Bridge in the summer sunshine, the glittering river and dull red brick, the throb of the heat from the tarmac – bowed to the primacy of that emotion and resolved themselves around Mr Swanson's unremarkable features, turned down towards me and expecting an answer. A bead of sweat made a break from my hairline.

'Ah, yes, I forgot them.'

'You forgot them?'

'Yes. But I had a basket of fruit, you see, so I thought I might as well deliver it.'

He looked at me, and to my horror a little smile crossed his mouth like a spider. It was clear that he entertained the notion that I was smitten with his wife. Smitten with his possession. I could see him stroking her on his lap atop his giant pile of money, smiling down at me. His was the triumph of the modern, the ignorant and the mundane. I wanted to throttle him there on the steps. I was prevented by the thought of how wonderful it would be when Claudia informed him that she had asked me to enter into regular tutorials.

'I'm going to go see her now.'

'Yes, of course. You must go. I have appointments myself. Have a great day.'

He entered the lobby, and I wiped the perspiration from my forehead.

# 9

I LEFT THE HOSPITAL, AND STOPPED OFF AT THE CHELSEA Booksellers on the King's Road for a copy of *Nineteen Eighty-Four*. They were all out, and I headed on to Daunt Books on the Fulham Road, who were similarly unprovided. At that point my desire to get hold of the thing overthrew my policy of never visiting chain shops, and I headed back, to the Waterstone's on the King's Road. Then another shop and another, and a final sweaty lunge to HMV (which I thought might feature the book as part of some sort of ridiculous 'rebellious youth' season). None of these outlets had it, and by that point I was gripped by the need to begin reading the book in the manner of a pregnant woman bent on a Marmite and marshmallow sandwich. There was nothing else for it. I returned home, and went into the kitchen to check if Cee was in. She was not. I ran upstairs to the library, and carefully removed my Mylar-bound first edition of *Nineteen Eighty-Four* from the shelf, and carried it reverently downstairs. I sat down at the table and read for over two hours.

Reading the first edition, which had sat on my shelf unmolested for almost five years, I felt the newness of the old ideas infuse me. Holding the sixty-year-old, £3,000 tome, I felt too a continuity with the past, with the author and also with the first generation of readers who had

had the good taste and foresight to read Orwell, and to recommend him to their friends. The words and the story and the style and the smell of the book folded into me as I read.

When Cee got home, she came over to me and stroked the back of my head absent-mindedly. Then she looked down and really saw the book for the first time. She picked it up and turned it over.

'Are you actually reading one of your first editions?'

'Yes. They are books, aren't they?'

'Yes, yes of course they are. It's just a surprise, that's all. You're usually so particular. You won't even let me open the curtains in the library.'

'That's true.'

'Don't get me wrong, I think it's wonderful,' she said, and kissed the top of my head. 'It really makes me happy to see you reading again. Maybe while I'm away on this trip you'll have more peace and quiet.'

She put the book carefully back down on the table and reached for my hand. For the rest of the evening I felt guilty about my intended treachery, in a way I had not in years. I cooked for Cee, something which I do not much like, but at which I am rather gifted. We ate together, and I asked her about her day and actually listened to her responses. Not since before the election-night dinner party had an adulterous liaison given me so much internal discomfort. And this one not even consummated!

Cee left for the hotel conversion three days later, and the day after that I had my first session with the freshly released Mrs Swanson. She looked much better than she had in the hospital, suggesting that the skein of ill-health that had lain over her on the wards had been largely the result of interrupted maintenance. Female beauty of even the most natural sort is something like the painting of the Forth Bridge – as soon as your work is finished at one end you have to begin again at the other, cycling from the painting of the toenails back to the plucking of the eyebrows. Sat once again on a stool in her kitchen, she looked radiant. The sight of her caused me to experience a confused impulse, pleasure at her recovery mixed with a renewed envy of her husband. When I asked her, she told me that she was entirely recovered, and that the incident had left no lasting damage.

We moved quite naturally into a discussion of the book. Claudia had the critical apparatus of the first three years of a four-year degree, a keen mind and an evident passion for literature. As our discussion gathered pace and complexity, it reminded me of an afternoon when I had watched two strangers begin to play a tennis match together from the balcony of Cee's family home in Hampshire. Each man had told the other they were not much good, and the first few balls found their casual way over the net to the mid-court, never troubling the opponent's return. When the first shot went awry, one of them leapt over to it and saved the rally with a tricky backhand, and it was then that the pace of the exchange began to change. Each of them sensed the false modesty in the other's claim to incompetence, and the ball began to move faster and faster over the net in the warm evening air, until at last the two strangers were sprinting across the grass, finding an unspoken consensus in their virtuosity.

At the end of an hour the two of us were flushed with mutual discovery. Conscious of a desire to be the first to call time, and not wanting the sensation to subside before I said my goodbyes, I told Claudia I had already taken up too much of her time. She smiled and nodded, but before

I rose from my stool at the breakfast bar I took the chance to ask her something.

'Look, I have to ask, what was the banned list about? I mean, you gave me that thing when I first came in, and I just thought, this is bizarre!'

I asked in a playful spirit. If I had known her better, I might have nudged her shoulder with a forefinger. But she took the question quite seriously, and looked at me searchingly before answering. I could actually feel the nature of our encounter changing with her decision.

'I wouldn't normally tell you this. Not because I think you'll judge me, though you might. Actually, I'm ashamed of it, I deserve to be judged. So I'm only telling you because you asked, and because I trust you not to be weird about it. A few years ago, I killed someone.'

'I know.'

'How do you know?'

'An old friend from Cambridge told me. She was a don there when you were studying. She didn't teach you but I imagine . . .' I didn't want to say I was sure it had been a common piece of campus gossip, but she understood and nodded.

'It was everything my dad could do to keep it out of the papers. So I was right to tell you. You won't be weird.'

'Did they . . . was there ever any question of your being in trouble?'

She nodded briskly, and scratched her nose. 'They held me and questioned me for a few days. They had very thick accents and I found it difficult to understand. But they couldn't work out a crime that fitted what I'd done.'

I coughed, and sat back on my chair.

'You want to know?' she said, and looked up at me from under her fringe. There was something slightly manic in the look, not that awkward pride that accompanies the confessions of the ex-addict, but rather a desire to tell me something that risked alienating me, that would either push me away or bind me to her.

'If you want to tell me, I want to hear it. Otherwise I don't.'

She looked a little disappointed at this. She had expected my curiosity to relieve her of responsibility. For a moment it seemed she might simply let the matter rest, but then she began to speak in the weary manner of someone assisting police with their inquiries, telling the same story for the fifth time, knowing they will not be believed.

'In Rome in my year abroad, I had a friend at college. We used to go out drinking together. She was . . . beautiful. Sweet. I kind of led her astray. We used to get so much attention, the two of us out together. We went to a party in this villa in the hills outside Rome in August. We both drank a lot, and Rose went off with this older guy who owned the place, and when she came back she said she was tired and she wanted to go home. She was so drunk she could barely talk. So I put her in the passenger seat of my Golf, blue, registration number SE5 7GH. I was wasted too and I couldn't be bothered to take her home, so I drove her to my place and parked on the little private drive outside. I think I tried to wake her, to get her to come into the house . . . but I didn't and all the windows were closed and when I woke up at midday it was thirty degrees and she was lying against the inside door and there was a fly on her tongue.'

'That's terrible. I'm sorry. Was Jim with you, during this?'

'I had been on a few dates with Jim just before I went off to Rome. I mean, I met him at the bank the summer before my first term abroad, and I liked him because he was so serious about what he was doing, he was really passionate about it, you know? Everyone I knew thought banking was boring, and I thought it was pretty boring myself, but it made a difference, to have someone in the office who really loved it and understood it. So I let him take me out to dinner a few times, and we had a kiss, but really I . . . I was seeing a few other boys, you know? And they were more fun. And then in Italy I could have had it easy because I'm not blonde, but I did the obligatory stupid northern European thing and fell for this complete dickhead with a Vespa, and then there were other men. It was the first time I'd really been abroad on my own, and I sort of went away from myself, just drinking and partying and taking drugs and . . .'

She frowned and shook her head.

'Everyone does that when they're young.'

'It made me . . . cynical. I didn't think much about Jim. But he kept on writing and writing, even when I hinted pretty strongly it would be over when I got back. I knew how little time he had in the office, so it made his emails a little bit more special, because he doesn't even stop for lunch. And he didn't do it in a creepy way, or a pushy way. He just obviously wanted to stay in my life, on whatever terms. All the same, I think I was actually pretty cruel by the end. I used to sit there with Rose and read his emails out loud and we'd giggle together, and she'd dare me to put in words in my emails back, like I had to use the word "badger" three times, and then after I'd sent it we'd lie on our backs on the balcony and smoke and talk about Carlo and Marco and Frank. Then this thing happened and I didn't want . . . For a long time I couldn't go outside. It sounds strange, but little things became unbearable. I mean, at first I really couldn't go out, I was in prison for about three days, and then the old guy who had had the party at his villa came and got me out. He just came and picked me up like it was a school and he was collecting me for a weekend out. He knew my name and he knew where I lived and he dropped me back at home and told me not to worry about anything. I hadn't told my parents because I was too ashamed, and when I came home I had to go to hospital for a bit, then back to Italy for the inquest, then I cut myself and went back to hospital. And there were other things, the smell of coffee, I had a cup of coffee in my hand when I found her . . . All the fun boys cleared off pretty sharpish when that happened. And my friends, the few I told, and my parents didn't really know how to handle it. Jim was the only person who was really there for me.'

'Your friends, what, they didn't talk to you?'

'No, they did, they did try, some of them tried really hard. It's just, they didn't really want to help me get better. They wanted me to be all right, which is a different thing. They wanted me to forgive myself and they didn't have the right, and that pissed me off. Anyway, that's where the banned list comes from. I was a real reader in Rome because I was supposed to be working at this school but I just never went. Rose was a bit better than me, she never skipped classes. So I just read and read and read in the days and went out at night. And with all my books I never felt alone. And all through the days when I wasn't with Rose I'd wander around the city thinking about those stories. Then when it happened I couldn't separate out the threads of feeling, you know? I had all these stories that gave me so much pleasure turning over in my mind, and this thing got mixed up in them, and it was like a thimbleful of poison in a great vat of the best wine, I had to just throw the whole thing away. I couldn't read at all for years after, not any book, let alone the ones on the banned list I'd actually read out there.'

'Is that where you got your scar?' I asked, not immediately considering its position.

'When have you seen my scars?' she said, laughing but
a little taken aback. More than one?

'You leaned down in front of me once to pour tea, and
I – I glanced.'

'You glanced?'

'I glanced.'

'Well, so long as it's only that one,' she said, laughing,
her hand going involuntarily to her breast. It was intensely
hot, even in the kitchen. I was aware of sweat tracking
down my spine inside the shirt.

'I felt so ashamed of what I'd done,' she said, touching
the place beneath her shirt, 'I could never let myself enjoy
anything. Any time I started to feel anything close to
happiness, I'd see Rosie in my dreams, and she would be
choking. I went out on one of my friends' hen night ten
months after getting back, and in the morning I tried to
cut myself to say sorry to her. The only saving grace in the
whole thing is that it preserved me from irony. So many
of my friends, they just seem . . . they can't feel anything
without making a little joke out of the feeling, as if they're
afraid that someone else will laugh at them if they don't
do it first. But, I don't know, when something really bad
happens, you can't hold life at arm's length any more. It,
you know, it grabs you and bear-hugs you and squeezes
the breath from your lungs; there's no space for irony to
weasel its way in between you and the experience. And
it brought me Jim. Jim doesn't make me feel bad. He was
there through the whole thing. You've got no idea how
much my parents love him! He understands that life is
important. He was born with nothing, and he wanted
something. No apologies, no qualifications, he wanted his
life and he went and he took it. That's why I love him so

167

much. It's not just some gratitude thing, although God knows I'm grateful. He sees life the same way I do.'

'That's wonderful.'

'Anyway,' she said, brightening, 'now thanks to you I'm reading again. And I can't tell you how happy that makes me. You've done a great thing for me, Matt.'

She smiled at me, and put her hand on my knee. I have always wondered, will always wonder, whether that was the moment to kiss her. She was not leading me on by touching me, of that I am certain. It was nothing more than a genuine expression of her desire to make me feel she cared for me. If I had kissed her, I would have been relying on the surprise of the shift in tone, on the intimate atmosphere of confession to carry us over the line, and not any signal from Claudia.

It was not cowardice that stopped me, but the force of a sudden revelation. It had been difficult for me to fathom the nature of the bond between that husband and this wife. I had tossed a pebble of enquiry into the well of their love, and listened idly for the quick 'plink' that would indicate the bottom. None had come. Now I understood why it was that Claudia was bound to Mr Swanson. She could not be with a man who made her feel joy, for with joy there came an unbearable wave of guilt. The same tragic events that had elevated her above the cultural dross of modernity had fused her affections to this unworthy object. The insight crashed through the walls of my consciousness like an aeroplane connecting with a downtown tower, leaving my internal world forever changed – my heroic act would be to free her from the burden of her duty. At the same time, I would cleanse my mundanity in the extremity of the action, become worthy of her affections. I had to kill Jim Swanson. In the moment of revelation, I felt like more than myself.

It was the same feeling I had had following the Italian into the alley, a comforting sense that rather than taking action myself, something greater was acting through me. Nemesis. The kindly ones. I dabbed my forehead with my handkerchief.

In case I had misread the situation, I asked her, 'What book shall we read for next week?'

'It's your turn to choose!'

'I'll choose the week after that. You pick next week. I can see you already have something in mind.'

She glanced at me quickly, pleased with my perspicacity. I held my breath as I awaited confirmation.

'OK, I do. It's a bit weird, but you know, I always had this thing about banned books.'

'Like the banned list?'

'No! Like books that were banned by the courts. They always have this frisson for me, you know what I mean? Have you ever read *Crash*?'

'I have read *Crash*. It's a very violent book, you know. Will that be all right?'

She looked at me with her dark little eyes. Her dark little eyes looked straight into mine.

'I'm sure it will be fine,' she said.

I exhaled. 'I understand what you mean perfectly. *Crash* it is.'

# 10

IT WAS AROUND THIS TIME THAT I BECAME AWARE OF someone following me. The fact that this awareness arose at almost exactly the same time as the necessity of killing Mr Swanson was not lost on me. I am, in moments of repose, a keen anthropologist of my own inner life. I approach this study not as one of those beardy professors of former polytechnics, convinced that female circumcision is quite the thing so long as it is performed by a woman in an authentic headdress, but rather with the prurient fascination of a Victorian explorer. When I find some new tribe of perversion deep in the blanks of the map, far away from the civilized hub of my conscious thoughts, I visit and I document, but I also judge, and when I present my findings to the royal society of my reason, I do so for the member's titillation. In many people a tendency towards self-analysis is considered tedious, and rightly so. However, to apply such a judgement universally is to miss the fact that the minds of individuals may be as different from one another as a selection of milk-bottle caps is from the Guggenheim, though both may be collections assiduously assembled. I am fascinated by the inner workings of my subconscious not because they are mine, but because they are fascinating.

With that in mind, it should not be supposed that the

possibility of my simply being paranoid, or of experiencing some manifestation of conscience, was not considered, especially given that the image of my pursuer presented itself to me from the first as a woman. I had in fact been actually stalked by a woman the previous spring, a client for whom Manches Interior Design had provided a new sitting room and, according to several thousand emails, letters and late-night phone calls, an illegitimate child. This allegation turned out to be completely untrue (to my great good fortune and assistance in persuading Cee of the general lack of merit in the woman's claims), but the experience had placed a certain strain on me which I frisked on suspicion of harbouring this fantasy.

There was no one incident in that first week which revealed my pursuer to me. Rather the details of her identity came slowly into focus by a process of unconscious compilation. As I became aware of being followed, I began to log the faces of women I saw in the street, or in cafés, or on the treadmill behind me at the gym. Three days of this scrupulous observation yielded no rewards, and it was then that I realized I would have to broaden my search from women to woman. My powers of observation had been tuned to a sexual frequency which excluded the presence of any girl who was too old, too young, or unattractive, and I had forgotten to reset it to accommodate my new parameters. It was this which finally convinced me that whoever was playing tricks on me, it was not my imagination – as a great student of myself, I knew that any female fury I conjured would be hot. I had an impression of poor, baggy clothes, lank hair and spectacles. If my pursuer was of below average attractiveness, she was real.

It was with unusual caution therefore, and quite against my better judgement, that I arranged to see Laura Rees one last time. I had already concluded that it was time to end the affair, not only because my obsession with Mrs Swanson had effectively eclipsed my feelings towards almost everyone else on earth, but also because I could sense that Laura Rees herself was starting to come apart at the seams, and our affair was no longer a help but an aggravating factor. One of the reasons I had been able over many years to conceal my habits from the world was that I tended to choose women who had more to lose from discovery than I did myself. This is the great mistake that many men make by choosing their sexy young secretary or personal trainer for an affair; if you pick someone single and without children, you put your card behind the bar for the entire tab. Pick a woman who's married, and she'll be scared of divorce. Plus if she gets pregnant you don't have to have any awkward conversations; the little chap already has a father.

Unfortunately a married lover is only an effective safeguard if they are capable of making a rational assessment of their options. If at any point they cease to be able to weigh up pros and cons and to act with a proper measure of self-interest, they become just as dangerous as anyone else. Laura Rees's phone and email messages (I had taken a small sample of both before deletion) indicated that she was not firm in her resolve to be normal. However, I was also aware that my lust for Claudia was threatening to occlude my charm. The only safe treatment seemed to be a course of sexual healing taken immediately before meeting her, which would leave me with enough post-coital confidence to make it through the afternoon. Cee was away on business (and was in any event an unreliable provider of uncritical sexual praise), and I had lately neglected to properly cultivate any other lovers. Laura was the least worst option.

She sounded pathetically grateful to hear from me when I called, which gave me cause for alarm entirely borne out by our morning's session. I couldn't get it up. Laura sucked frantically, but to no avail. Strangely, she was as desperate for the thing to work as I was. Indeed, the sheer Stakhanovite work ethic with which she addressed herself to my genitals completely effaced any last remaining shreds of eroticism. In the end I had to prise her bodily away from my groin and lift her up the bed by her shoulders. As she lay there panting I could feel the flaccid little traitor, slick with her spittle, cowering down further between my thighs. He made all sorts of protestations. Tiredness. Stress. For the last few nights I couldn't sleep, and when I finally did, I woke up screaming from dreams I couldn't remember. All true, but I knew what had really happened. He had gone over to Mrs Swanson. I understood that I had lost my heart, I was beginning to feel that I had lost my head, but of all the organs I had really thought my cock might hold out some little store of independence. This failure of my erection was a failure of my autonomy.

The fact filled me with an instant and potent shame. Laura clung to me as if terribly frightened by what had not happened. I switched on the TV, and tried to turn away from her on to my pillows, but she came with me like a Siamese twin whose organs are getting all the nutrients. Her not being Claudia annoyed me deeply. I had intended to break up with her by phone some time in the next week or so, but my impotence stimulated me to do it then and there. I flung the bedclothes back from the bed and walked over to the bathroom, closing the door behind me. I gripped the edges of the sink and watched the naked figure in the mirror breathing heavily.

'Is it . . . has that happened to you before?' she asked

through the door. She wanted to be reassured about her own performance, her own attractiveness, but I did not exactly have reserves of reassurance to give away.

'No.' Which was, surprisingly, pretty close to the truth.

'Was it . . . did I . . .'

'It was and you didn't. Think of yourself as the trauma specialist emerging grey-faced from the operating theatre. You did everything you could. No one blames you.'

'Oh. Thank you.'

'My displeasure.'

There was silence from the other side of the door.

'The fact is, Laura, I'm going away on holiday. I'm leaving for quite a while actually. Probably the whole summer. We won't be able to speak when I'm away, I'll be with Cee the whole time. And I won't have access to my email. So I think really, given that this is where we are, and given that I won't be here for some time, we should stop all this. I mean, I've got my wife, you've got someone else's husband. I'm sorry, that was uncalled for. I don't mean that. I just think – Laura?'

I wrapped a towel around myself to conceal my shrivelled appendage. I came back from the bathroom and found that the bed was empty. This fact filled me with a sudden dread that completely obliterated my meanness. It was as if I was a mother returning to an empty crib in expectation of a full one; I could think of no safe way in which Laura might have removed herself from the tumbled sheets. There was something instantly different in the atmosphere of the room which raised the hairs along my bare arms. I stood still, but I could not determine what it was. I called out her name, and received no reply. The television was on, and her handbag was still on the bedside table, showing its contents with all the casual disloyalty of a gossipy friend. The sound of canned laughter was eerie in the silence. Although it was not quite silence. As I stood holding my breath, frozen in mid-step, straining to identify what it was, that strange thing that made the air different, I became aware that where before there had been only the white-noise hum of the air conditioning, now there was something else. Then I heard the distant horn of a car, somewhere down in the London streets many floors below. Someone had opened the door to the balcony.

As calmly as I could, and still wearing my towel, I walked into the main part of the suite to where the balcony door led out on to the terrace. I stopped in the middle of the room, and Laura turned and smiled at me. My blood ran cold. I thought of Marcus's party, right at the start of the summer.

'You were saying about holidays?'

'Oh, yes. It doesn't really matter now.'

'No, come on, tell me if it's important.' She smiled brightly. 'I want to know what's going on in your life. We are, like, friends, right?'

'Yes, we are.'

'And friends tell each other stuff.'

'OK, yes, of course. Me and . . . I'm going off on holiday for a while.'

'Without Cee?'

'Sure, without Cee. Just me. Cee's busy with all this work in the countryside.'

She nodded as if that was to be expected, and looked back out across Hyde Park.

'Where are you going?'

'St Lucia.'

'That's really nice. Are you staying in the Sandals there? It's really nice, Geoff took me there once. They

don't allow children though . . . You can't have children.'
Her smile faltered.

'I hear it's really nice. Listen, Laura . . .'

'How long are you going for?'

'Oh, I don't know. Not long. Listen, Laura.'

'Yes?'

'Do you think you might come down from there?'

'Down from where?'

'From there.'

Laura looked down at the chair upon which she was standing, as if seeing it for the first time. Her hand, with its diamonds and long slender fingers and careful manicure, was placed high on the wall beside the railing, the top of which was level with her shins. Her other hand rested palm up on the underside of the balcony on the floor above. One small foot stood on the hot metal of the railing. I was surprised she could take the heat on her sole. The other stood on a chair she had hauled out through the sliding glass doors. She was completely naked, framed against the hot blue sky. Her torso was at right angles to the drop, her breasts in perfect silhouette. At this height, even on such a still day, there was a breeze to stir her golden hair. She looked slightly unreal, like a model posing in a fashion magazine.

'Oh!' she said, and laughed. 'I'm sorry! I just so wanted some air, you know, I suddenly felt all trapped and stuff and I had to get out in the air, you know when that happens.'

'Yes, I know that feeling very well.'

'Yeah, it's been so hot . . .'

'Laura, come down.'

Thoughtfully, she brought the foot off the railing. The chair had a soft cushion seat, and with both her feet planted so close together it made her wobble in the middle. She giggled and caught the wall, and fell rather than stepped down on to the metal boards of the balcony. I walked over to her and picked her up, and brought her back into the room. I closed the balcony door and wrapped a blanket around her. I stayed with her for the rest of the morning, asking her questions about her husband and the kids, which she answered quite happily. We watched TV for a while (Laura asked if maybe we should watch porn to help me, but I declined). When I left I told her I would see her again soon.

# 11

IT WAS NOT, IN MANY WAYS, THE IDEAL PREPARATION FOR my meeting with Claudia. I had intended to meet her calm, collected, with my recent orgasm in one pocket and three of Laura's in the other. Instead I left the hotel in something akin to mild shock. My only consolation was the encounter with Laura had been sufficiently disturbing to keep my mind off Claudia for as long as it took to ride the tube to Oxford Circus. I was still trying to work out how to get her to a good psychiatrist without alerting her husband when I alighted on the platform.

We were to meet in a café in St Mark's Square, just behind Oxford Street. It was intended in general that our meetings were to take place in her home, but that day there were works scheduled which would create so much noise and disturbance in the house that the Swansons would have been advised to spend the whole day out in any event. I happened to know, having organized it, that the scheduled works involved the removal of certain features (such as a state-of-the-art changing table mounted on the wall, and some cheerfully patterned wallpaper) from the nursery, converting the space back into a conventional guest bedroom.

I knew that St Mark's Square would be busy, and I turned up at the restaurant almost two hours early to secure a decent table. When Claudia arrived she sat down and arranged herself in her chair, fetching the book from her bag, placing her dark glasses down beside her water glass and, having checked her phone, returning it to her handbag. I was deeply gratified that she did not leave it on the table. Her presence made the morning's experiences seem as flat and distant as a photograph of someone else's holiday.

'God, I should start with a grovelling apology,' she said when she was settled.

'How do you mean?' I asked, afraid that she was going to say that she hadn't finished the book, or that she would have to leave early.

'First of all I berate you for giving me a book to read with too much sex in it, and then I ask you to go away and read what was frankly the most disturbingly pornographic thing I've ever read in my life.'

'Oh, I think you'd be hard pressed to read the sex in Ballard as flirtation!'

Though of course, in this case, that was exactly what it was.

'Maybe you're right. Although it never ceases to amaze me what people can construe as a come-on.'

'So what did you think of it?'

'Well, I thought it was a better idea than it was a book,' she said.

'How do you mean?'

'At first, you see, I just thought it was terribly written. I mean, I think a writer should probably think twice before using "pubis" in a book, and several times before using "natal cleft", but in *Crash* there's about ten pubises and another dozen natal clefts in the first ten pages.'

I smiled. I loved the age-old artistic privilege of discussing pure filth with someone one fancied without the slightest admission of strangeness. It was as if we had entered a sauna of the mind, and we were both to remove our towels and sit in the clear heat without comment on our glistening nudity. It was all terribly, terribly grown-up, and I folded my brow to make it clear that I received no more pleasure from hearing her utter the word 'cleft' than I ought. She was gloriously complicit in this, and continued to talk as if things between us were entirely platonic.

'But then I guess I kind of saw what he was doing. I mean, by enumerating the body with all these artificial, vaguely medical words. Because at the same time you've got all those technical car terms, like "binnacle" and "steering column". He's trying to use language that reduces human beings to little bits and pieces, so he can build them up again with the cars.'

'I think that's right. And then the pornography itself ties in with the voyeurism, the sex act mediated through the lens of a camera.'

'Yes, that shady figure on the overpass, taking pictures of the lovers in the back seat of their car . . . There's something in the idea of car crashes though. I can see what he means about that. I mean they're supposed to be functional really, aren't they, cars? They're supposed to be real things that take you from one place to another. But they've become this weird symbol, this thing that was supposed to free us has also become the main cause of our violent death.'

She was a little too casual. She was daring herself and me to declare this line of thinking inappropriate in the light of her confession.

'The betrayal of our secret desire for death in the traffic accident?'

'You know you're not supposed to call them "traffic

accidents" any more? The police have started calling them collisions.'

'Why?'

'Because "accident" implies there's no one to blame. There almost always is someone to blame, when someone dies on the road. Funny that, isn't it, how words have the power to change the nature of the thing they describe?'

I put my tongue out to taste my lips, and found them dry. Mrs Swanson smiled at me, interested to hear what I had to say. I found her unnerving. God, the pleasure of conversing in expectation! Like the pleasure of reading, how had I forgotten it?

'I think maybe that's part of what Ballard means. He really believed in the power of the imagination to shape, even supplant, external reality. In one of his short stories he has a narrator who writes people's deaths into his diary, and then the people he's written about die as he's described in the book. Then at the end he tells the reader that they too will die as a result of having read the story.'

'What a wonderful idea! Although, of course, rather self-defeating.'

'How do you mean?'

'Well, presumably the point of the fiction is that the written word has the power to directly alter the lives of men. But at the end, the reader doesn't die. So if you're setting out as a writer to prove that the written word can escape the page and get out there into the world, surely it would be better to choose a set-up which isn't going to prove the exact opposite?'

No, not the pleasure of conversing. The pleasure of conversing with her. The pleasure of reading with her in mind. The only thing between me and complete absorption in her intelligence was the heat, and the sense of her imbalance. I was aware that I was sweating, the drops forming on my brow, but dared not draw attention to it by attempting to wipe it away. She crossed her legs. As she did so, one of her bare ankles brushed my calf. I started back, and she said, 'Was that you? I thought it was the table leg.'

'That's OK. So you don't agree with Ballard then? That the world, with the universality of adverts and films and computer games and spin, has become a fiction, and,' I opened my copy, and read aloud, '"the one small node of reality left to us is inside our own heads"?'

She frowned and, as was her way, considered her response in the light of the question that had been put to her. I was in awe of her admission that the mind moves slower than the mouth. At last she said, 'I think it's a dangerous way to be. But sometimes I feel it is.'

We continued to talk about the book for more than an hour, discussing the role of the car crash and of the mechanization of violent sexual desire, and over the course of our lunch it dawned on me what was happening. She was communicating to me the means of her husband's murder. She was placing the weapon in my hands. Not consciously, of course, but by the only means allowed to her by the repression of her desires for freedom in the face of her obligations. I thought of the yellow Cayenne I had seen sitting outside their house on the day of my first visit. Was it possible that she was sensible, at some level, to the pure vulgarity of this hideous vehicle? Could it have been for her, by virtue of its prominence in the bookish repose of the London square, an unconscious symbol of her husband's unworthiness, and of the insurmountable distance between them? I had to wrestle to control my thoughts, which strained at the leash to pursue this enquiry, to focus on the conversation with Mrs Swanson.

'I should really let you get on,' she said, as we finished

our tea. 'I've kept you well after time. We'll have to add a little bit extra on to your fee.'

'Oh, no, come on, please, please.'

She smiled. 'Well, all right. But I'm paying for lunch.'

'No, let me! You always have me to your house, drinking your tea, let me . . .'

'But you're doing this as a professional,' she said. 'I wouldn't expect my hairdresser to pay for sparkling water when he comes round to do my hair! Or, ah, my doctor, I wouldn't ask my doctor to pay if he came round.'

'Let me pay,' I said, aware of a hint of desperation in my own voice.

'You pay next time if you want,' she said.

'But next time we'll be at your place.'

'Oh, this is ridiculous,' she said, shaking her head and going into her bag. I responded by digging about in my pocket for my own wallet, which turned out to be twisted round in the lining. I wrestled with my trousers as she calmly opened her purse, and eventually extracted it with a bark of triumph.

'All right, all right, fine,' she said, and sat back in her chair. She looked away from me across the square. To my great regret, I was suddenly aware that the little incident had approached the threshold of hysteria, and that I had made a fool of myself. The bill had not even been requested from the waiter and here I was, panting, with my wallet in my hand.

We sat beneath the awning with our copies on the table between us. After a silence of some moments, she said, 'To be perfectly honest, I don't really want to go home.'

'Why not?'

'I don't want to get back before they've finished.'

I nodded, not knowing what to say.

'You know what you were saying about Ballard, about

the real world being fiction and the mind being fact? Well, I feel that sometimes with Simon.'

'Simon?'

'Simon was his name. I mean, I can admit that now. He only existed in my head. But he was more real than almost anyone I can actually touch or see or talk to. Only I'm not allowed to mourn him, because he wasn't real. I'm only allowed to mourn him in my head.'

I rose to kiss Mrs Swanson goodbye, and I was conscious as I entered the penumbra of her scent that it was something to which I had been looking forward, as a child asked to move the presents from under the tree a few days before Christmas may enjoy a furtive squeeze of his gifts, and speculate on their contents. I lied and said I wanted to stay at the café and read in anticipation of an appointment in central London. She left me to settle the bill. I sat at the table and tried to collect myself. I found that, in the heat, and with her so close to me, the need to maintain a veneer of light and reasonable behaviour took all my strength.

About a minute after her lovely figure had departed, I felt the child instinct tug at my sleeve, and I glanced at the passageway leading from St Mark's Square back out into Regent Street. In the sunlight that fell on the square, the slice of shadow between the two buildings was deep and velvety as deep clear water, but I could distinguish within it what looked like the barrel of a camera directed at our table. The lens of the camera, if camera it was, was framed by an impression of lank brown hair falling to shoulder height on either side.

I leapt up from my seat, causing my chair to spill over behind me. The clang of the metal hitting the pavement disturbed the placid surface of moneyed lunches, and the waiter, who had been fawning over a table of Italian women, looked up. I cried out to the figure with the camera, but my rising had frightened her back into the depths of the passage. I pushed the table aside, and vaulted the absurd little trough of foliage which demarcated the café's al fresco dining from the common square beyond. Behind me the waiter, apparently under the impression I was absconding without paying and keen to impress the signorinas with a display of athleticism, gave chase himself.

Two decades-worth of slavish attendance at the gym, whilst undertaken purely as a reflex of vanity, had had certain ancillary benefits. I was across the square and through the backs of the shoppers milling around the menus before the waiter could disentangle himself from the guy ropes of a parasol. I plunged through into the little alley, shocked for a moment by the transition from blinding light into shadow. The photographer had gone, but at the end of the passage, where the darkness changed again for the light of Oxford Street, the turned heads of two tourists, stopped on the pavement in an attitude of mild outrage, were the telltale ripples of a rapid retreat. I ran down to the high street and emerged into a sweating migration of shoppers, a vast transition of biomass from shops to offices stimulated by the end of the lunch hour. Left and right, left and right, there was no further clue as to the direction the woman (if it was in fact a woman) had taken. Indeed, she could have run six feet from the end of the alley and sat down on the pavement, and in the long grass of consumers she would have been instantly invisible.

Then suddenly a horn blared further up the street, and the traffic which had been moving slowly in one direction stopped, and I heard behind me the shout of the waiter rapidly approaching. I vaulted the black iron railings, and found myself embroiled in the lethal kinetic chess match of the traffic, running round the fume-belching back of a red bus into an oncoming motorcycle, reeling back into the path of a cyclist, who furiously dinged his little bell as I stumbled on to the sacred green strip. I flattened myself back against the railings and the bus moved on, and the bicycle sailed by with a cry of 'Wanker!', and over the other side of the road I thought I saw a dissipating ripple of interest as the stream of shoppers absorbed my fugitive brunette. Then I gasped with shock as the hands of the waiter descended on my heaving shoulders.

'Hey, mister, you didn't pay! What the hell you didn't pay?'

'Yes, yes all right, get off,' I said, shaking his hands off my shoulders. He stayed suspiciously panting beside the barriers, prepared perhaps for me to make another break, but allowed me to climb back on to the pavement of my own volition. He was wearing the traditional uniform of his trade, black trousers and a white shirt, and still carrying a small white cloth. He was a little overweight and perspiring in the heat, undone by the pursuit. Hived off from the restaurant itself, he cut a comical, almost a pathetic, figure, waiting alone on the pavement. Then I strode off ahead of him back towards the restaurant, and he, clearly desiring to collect the bounty of honour due for reclaiming a fugitive patron, ran up alongside me. Feeling an odd moment of pity for the way he had seemed in the middle of Oxford Street, I slowed to allow him to catch up, even bowed my head a little to imply he had really caught me. He must have sensed this, for as we neared the end of St Mark's passage, he said in a friendly manner, 'So why you run away, eh? Do you not have money?'

'No, no, it's not that,' I said.

'You wanted to catch your friend?'

'No . . . I thought there was someone following me.'

'What?' the waiter asked, stopping just as we reached the square, where the al fresco diners watched our return with interest.

'I thought there was someone following me. Taking photographs,' I said.

'Many people take photographs in the square,' he said comfortingly. 'Tourists.'

'This person is following me. Just photographing me,' I muttered, looking back over my shoulder as if they might have crept back to the head of the alley.

The man's solicitous air receded, and he gave me a look which initially I could not place. It took me a second or two to realize it was one I had sometimes had cause to give, particularly around Oxford Street, but had never until this moment received – it was the expression one adopts when dealing with someone who is perfectly sweet, but may not be in their right mind. I paid the bill, leaving a large tip, and pondered without enthusiasm the import of that look as I wandered over the sunlit pavements in search of a taxi, the sweat once again rising on my skin.

# 12

AND SO, WITH CEE AWAY AND THE HEATWAVE TIGHTENING its grip on the city, we read *Brave New World*. And *Jacob's Room*. And *The Famished Road*, and *Middlemarch*, and *Porterhouse Blue*, and *Generation X*, and *Some Hope*. I was reading more than I had as a teenager and, as with so many teenage pursuits, wondering what spurious notion of maturity it was that had stopped me in the first place. Sometimes the books contained messages for me, communications about the ideal means and timing of the impending tragedy, and sometimes they did not. We met once or twice a week, always in Vincent Square. It would be wrong to say that the books provided an excuse for seeing one another — indeed, I had seldom in my life wanted so greatly to measure my readings against another opinion, and to explore my judgements in conversation. It was clear from that first afternoon in the hospital that my sessions with Claudia would be dialogues. Her taste was so keen that I actually began to feel nervous excitement in expressing my opinions, for when she approved I was silently elated, whilst her disagreement left me downcast.

The critical discussions could not exist in a vacuum, any more than the books could be discussed in isolation from the relationships they described. Always after three-quarters of an hour the talk would move quite naturally into the arena of personal disclosure, and in this way we came to know one another. The more I knew of her, the more I wanted to know. As for her feelings towards me, I can only say that she listened without judgement. I found myself telling her of affairs, and of some of the nastier things I had done to conceal them. I realized at some point that the implication of making such confessions was that I was ashamed of my behaviour, and intended not to repeat it. Fine, I would not repeat it, once the two of us were together. She made me feel I must be all right, because she liked me.

I would say for my part they were some of the most honest conversations I had ever had in my life, and unless Claudia was compulsively frank with her general acquaintance I think they were the same for her. There was, however, a curious paradox in place, for with each further disclosure, with each extension of trust, the baby elephant in the room grew a little nearer to full-tusked maturity. It suckled greedily at my talk of past affairs, and of her hopes and fears for her marriage. As our talks became more honest, more intimate, ignoring the fact of that intimacy became more artificial. It was the one thing neither of us was prepared to discuss.

There was something almost deliberate in our meeting alone in her house in the afternoons, a kind of perverse proof of innocence in the brazenness. Under the effects of this protective charm I even mentioned to Cee that I was discussing the specific content of the library with Mrs Swanson, and sure enough she expressed no suspicion, only pleasure at my having found a receptive client. It would have been just as easy and perhaps more convenient to meet in a restaurant or café somewhere around Victoria, but whenever I suggested such a venue Claudia laughed it away with some excuse. For this I had reason to be grateful, for as my plans for the tragedy that was to befall Jim Swanson progressed, I was able to take a useful inventory of the raincoats and umbrellas stashed in the downstairs cupboards whilst Mrs Swanson was on the phone in the kitchen.

As the first fortnight passed, our conversations became more personal. I even allowed myself to believe that they might be a source of comfort to her. She talked of her feelings following her miscarriage. She articulated to me her grief, and the biological snub to the mourning process, for her sense of the humanity of her child had outstripped its development in the womb. I listened as best I could, and knew enough not to pretend to understand. At the same time, the means she employed to confine our relationship became more abrupt. We had agreed at the outset that the sessions should be priced by the hour, but for the first few neither of us kept track. Claudia began to make a note of the duration at the conclusion of each session in a small pocket book kept by the stereo in the kitchen. Sometimes to ram the point home she would ask me to confirm the time, though the stainless-steel door of the oven was inlaid with the green glow of a little digital clock. This habit left me with mixed feelings as I walked out into the street in the shortening summer afternoons, a residue of peace from the preceding hours mixed with frustration at the insult of the last five minutes.

She would also occasionally insert the blade of her husband's name. We would be discussing something, generally some topic of a particularly personal nature, or else we would have hit on some new reading that made a geyser of ideas spurt up from the page, and she would say, apropos of nothing more than the moment, how Jim had reacted to her account of the previous week's session. These asides were deftly managed; she always found some clever line of thinking to tie Jim to the matter in hand. Through these references, Claudia made it clear to me, and I suspected to herself, that there was no illicit content to our friendship – how could there be, when the whole thing was laid out so casually before her husband? Only the very deepest places, her stories of her grief, were free from these chance little encounters with Jim and his opinions, and from that I inferred that her accounts to him were not complete. It was understood also that my own confessions were private. As to the general tone of our conversations, Claudia could only relate to him the things she was willing to admit to herself, and I imagined Jim might be inclined to read between the lines. Still, he never asked her to stop seeing me.

Bearing these temptations was a great deal easier than it might have been, knowing that I was going to murder Mr Swanson. The thought of his death was a *calmant*. Sometimes I would find myself after my appointments with Claudia in a strange part of London – I would be in Battersea Park when I was expected in Shoreditch, or Muswell Hill when I had an appointment in Fulham. I invariably had no idea how I had come to be there. When this happened it frightened me, and the only way I had found to relax that fear was to focus on the idea of his death. I had no intention of being caught or involved in any kind of criminal consequence, and any hint of suspicion on Claudia's part would have ruined my chances with her, as well as spoiling the gift of freedom I sought to present to her with a measure of guilt. It took me some weeks to come up with a plan that fulfilled these criteria, but with the hints provided in our discussions and materials I was eventually able to concoct a scheme that satisfied them.

There was only one conversation which threatened to

shake my purpose, for it suggested to me a foundation for the Swansons' marriage which went beyond my analysis, and thus cast some doubt on the righteousness of my cause. The book for that week, which had been chosen by Claudia, was *Bleak House*. I would never have chosen it myself, for it required at least a week to read, which reduced the frequency of our meetings. I took some comfort from the fact that I liked the book, would enjoy rereading it, and that it would take at least two hours of discussion to do it justice.

We were sitting on the high stools in the kitchen, and had come to the point of the death of Lady Deadlock's vanished son, when Claudia moved abruptly from the particular to the general. At the same time her voice took on a kind of off-hand quality which I had learned to interpret as a sign of impending confidence.

'Why all these books about foundling children? I mean, it's always coming up, in Dickens and Fielding and Rushdie and Shakespeare and Eliot. Again and again you have these children who get brought up by peasants and turn out to belong to someone posh.'

I was careful to match her casual tone, knowing that any attempt on my part to pre-empt intimacy would likely banish her revelation.

'It's usually a critique of social division. Or it was with Dickens, anyway. The concept of heredity is one of the greatest barriers to a compassionate society. In England, we still basically believe that your family defines your life chances, and that to a certain extent that is the way things should be. If you can write a convincing story in which dear baby Tarquin gets stolen by brigands, or stranded by a storm, and it only becomes clear years later that he should have been a prince, then it's a very powerful message. It reminds people that class is an illusion, that when you kick the chimney sweep you might just as well be kicking your own child.'

'Jim wants to adopt.' She didn't look at me when she said it, but frowned down at the book, continuing to turn the pages, as if the really important thing was finding a specific passage she had just remembered.

I felt pressed back in the seat as my heart began to accelerate, the way it always did when I sensed I was about to get a glimpse of her inner life.

'Does he?'

'He mentioned it again the other day, in his sweet, clumsy way. We were watching *EastEnders*. Do you watch *EastEnders*?'

I smiled, not wishing to admit that I didn't, and indeed that had she been anyone else I would have thought less of her for doing so herself.

'There's a character in it who has an adopted child, and I said how hard it must be, and Jim said not that hard, not if you have a loving home.'

'That could mean anything.'

'It could. But it doesn't.'

'I thought . . . forgive me, but I thought you would have no difficulties . . . that you had completely recovered.'

'I have. Or I will eventually. I just don't want to try again yet. And Jim was in care growing up.'

'I didn't know that about him. I thought he had some family?'

'Plenty of the boys in homes have families, Matt. He's got a sister he sees sometimes. And I know he's paying some money to somebody else in Brighton – it goes out of his account every month – though he's never told me who, and he never goes down there or calls.'

'I can't imagine that.'

'What?'

'Jim in a home. Jim without all this.'

'I remember, it was our third date, after getting back from Rome. I wasn't ready to go out in public, I couldn't see people, so Jim hired out the whole restaurant so we could be alone. It was the basement floor of the Bleeding Heart.' She smiled at the memory, and I gritted my teeth. 'And then afterwards he asked if he could show me something, and I said sure. So he drove me all the way out to Hackney Wick, and we parked in front of this weird old Victorian building that looked like a brickworks. And he said, "This is where I grew up." I got out and went to look through the windows, and on the ground floor you could see this really lovely-looking day room, with the walls covered in pencil drawings, like the ones you get in the corridors of secondary schools, everyone's art GCSE projects. Jim didn't get out, and when I got back in he was crying. Do you know, that's the only time I've ever seen him cry. And I said it looks nice, and he said it didn't look like that twenty years ago. Then he drove me back to my parents' house, and we had our first real kiss before I got out of the car. No one else knows, I think. I'm pretty sure he's never told his friends at work.'

'How on earth did he wind up at the bank?'

'Oh, he got a job in the post room of a start-up hedge fund when he was sixteen. He worked out a new way of distributing the letters around the building that meant everyone got their post half an hour earlier. One of the MDs paid for him to do his A-levels and then gave him a job. He was the youngest trader they had, and then the youngest team leader.'

I baulked at the pride in her voice. It reminded me of something it was easy to forget. Behind the home counties accent and the English education, there was the shadow of the immigrant mother in her, the Eastern European pride in self-reliance and hard work over the settled privileges of the indigenous caste system. English blood cools alone in the marital bed. It needs the proximity of another body to keep it warm. A native wife would be raised by a thousand films and magazines to see Jim's work ethic as an insult. She would have friends and coffee mornings to reinforce her views, and to convince her of the legitimacy of her outrage: 'He spends more time at that desk than he does with me! Am I not beautiful? Don't I deserve a little bit of attention?' Long hours would be the neglect that justified the affair.

The immigrant mentality would cast the thing in a completely different light. I remembered at Marcus's cocktail party how I had tried a little joke at Jim's expense, saying that he was distracted by a higher purpose, and Claudia rather than laughing or taking offence had simply nodded in sober agreement. It had not occurred to her that I was being anything less than serious. The hours of toil were an offering laid at the hearth. A Slovak wife might be understanding, grateful even to her husband for devoting himself to their mutual betterment. She might even pity him for the time they were forced to spend apart, and love him the more for his sacrifice. I wondered what model Claudia had taken from her own parents, the ever-on-duty of the British ambassador, the fixed smile and long exiles of the diplomatic wife. The insight revealed itself to me in an instant, but it had been long in the making. It was as if a sculptor had dropped the sheet from his creation. It took some effort to tear my eyes away from it, and to return my attention to the present moment. I waved the book in the air, and said something about how Jim's career path itself was quite Dickensian, more *David Copperfield* than *Bleak House*, and we went back to decrying Tulkinghorn.

The conversation came back to me forcefully two weeks later when I was going through the Swansons' bedroom. Our session had overrun, and Claudia had been hurrying off to meet her mother. I had told her I wanted to look over the works, and would lock up and set the alarm when I left. When she was gone I went up to their bedroom, and stood in the space hollowed out by the sunshine, smelling the private air. I had not been into the bedroom for almost eight weeks, and was fascinated to see that it was much as I and my wife had designated, right down to the sheets on the bed. Beyond a photograph of Claudia's parents in a silver frame, a number of electrical gadgets for grooming sitting on the floor in front of the dressing table and a line of expensive-looking toy cars on the window sill, the Swansons had made almost no visible contribution to the space in which they lived. It was as if they had purchased some historic castle complete with beds in which kings had slept, and mirrors which had held the beauty of queens, and found themselves now afraid to compromise its authenticity.

I began with the bureau. The top drawer was the glorious berth of Claudia's underwear. In a more conventional affair I might have helped myself to a frilly something, but the delicacy of my feeling restrained me, and I closed the drawer tight.

That first success, however, proved misleading. As I went down through the drawers, and then through bedside tables, medicine cabinets, cupboards and files, I could find no other source of insight. I was aware that the equivalent process in my own bedroom would quickly yield sex aides, pornography, some ill-advised items of clothing from a brief goth phase shortly after university, love letters (mine to Cee, hers to me, both of ours to other men and women), some rather purple poetry, old drug wrappers and probably somewhere at the back of a cupboard a mouldering double portrait of myself and Cee looking wizened and corrupt. The Swansons' vices, if they had any, left no trace behind. I had almost given up looking when I found it.

The fitted cupboards presented a mirrored surface that doubled the size of the room. When I first slid them open, Claudia's scent enveloped me, and I put my hand into the soft folds of her summer dresses. On the parallel rack hung a line of Jim Swanson's suits, as grey and glum as a queue of deflated accountants. On top of the cupboard was an old laptop case, black wire guts hanging from the open zipper. As I stood on tiptoes to observe it, I realized suddenly that Jim or Claudia would only be able to reach it by standing on a chair. Something about its inaccessibility alerted me, and I reached in and pulled it down. As I did so, a strange musical jangle emerged from inside, faint but unmistakable in the silent room. I could not place the sound, but it was familiar to me, calling back to me across the space of many years, its message rendered indistinct by distance. I pulled out a charger and a dongle, and behind them found a box wrapped in tissue paper. The box was duck-egg blue, and I knew what I would find inside before I opened it. Behind the Tiffany's livery there lay a tiny gleaming rattle, with a smooth handle shaped like a heart, safe for an infant mouth. Engraved across the circumference were the words 'Simon Jim Swanson, born', and there the inscription ended, a desert of polished silver waiting for the date that would never come. It was bad luck to have begun such a thing; the salesman must have told Jim Swanson it was not traditional, and he must have insisted. Perhaps it had given him the sense that his happiness was secure, holding the engraved toy. I understood the impulse from a man who had daily to contend with the great uncertainties of the markets. He must have known he was punching above his weight with Claudia. That she should bear his child would have seemed a suspicious portion of luck. He had sought to fix his gain by having it carved in metal. I pitied him his hubris, and for a few moments that sense I had of being the gods' tool was shaken. Had he not had his fair portion of suffering? The rattle made mournful music in my hand.

It was a great risk to have kept it, after every other trace of the absent child had been expunged from the house with such care. If Claudia had ever come across it, she would know of the depths of her husband's grief, of the falseness of his professed peace. That he had kept such feelings from her was a reproach, for it implied he thought her unequal to the task of helping him. Women are apt to take that kind of insult to heart. I took the rattle in my hand, and lay on the marital bed, looking at the ceiling. I tried to imagine the thoughts that went through Jim Swanson's mind as he lay there next to his beautiful, damaged young wife. It seemed so uncharacteristic of him, to want to adopt. I had assumed he was the kind of man who would view a biological child as evidence of his potency in the first instance, and a source of harvested pride thereafter, a father who talked up his son's A-level results with the same forced nonchalance he used when listing the specs of his car. It takes a more evolved sensibility, to trust one's capacity for unconditional love in the absence of genetic obligation. Perhaps he simply felt the need to preserve another human being from whatever suffering he had experienced in his own boyhood. Whatever his motive, I was impressed that he thought he could love in the abstract. I knew it was beyond my powers, though Cee might have made a go of it, had she had a different husband.

The cold metal of the toy had grown warm from my skin by the time I returned it to its box. I had lost track of time, and was vaguely fearful that either Claudia or Jim himself might possibly come home. Nevertheless I sensed that Jim would detect any minute adjustments in the configuration of his secret package, and I took the time to restore both tissue paper and wires just so, before reinterring the case and its withered dream at the top of the wardrobe. When I finally left the house, the need I felt for Claudia became so strong that it was almost physically insupportable, and I had to light a cigarette with shaking hands.

I felt almost sorry for Jim Swanson – he had spent the early part of his life ignored and mistreated by society, a drain on resources only, and the kind of vulnerable child to whom every colour of politician imaginable would pay lip service. He had through his own vigour and determination forged himself a success of sorts, only to find that his profession made him as despised as he had been at the beginning, a despicable banker whom every politician would rush to condemn. If he had been contented with a woman less like Claudia, I sensed I might have liked him, felt gratified by his success. I had an instinctive affection for anyone whom society looked down upon for being born too poor and winding up too rich. If he had only sought out the big-titted young blonde that his profession and his car seemed to presage, I would have left him alone to enjoy the spoils of his victory over privation.

As it was though, he had chosen Claudia, and the union threatened my sense of order. I could make out the shape of her need for him, but not the other way round. What did he want with her? She was insufficiently shallow to worship him as a provider only. Was it simply that he could sense she was worth more than the usual banker's wife, even if he lacked the capacity fully to appreciate the reasons for it? Was he able to feel comfortable with her? She was too sophisticated, too subtle. And the thought of them making love . . . My resolve was restored. It made me feel, for the sake of civilization generally as much as for myself, that something must be done. In that sense, his murder would be a crime of necessity, and if he felt untold suffering at the loss of his son, at least that suffering would be ended.

I had finished my cigarette and was about to head home when I put my hands in my pockets and discovered I had a pair of women's pants in one, and a miniature MG two-seater in the other. I ran back to the house to replace them, and afterwards mislaid my breath. I had to go and sit on a bench on the green for twenty minutes until my heart slowed down, and I was late for my next appointment.

# 13

THE WEEKEND BEFORE SHE WAS DUE TO RETURN TO LONDON, Cee called me on Saturday morning to inform me that the project would likely run over. She would be away for a further two weeks. It was always a little strange to have reality give such blatant confirmation to my sense of tragic destiny, but I accepted the news of her continued absence with all the correct noises of regret. We discussed the project, the schemes she was considering and the outcome of the tender for the builders' quotes before the conversation turned to the Swansons.

'So how are your little sessions?'

'What sessions? Oh, the consultations.'

'Yes, the consultations.'

'They're fine.'

'Tell me she's as stupid as she looks.'

'All right.'

'So tell me.'

'She's as stupid as she looks.'

'You have to mean it. Put some feeling into it.'

'Listen, darling, I have a lot of work to do . . .'

'I know, I know. Have you at least brought their billing up to date?'

'Yes.'

'Are you lying?'

'Yes.'

'For fuck's sake, Matthew. You do know we're running a business, don't you? At least tell me there isn't much outstanding.'

'There isn't much outstanding.'

'Are you lying?'

'No.'

'Look, just forget it, it doesn't matter. Oh, by the way, I've had some rather sad news.'

'What's up?'

'Do you remember that couple we did the drawing room for, the Reeses?'

'No, I don't remember them.'

'You must do, it was one of yours in the end! It went on and on, they kept changing the spec. I thought Vincenzo was going to kill us, he had to reapply for planning permission . . . He was at Core Private Finance, she was some kind of waitress?'

'Oh, yes.'

'Well, anyway. I called his personal assistant this morning, to settle their final bill. And she told me that Mrs Rees threw herself under a train two days ago. Isn't that horrible?'

'Was she, could it have been an accident?'

'No, apparently she'd been depressed for ages.'

'What, and the PA told you that?'

'I asked her if it was an accident, and she said definitely not.'

'Jesus Christ, you shouldn't ask his fucking secretary questions like that.'

I stood still in the middle of the kitchen, holding the phone to my ear. Cee did not respond, but I could hear her breathing.

'Is there something wrong, sweetheart?' she asked.

'What do you mean?'

'Only it seems . . . I just want to know what's happening in Matt-world. It feels lately like you've gone off for a party in your head and I'm not invited.'

'Of course you're invited.'

'You say that, but . . . I don't think I am. Not for weeks in fact, not since the night we had that dinner with Don Joan and Hugo. Did Hugo say something to upset you?'

'I'm not upset.'

'Are you seeing some hussy?' she said, in the accent of a southern belle. 'Are you going to run off and leave me? I should die if you were having an affair, I should simply die.'

Tradition dictated that I should respond with my own Cajun accent, but I simply said, 'I'm not having an affair with anyone. It's the heat. It's making me feel lethargic. That's all. It makes me feel like a hippo.'

I waited to see if she would swallow that, or if I would be obliged to discuss the matter further. I sat stubbornly through her silence, and was finally rewarded with a sigh. I imagined her nodding as she sometimes did on the phone, as if completely oblivious as to how the medium worked.

'All right,' she said in her own voice.

'All right. I'm going to go play with my library now.'

'You go play.'

'Will you call me again to let me know how things are going?'

'Of course, Matt. Have a good day.'

'And you.'

I climbed the stairs to my study. I closed the door behind me, and turned the key very slowly and softly (force of habit, so that Cee wouldn't hear the mechanism catch). The curtains in my study are always closed, to keep the sun's grubby paws off my books. I opened them, and daylight tumbled into the warm dry room, with its smell of wood polish and ageing leather. I removed the purple cloth that sits on the display case which houses my greatest treasures.

The jewel of my collection was the 1498 Wynkyn de Worde edition of Chaucer's *Canterbury Tales*. The book itself is a giant thing, ten kilos with a cover bound in calfskin and metal, and an ornate clasp across the book's open page ends. The book contains the very first proper expression of modern English, when the blooming stem of Norman French had been grafted to the thick roots of Anglo-Saxon, producing a hybrid language that would grow to seed the mouths of the world. It had come from the final sale of the greatest private collection of manuscripts of all time, that of Sir Thomas Phillipps. Sir Thomas was a baronet and bibliomaniac of the nineteenth century. His library had once contained over 80,000 books and manuscripts, making it the largest ever amassed by a single man. In one of his earliest catalogues, he recorded that his desire to accumulate documents was 'instigated by reading various accounts of the destruction of valuable manuscripts'. He had read at Oxford of the sacking of Rome, and the burning of the library at Alexandria, and the image of those flames had licked like a fever up the walls of his brain. There is no doubt that he himself saved hundreds of ancient documents from such a fate, for many of his early acquisitions came from the dispersal of the monastic libraries of France in the years after the Revolution. In his lust for the printed word Sir Thomas was to bankrupt himself and several booksellers, and to reduce his wife and daughters to living like tramps between the great stacks of vellum that obstructed the rooms and passageways of the family seat at Middle Hill, and yet it was all begun with this ideal: that the sum of human learning should be preserved from the worst of human nature, and from the ravages of time.

Sir Thomas had sought to do two generous things with his library: to open it up to visiting scholars during his life, and to leave it to the British public on his death. The first of these faltered when he admitted a young student named Halliwell to Middle Hill to examine his collection. The man fell in love with his daughter Henrietta, and when he was refused permission to marry her the two of them eloped together and returned as husband and wife. After this betrayal, the welcome extended to visiting scholars was revoked. Sir Thomas cut himself off from his child and her husband, and when it became clear that under the terms of the family trust the young couple would inherit Middle Hill on his death, he removed himself and his great library from the family seat and left it to rot, until the roof gave in and the ancient halls were filled with weeds and rain.

The second was to consume the latter half of his life. Many times he tried to sell his collection to the Bodleian or the British Museum, but each attempt was thwarted by the impossible conditions he placed on the sale. Sir Thomas had a hatred of Catholics, and he would only part with his collection on the understanding that no Catholic should ever be allowed to view it. Finally he tried to bequeath it, but the anti-Catholic terms that governed his will were deemed by the Court of Chancery to be too restrictive. With no sale and no successful bequest, the collection was broken up and sold by his executors. The process of dispersal was to take over a hundred years. The copy in my possession had come from the very last catalogue to bear the name 'Bibliotheca Phillippica', circulated in 1977. It was a memento of a life informed by a grand battle between the angels and the demons of human nature. Sir Thomas had sought to preserve the culture of man, to accumulate it in a single place, to pass it on to the public for the glory of the nation and so to secure his name for ever alongside that of Elgin and Tate. In the end, however, overwhelmed by his hatred of Halliwell and of the Roman Church, he could not find anyone to whom it could be given, and so the thing had been smashed by the auctioneer's hammer into ten thousand smithereens, one of which had come skidding across the tiles of history to rest in a Chelsea townhouse, in the study of a Catholic philanderer and interior decorator, in this philistine first decade of the new millennium.

I thought of Sir Thomas, and of the book collector's curse – to obtain the thing you love, and never to open or share it for fear of compromising its quality. The thought of Laura Rees's death, unloved and muddled in front of a hundred strangers, made me suddenly terrified. If there was a rational part of me still holding back, still insisting upon some small qualification in my feelings for Claudia, or my intentions towards Jim, I felt it let go. A man can hold on to a cliff by his fingertips alone, and yet stay stable. It is the final release of that tiny point of contact, insignificant in the scale of the whole, that presages disaster.

The window in my study looks out into a small cobbled mews behind our house. I held the book open in my arms and stood before the window, smelling the scent of vanilla that rose from the warm and ancient pages. Outside in the street the refuse lorry was passing, the binmen swinging their cacophony of bottles into the back in orange recycling sacks. I got a hint of the sweet rot of the rubbish, and the smell mingled with old pages recalled me to the bookshop on Berwick Street where I had worked as a teenager. I felt a deep yearning for that world of lost significance. The heat was so great in the street that it made the distance shimmer like an African road. I started to sweat with the sunshine falling through the open window. I realized quite suddenly that my arms were trembling with the weight of the book. In fact my whole body was shaking. I held the book away from me instinctively to protect it from the tears I felt coming from my eyes. Taking care, I put it back in its display case. Then, by way of an apology to Laura, I placed my hand in the drawer of my bureau (a rather fine Edwardian writing table upon which Leonard Woolf used to write his letters) and slammed it closed on my fingers.

# 14

THE TELEPHONE CONVERSATION WITH MY WIFE HEIGHT-
ened a tension that had been building during her absence.
With Cee I had for some time been lying outright
about my meetings with Mrs Swanson. Not about every
session, but certainly about their frequency. There was a
recklessness in this, for as neither Claudia nor Jim knew of
her ignorance there was always the chance that they might
disclose to her an unknown visit. I was helped by the fact
that I had taken over the decoration of the entire property
and Cee was out of town, greatly reducing the risk that
they might ever need to speak, but the chance remained.
In truth, I simply did not want to stop seeing Claudia.
There was no way I could justify to Cee seeing her so
often, and so I took the plunge and just plain lied. The
figure of my pursuer had receded into the background
– I had not been aware of her since the brief cat-and-
mouse of St Mark's Square – but I began to feel a fugitive
nonetheless.

I was not in the habit of lying to Cee. I was in the
habit of obfuscating, twisting, shifting, backdating,
emphasizing, de-emphasizing, digressing, editing and
diverting. These were tactics better suited to the evasion
of her particular brand of instinct, like crossing a river
to break a scent. I was not sure how good I would be at

lying, or even how much I wanted to do it. It makes a difference to a man's conscience, whether he lies or omits the truth, even if the net effect is the same. All the reading didn't help. There's only so much moral truth one can consume without getting a taste for the stuff. The very idea that there might be such a thing as truth was a new and unhelpful notion, sprouting up amid the rubble of my relativism. Hence the jump from *Middlemarch* (her choice) to *Porterhouse Blue* (mine). Sitting opposite Claudia in her kitchen, Sharpe's exploding condoms were somehow a great deal less embarrassing than Eliot's perfect diagrams of the human heart in motion.

The situation could not continue indefinitely. I was aware that Jim might expect to see some practical progress in assembling the library, and in the accomplishment of the remaining works. The latter were coming slowly – I had a suspicion our painters, usually reliable, were eking out the job for want of a follow-on. However, they had managed to finish the guest bedroom, and the recarpeting of the hall had been brought forward in the wake of Claudia's miscarriage, the stained original being discreetly removed before she emerged from hospital. I had located for Jim a reprint of *The Wealth of Nations* published in the same year as the original, and finely re-bound by the Chelsea Bindery, and was negotiating a price. I had also got hold of *Liar's Poker*, and I had decided to telephone him to give him an update, though the call was continually postponed by the secret hope that his death might overtake it.

Things with Cee were more difficult. She mentioned in a call one night that, contrary to my earlier statements, the Swansons had now run up a sizeable bill on credit, and began to question me as to when we might expect settlement. The real figure was almost double the one she quoted (which was an estimate based on bills from our suppliers), as I had neglected to keep the account up to date. She was dogged in her pursuit of the subject, mentioning it on two subsequent occasions, and her very diligence informed me that my deception was beginning to take on water. I did not know whether she had specific suspicions, or whether something in my general manner had betrayed me, but relations between us deteriorated as the long summer dragged on, until even small exchanges by text message seemed clenched with the agony of a costive bowel. I was aware for the first time in our marriage that more than risking her happiness, I was actually making her unhappy.

It is surprising how long things that can't possibly go on do, and for the last two weeks of August I found myself plunging from one emotional state to the next in the manner of a fanatical Roman bather staggering between pools, from the caldarium of the Swansons' kitchen to the frigidarium of my own, with the tepidarium of London days in between. I had decided by this time upon the final method of Mr Swanson's murder, and waiting for the necessary circumstances left me in terrible suspense. Claudia and I were by that time meeting twice and sometimes even three times a week, and it was after one such session, the last before the start of September, that the event occurred that signalled the beginning of the end.

I had emerged from the Swansons' house in a state of contentment. Claudia had made no mention of my fee at the end of the session, a leaden fact which was transmuted into a golden promise by romantic expectation. She had also rejected my proposal of *The End of the Affair* as the next week's subject, which suggested to me a growing acknowledgement on her part of the state of things between us. She had claimed it was too depressing, though I suspected that in truth it was simply too close to the bone. The cheerfulness lasted me all the way out through her garden gate and on to the street, where my nemesis was parked on the opposite side of the road.

The woman was there. She was sitting outside the house in a red Volvo estate, parked about ten metres from the door. She was as least as unremarkable as she had been in the hospital waiting room, if indeed I had seen her there at all. She wore the same T-shirt, and the same baseball cap pulled down over a greasy brown ponytail, which makes me think that perhaps I have simply transposed her image from one negative to the next. Had things been different, I would not have noted her and she would have noted me. As it was she was turned around in the tangle of the driver's-side belt (unplugged from its socket but not removed from across her shoulder), struggling with something in the back seat. The dashboard of the car was strewn with the detritus of either a very long journey or an incredibly slovenly driver – there were crisp packets and maps, and a paper milkshake cup with the straw poking out rolled sideways into the gap at the bottom of the windshield. An unholy racket, audible even through the closed doors of the family saloon, announced the presence of a baby in the back seat of the car. I always try to take note of such displays as a preventative against the temptations of procreation (although I have never quite been able to countenance the idea of raising children, I find it appalling that the world might be denied my genetic legacy). With that in mind, I made a point of crossing the road to get close to the car, to experience with as great an immediacy as possible the awful effect of the angry, senseless midget strapped into the back.

As I passed the window, the sound was not disappointing. The scratched doors of the car seemed actually to buckle out under the internal pressure. The tiny pink lungs beat on the bodywork with the force of a clapper in a mighty bell. The unfortunate mother (I knew she was a mother, as any disinterested professional would long since have abandoned the driver's seat in search of another career) was twisted completely around, and so I risked bending down for a look inside. I peered in, and sure enough in the far corner of the interior there was a face suffused with the complete conviction that whatever temporary ill it was suffering, no creature in the universe had ever experienced anything half as bad. Against this epic and implacable conviction, the brown-haired woman had raised a small and heavily soiled toy meerkat, which she jiggled. I grinned to myself, and before turning away I glanced at the passenger seat. On it was a digital camera with a long lens, such as one might use to capture twenty-something starlets descending from the yachts of married men. There was also a photograph of myself, a good and detailed likeness taken as I exited the front door of my house, and a printed piece of paper on which I had time to distinguish my name, before the woman in the car dropped the stuffed toy, causing me to jerk away from the car as one placing a hand on a hot pan. She bent down into the footwell to quest blindly for the animal with both hands, and I turned away from the car and walked quickly to the bend in the road.

I kept on walking for almost four hours. I walked along the river, away from Chelsea towards the City, and I crossed over the river to the south bank along the Millennium Bridge. All the time, my mind was in utter turmoil. The sunny day seemed to mock me with its rabble of happy families and carefree joggers. In my long career as an adulterer, I had had good cause never to enquire too deeply into the degree to which Cee might be aware of my affairs. If you still care about your wife, there is a certain delicacy of feeling which prohibits the consideration of whether or not she knows. If she does know, and stays with you without complaint, she will be lowered for ever in your esteem, for such pliancy seems gutless. If she does not know and for many years continues on oblivious with the hymen of her pride intact, then she has displayed a lack of acuity which does not sit easily with a sense of her intelligence. This is in fact one of the single most emotionally destructive aspects of long-term infidelity (it's fine for a one-nighter – you can tell yourself either that you got away with it because as clever as your wife might be she trusts you, or that she sussed you but out of love forgave a single indiscretion). It is only a particularly unpleasant type of philanderer, one totally lacking in proper respect for his spouse, who gives the question the full weight of his consideration, and comes to a conclusion one way or the other. Of course there must be an answer – the two conditions, knowledge and ignorance, are mutually exclusive. But as long as the question remains unposed, the two contradictory possibilities can exist in mutual peace. She can remain both intelligent and dignified despite your actions, like Schrödinger's cat, simultaneously dead and alive until you open the box.

The presence of the private investigator threw me into complete disarray. Not only was it an upsetting and vexatious discovery in itself, it also upended the box over me, dropping a dead cat in my lap. So, Cee knew, or at least suspected enough to have hired someone to catch me in the act. It dawned on me suddenly that the timing of this long business trip, which I had taken for the fates assisting me in the assembly of my tragic climax, was in fact a lump of cheese in the trap. She had left me feeling completely unobserved, the better to catch me in the act. But why now, after so many years? And what would she do with the information once she had it? Was she intending to divorce me? Do you still need evidence of infidelity to divorce someone? My understanding was that you just declared them a bastard and hired a lawyer. To confront me with cast-iron evidence of my misdemeanours and force me to change my ways? Whatever her reasons, her timing was terrible. At almost any point since the late nineties my life might have furnished a hidden cameraman with a pornographic showreel sufficient to found his own internet site, and yet Cee had chosen the one occasion of a platonic friendship to loose this woman upon me.

Then there was the practical question of what to do. The woman did not know that I had spotted her; she had been fully engrossed with her explosive offspring, of that I was certain. Perhaps, if I simply continued on as I was with Mrs Swanson, these innocent and properly scheduled meetings where I drank tea and talked books and struggled to contain my growing lust, she might eventually report that I was as celibate as a visiting vicar and the whole thing would simply go away. By the time Jim met his end, and Claudia was finally free to acknowledge our love, it would be irrelevant what Cee did or didn't know. I would save her the overtime and tell her myself. That thought whirled me along to the next, even more disheartening, one: how could I accomplish my crime under covert observation? I thought it safe to assume that the woman had been watching me at some time between this chance encounter and the chase on Oxford Street. That she had done so without detection raised the terrifying prospect that she might be there watching me at any given moment.

I walked and walked, up the south bank, under Waterloo Bridge where the booksellers at the market were packing up their wares, past the bikers doing tricks on the concrete ramps by the National Theatre, past the Oxo Tower, heading further and further east, but the process of striding through London which was my usual respite from inner disturbance only led me further and further into confusion. In the end the sun went down and my feet started to hurt, and I caught a cab back home. By that time the hottest of my notions had cooled, and I was determined at least that until I knew what I should do, I would do nothing more than stop lying about the frequency of my meetings with Mrs Swanson. I would mention nothing to Cee in our phone calls, and I would take greater precautions in arranging for Mr Swanson's demise.

This last point was becoming for me a source of general frustration, but I was powerless to hasten its coming. There is a literary term for the attribution of human emotion to meteorological event, known as 'pathetic fallacy'. It is a trope that has fallen out of favour in modern writing; it is thought of as rather gauche, quite old hat, to have sunshine break through the clouds upon the lovers, or a storm gather over the laminate roof-tiles of the suburban semi in which the skeletons are about to dance from the fitted cupboards. My own theory is that the fashion for literal Sturm und Drang to accompany literary climax passed away with the popularization of antibiotics. When Austen sends Marianne out into the wild parts of the estate in wet shoes and stockings, or Brontë sends Catherine hurtling across the moors, the melodrama inherent in the recent/attendant rainfall is offset by a genuine sense of consequence – young ladies could, and quite often did, die from chest infections occasioned by exposure to the inclemency which just happened to reflect their inner turmoil. In an age where a quick visit from the local GP, Lemsip and a course of penicillin will do for a heroine with a chesty cough, it also rather does for the romance. With the seriousness of consequence removed, it began to seem artificial, heavy-handed, to externalize the character's interior landscape in storms.

It's a shame really, because, as literary devices go, pathetic fallacy is actually one of the least artificial. The weather shapes personal and historical events far more readily than, say, conspiracy, or madness, or amnesia, or any of the other constructs that novelists seem happy to wield when bludgeoning the narrative arc into submission. Indeed, some of the most fantastical conjunctions of weather and metaphor are no more than reported fact: when García Márquez tells us in *One Hundred Years of Solitude* that the climate changed in his fictional South American country following the rapine of the land by the conquistadors, resulting in the sky weeping a constant rain of tears, he tells us no more than the truth. The deforestation required by the heavy mining and agriculture of the Spanish altered the pattern of rainfall in some coastal areas, causing towns and villages at high altitudes to be caught in a novel deluge. Of course, one may doubt whether the drops were salty, but their falling is a matter of public record.

I had ample cause for reflection on this strange conjunction, since my plan (such as it was) was for the murder of Jim Swanson to take place under cover of a storm, or not at all. The increased reliability of weather forecasting has given us all the power of narrators in our own little dramas; if we wish the sun to shine upon our proposals, or the rain to cover our tears, we stand a good chance of being able to orchestrate both. By looking at the BBC five-day forecast I was able to predict with some accuracy what days were likely candidates for a morning downpour.

The storm was not intended to provide me with an emotional correlative to the deed, but rather to act as a sheepdog to the morning commuters of Pimlico, the bark of thunder herding them down from the pastures of pavement into the narrow corral of the northbound platform of the Victoria Line. Not only would a deluge of sufficient vigour cause people to abandon bicycles, buses and umbrellas in their daily schlep, it would also provide me with an opportunity to wear a hood and cap on the platform itself without appearing overly conspicuous. If I was lucky it might even cause delays on the line, which would increase the bottleneck.

My plan was, quite simply, to push Jim Swanson under the wheels of an oncoming train. In this I was indebted both to Claudia (who had started me thinking about the lethality of modes of transport) and Laura (who had led by example), and it was my intention that this should be construed as an accident. Indeed, I had an inkling that with time I might be able to tell myself it *had* been an accident. It was difficult to see myself being a murderer in the long term. There were only two obstacles – the fact that Jim drove to work, and that on a sunny morning the northbound platform at Pimlico was not especially busy. The plan therefore required first that Jim should be denied the use of his car in making the morning commute, and secondly that the train platform should be extremely and unusually crowded with jostling bodies in order to provide cover for my assault. The more people there were at the scene of the crime, and the more slippery the surfaces, the greater the plausibility of an accident, and it was these two factors that made a rainy day essential.

The heat in the city was oppressive. Every day it bore down upon my shoulders like the world upon Atlas. The meetings with Claudia continued, and I began to feel that they never stopped. Our actual conversations, over the breakfast bar in Vincent Square, were only the visible parts of a communion that continued every moment of the London summer. They were like a series of tropical islands which when viewed by the tourist coming in to land appear no more than scattered scenes of pleasure, but which are in fact the peaks of a range of mountains, their mammoth sides and deep-groined chasms submerged beneath the sea. Sometimes I did not sleep for two days at a time, lying on my back in the furnace of my room, the windows open to the sounds of sirens and drunks, replaying our conversations, and even conducting the new ones we would have when together. But although the meetings went on, and the heat went on, and everything went on as if it meant to go on for ever, I knew that the weather would have to break. Sooner or later, the weather would have to break.

In the first week of September I received a call from someone I initially assumed was Jim Swanson's secretary, but who when I said as much informed me in no uncertain terms that she was in fact his personal assistant. My first feeling was one of panic that I had somehow been discovered in my plotting, and that Jim had deputed her to sack me and to telephone the police, but I managed to restrain myself from a confession for long enough to discover her real purpose. She asked if I might be free for a lunch with our employer. Along with relief I felt my toes curl with dismay at the prospect, but somehow it was so much more difficult to refuse her than it would have been to fob off Mr Swanson himself. The prospect of his imminent demise did not make the idea of lunch with him any more attractive. The PA had the bright directness of someone used to making things happen, and none of the awkwardness that might have served to throttle the issue between Jim and me. On the other hand, I reasoned, if I could time the lunch to occur after the first day of rain, it was an obligation I would never have to fulfil. So it was that after several dates had been proposed and rejected I eventually agreed to lunch the following Wednesday in Canary Wharf. The Swansons were to be in Hertfordshire over the weekend visiting Claudia's parents, and personal conversations over the telephone were not in our repertoire, so I could not discuss the lunch with her in prospect, and if things went to plan there would be no retrospect to speak of. Six days seemed more than enough time for the elements to get their act together.

As Sunday and Monday passed, my confidence wilted in the sweltering heat. The five-day forecast kept on making promises, but they were never kept. The sky was free from clouds, but not clear – rather a skein of haze lay over it like a cataract over a bright blue iris, and the city stayed hot. The fabric of London seemed to be giving way beneath the onslaught. The Albert Bridge was closed when it seemed the Victorian girders might buckle, and my beautiful shoes sank in the black, glistening surface of the streets. I could not sleep at all on Tuesday night, but lay naked on my duvet, staring at the ceiling.

On Wednesday morning I found I had the butterflies one associates with a stage performance or a public speaking event. In addition, I was peevish at having to travel the hour or so across London to get to Jim's bank in Docklands. I do not mind confessing that I find the City and Canary Wharf, the bastard son that has grown up to steal its inheritance, to be disorientating to the point of nausea. London contains many Other Londons, a result of its habit of expanding not by organic accretion, but by the encirclement and eventual absorption of existing communities that would before have claimed a separate identity. From Covent Garden and Bloomsbury in the seventeenth century to Harlow Town and Stevenage in the 1950s, the history of urban planning in London is that of architects seeking to create satellite communities beyond the reach of the urban sprawl, only to find that the relentless growth of the city consumes their pet projects and adds them to its patchwork of disparate geographies. Canary Wharf was to me the most forbidding and unfamiliar of the Other Londons, more foreign than Paris or New York.

The names of the streets on which the new economy has established itself tell the story of a glorious past based on trade and manufacture. Canary Wharf took its name from the ships that docked there from the Canary Islands, unloading sugar cane and coffee. All that they now unload on the wharf is debt, savings flowing from the East to borrowers in the West. I know that the unions had to be broken, and that Brazilian steel is cheaper to smelt. I know about outsourcing and globalization and free movement of labour within the EU as a foundation principle, and that in the unlikely event that we ever need to rustle up some new Spitfires we can just get the Chinese to do it or, if it's them we're fighting, the Indians, and they'll probably be better made than our own. But I can't help feeling an almost superstitious attachment to the material, to the thing that you make and see in your hand. When the financial crisis got into full swing, I felt the same sort of mean, vague vindication that a set of religious villagers might have felt when the new supermarket that had started opening on Sundays burned to the ground. It was the confirmation of an atavistic sense that an economy made of paper could never be as strong as one of bricks, guns and widgets.

The journey reminds me too of my parents. The last time I saw my mother she was heading down onto the eastbound District and Circle line platform to attend the picket line at Wapping, there to be squashed by one of the vans delivering strike-breaking copies of the *Sun*. She was a bit of a left-wing martyr for a while, though because no one remembers the printers' strike any more her legend has rather subsided. Most people now read their papers online. The present condescends to her socialism, makes it seem almost quaint, like a seventies haircut. I have missed her every day of my life, but in some ways I'm grateful that she never lived to see her ideals not only fail, but become an irrelevance. No one today would dream of suggesting that human beings should be expected to share. If they did, a weekday lunch in Canary Wharf would disabuse them.

After forty-five minutes on the Underground and the Docklands Light Railway, I rose out of the earth in the centre of the plaza, the long escalator delivering me up like one of those conveyor belts that used to haul coal up from the mines. As I rose towards the sunlight, I passed through the subterranean layers of the shopping centre that stands beneath the garden in the middle of the square, a place stocked entirely with shops catering for the transitory needs of a daytime population of office workers. As a result I saw no bookshops, and counted seven different places to buy coffee. At the top of the escalator a man walked straight into my chest, looking up from the document he had been reading long enough to tell me to watch where the fuck I was going. All round the square, men and women in suits hurried hither and thither, drawn quickly across the clean concrete on little chariots of self-importance, holding the reins of their BlackBerries before them.

I spent a few weeks in Florence once, on a doomed attempt to acquire some of Elizabeth Barrett Browning's papers, during which time I became quite friendly with a young teacher at the Charles Cecil Studios. I was sitting with him one evening outside a bar on the Piazza Santo Spirito, drinking beer and watching a young couple sitting on the stone fountain, the boy running his hand in the water as the girl looked around listlessly. Quite without warning the two of them began to share a passionate kiss, the sort of thing that would have been faintly disgusting had they been less prepossessing, and I remarked to my Italian friend how much more romantic were young Italians than their English counterparts, and how many couples I had seen embracing in the street since my arrival. He laughed at me, and said, 'These are not romantic. These are horny. But they live with their parents, they cannot go home, so they,' and here he clapped his hands, 'all over the streets!'

I think of that moment whenever anyone describes London as a tolerant city. It is an example of how completely one may misconstrue the character of a place by importing assumptions from one's own culture. French, Americans, even people from other parts of England, praise the city for its tolerance. London is not a tolerant city. London is indifferent. It's not that it accepts you, it just doesn't give a fuck who you are.

At the top of the escalator I had a cursory look around, checking for the woman I had seen in the car. It had become a habit of mine to seek her out in any idle moment, but I had not seen her since the afternoon in Vincent Square. I found the restaurant eventually with the assistance of a colour-coded map mounted on a steel stanchion beside the exit from the Underground. The dining room was a light and airy space filled with men and women in suits, the menus had no prices, and the table to which I was shown was excellent, positioned next to a plate-glass window beyond which the Thames and the wide blue sky made empty promises of freedom. Jim was on time to the minute, entering the restaurant at precisely 12.29 p.m. He wore a suit without a tie, and the hairless slice of his breastbone was visible between the lapels of his jacket. His BlackBerry was in his hand as he approached the table, and before he had pulled out the chair he placed it next to the knives on the white linen tablecloth as if it was an article of cutlery his particular dish required. I had not seen my victim since our meeting on the steps of the hospital, and was rather thrown by his reality. I tried to rise from my seat to greet him, but my thighs became trapped and I only managed a kind of trembling squat. He gave my hand two pumps, as quick and masculine as two sporty sons. I had the unnerving idea that he had grown taller since our last meeting, until I realized that he stood on the shoulders of the location. This was his turf, his postcode, his gang colours in the surrounding pinstripe. He was closer to the source of his power, and the ironic little sense of superiority with which I enfolded myself in west and central London provided me scant protection in the east.

He sat down and yanked the chair forward with his hands on either side of the table. As soon as he was seated he opened the menu. He frowned as he consulted it. His whole air gave the impression that his time was a scarce commodity, that this lunch with him existed in a tiny alleyway sandwiched between the great edifice of his last activity and the grand structure of the next.

'So how are things in the markets?'

'Shit. But we're making money.'

'Ah. I read something in the papers about another building society going bankrupt.'

'Not bankrupt. Nationalized.'

'You'll have to forgive me. I don't really concern myself with economics.' I caught the tone of my own voice. It was completely inappropriate to a meeting with a client. What I had meant to convey was a wide-eyed naivety in matters where he and his friends strode around in suits and worldly confidence. Instead I had managed to imply that I thought I was better than he was and that what he did for a living was beneath me. Jim looked up at me sharply.

'Yeah, well, you're forgiven.'

'Aha. Thank you. Of course it's fascinating and I follow the news when I can, I just don't seem to have the time. And it's all so complicated.'

'The economy's like gravity. It doesn't matter whether or not you understand it, or even whether you think about it at all. If you step off a building you're still going to hit the street.'

I wondered where he had picked up this little morsel of wit. I expected him to look to me to check that I had registered his cleverness, and I had my appreciative nod prepared, but he ignored me and continued to read the menu.

'I often find myself thinking, where has all the money gone? I mean, it was there before, and now it isn't.'

'The money hasn't gone. It was just a crisis of values. Nobody knew how much they were worth,' he said, and hailed the waitress.

'Yes, sir, can I get you something to drink?'

'Yeah. Get us water, please.'

'Still or sparkling?'

'Tap. Tap's OK for you, yeah?'

'And will you be having any wine with your lunch?'

Jim looked to me and raised his eyebrow.

'Not for me, thank you.'

'Come on. We're supposed to be celebrating.'

I was a little taken aback, but I smiled.

'That's very kind, but I'm afraid I have things to do this afternoon and I'm useless after a glass of wine.'

'What things?' he asked.

As he looked at me across the table, I felt completely unsure of myself. I had a sudden and horrible suspicion that I had plans to see Claudia. I knew that I was not due to see her with the same certainty that one feels when asked if the iron was definitely turned off before leaving the house; the asking of the question shook the foundations of the answer. As this suspicion lurched suddenly into view, it dragged behind it a question – even if I was to see Mrs Swanson, why should that make me feel so struck with guilt, given the complete physical innocence of our meetings? I had never conducted a professional relationship so far above the board. I wanted to pull my iPhone from my pocket to refer to my calendar, but I was aware that that would look like a desperate lunge for verisimilitude. I opened my mouth, hoping that this might prompt memory to action, but nothing came, and Jim continued to look at me. I was still floundering when he turned away and said to the waitress that we would be having both white and red. The list and the corresponding glasses were brought to our table.

'So what are we celebrating?'

'You found those books, didn't you? The ones you decided I'd want. I reckon that covers the first bottle. And now you've done all the hunting and the buying the project's almost complete. I'll take that for the second.'

'Aha, thank you. But of course, the second bottle might be a little premature. I mean, we do have to decide on an arrangement for the shelves . . .'

'But you probably don't do that, bossman like you. That's probably left to some unpaid intern, actually sticking books on shelves.'

'Oh, I like to involve myself in all aspects of the thing, you know, really provide a complete service . . .'

He did not look at me, but kept scanning the wine list.

'That's not a complete service. A complete service involves delegation. I work in a service industry. I have clients. And they'd be fucking disappointed if I charged them for stuff my secretary could do.'

'Ah yes . . . the division of labour,' I said, not really sure of what that might mean.

The sommelier came to my rescue, and asked whether Jim might like some assistance in choosing. He shook his head, and with the help of his finger ordered 'one of those and one of those', before snapping the list shut and turning his attention back to me. By that time I had thought of something useful to say.

'Also of course there's more to do than just the library.'

'I know you've been giving her . . . what are they? Lessons or whatever. But I think she'll be stopping those. Not that I think you're overcharging, but I hate the idea of paying for stuff you can get for free.' He tapped his tap water.

'Well, I would be very happy to go on a reduced rate.'

'Cheers, but no. We don't see enough of her friends as it is, so I rang round and set up a bit of a book club for her. Turns out they have one already, so she's going to go to that.'

Jim stared at me in a way that appeared almost overtly confrontational.

'Then there's the guest bedrooms, and the furniture and the curtains in the library itself.'

'Your wife's doing all that.'

'Well, she was, yes, but she's got so much else on at the moment that we've shuffled some of our properties. I've taken one or two off her hands, including yours. So I expect I'll be around for a while yet.'

Jim stared at me.

'Does Claudia know about this?' he asked.

The question brought me immediately back from the clashing of antlers. I had no desire to get Claudia in trouble, not least because if everything went according to plan then Jim would soon be in no position to impede our little get-togethers. The last thing I wanted was to sow discord in their house – I would never wish on Claudia the burden of having exchanged angry words with her husband the evening before his accident.

'I . . . uh, I don't know.'

'That's not what we paid you for. We paid for your wife to do the decorating because Claudia loved what she did to Patrick Massey's place.'

'Ah, look, I really am sorry. But I assure you, I am fully qualified,' I said, as if that was what this was about. 'I started the business with Cee, we do all our design work in tandem anyway. It's just that I will take day-to-day responsibility for the implementation.'

Jim's BlackBerry buzzed. He looked at it, not registering the content of the message, merely its presence, and the office seemed to reach out and puncture his resolve. He deflated slightly, and looked down at the bare white tablecloth between his cutlery.

'I'm going to have to talk to Claudia about it. I don't

know if that's what she wants,' he said, and left it at that.

The remainder of that lunch was so exquisitely awkward that it made me feel like a teenager, as not since my identity began to firm up in my first year at university had I ever felt an embarrassment so acute. It was an embarrassment at a profound level, not of the kind that results from having been caught out in some social solecism or hypocrisy, but of the gut-wrenching variety that comes when you see yourself from the outside, pretending to be someone you want to be but secretly know you are not. Jim ordered a starter, obliging me to do the same, and when the wine arrived he drank an entire glass before the waiter could produce the basket of freshly baked rolls.

Conversation was stilted at first, as it must be between two men who not only share a mutual antipathy but whose only point of common interest is a contested woman, a subject that must be avoided at all costs. When he had consumed the first three-quarters of a bottle of wine, however, Jim's manner changed completely. He became garrulous, and began to tell me anecdote after work-related anecdote about banking. These stories were filled with characters identified only by their first names, who I was apparently expected to know. My gratitude to him for filling the silence outweighed any critical judgements I might otherwise have exercised regarding his skill as a raconteur. I simply ate and smiled and tried not to feel the slow progress of the minute hand.

There is also, I discovered, a hidden dimension of social awkwardness of which only a tiny portion of the human beings who have walked the earth can ever have been aware. It is the particular tension that exists between a murderer and his unwitting victim. Or rather, a tragedian and the subject of his tragedy. Whenever Jim diverged from matters of the past and projected himself quite innocently and with complete confidence into the immediate future – say, with a story about where he and Claudia were going skiing in the autumn (a topic which would have been particularly distasteful to me in any case) – I found myself thinking, oh no you're not, boyo, and the urge to say as much became almost overwhelming.

I had expected the lunch to be a short affair, remembering Claudia's account of how hard Jim worked during the week. And indeed he never seemed to be in a state of leisure – his BlackBerry buzzed several times, he excused himself once to return a message, and I frequently caught him looking at the screen as he spoke as if anxiously registering the time. Yet despite this evident pressure, the lunch was allowed to drag on and on. He kept telling stories, and he kept drinking, and after the main courses were finished he asked for the dessert menu with all the enthusiasm of a man on death row selecting the method of his execution. I said I wanted nothing more to eat or drink but Jim decided he would like a chocolate moelleux with organic vanilla ice cream. It was after the arrival of this dish that I ceased to collude in my torture, and stopped supplying the little grunts of acknowledgement that had allowed Jim to shore up the unwieldy structures of his anecdotes. Without my assistance, we eventually lapsed into complete silence. After a few moments tracking his spoon backwards and forwards through the melted chocolate congealing on the plate in front of him, he said, apropos of nothing, 'How long have you been married?'

'Almost ten years.'

'Do you love your wife?'

'Yes, I love my wife.'

'How do you love her?'

'Would you like me to count the ways, Jim?'

He stared at me. I remembered Claudia telling me, when we had been discussing Hemingway, that her husband was not a big drinker. He blinked twice and sat back in his chair.

'Because I have this theory. That it's not just about love. It's not just about that . . . love.' He picked up his BlackBerry, and began turning it absently end over end on the white cloth. 'You have to love them in the right *way*. You have to keep . . . you have to keep a little of yourself back. You have to make this room in yourself they can't go in, because they all say they want someone to love them completely, to give them everything. But actually if you give someone everything, they start wondering what else there is out there to get. It's human nature. If you really love somebody, you have to hold something back, for their sake, to save them from the wondering.'

I looked at Jim, and thought how much you have in common with a man when you both love the same woman and she is somewhere in between the two of you. That is perhaps the closest state of kinship two men can attain. It's only when she makes her final choice that one man goes to heaven, and the other plunges down.

'It's an interesting theory,' I said.

'Does she talk to you about losing Simon?'

He looked at me, waiting for an answer. He skewered me with the intensity of his waiting. All the nervous energy which had jumped through the encounter, the drinking, the time checking, the fiddling with cutlery resolved itself into that one question.

'I don't . . . I'm your decorator, Mr Swanson.'

He kept looking at me for a few more seconds, but the silence was unsustainable. I felt ashamed of myself, given the courage it had taken him to muster the question, for deflecting it. I thought suddenly of the little silver rattle lying unshaken in its shroud of tissue paper.

'She won't talk to me about it,' he said.

He took a sip of water. I cleared my throat.

'You know, if Claudia ever went away from me, I'd kill myself,' he said.

I looked across the restaurant and caught the waiter's eye. He started to come over and I smiled and nodded at him.

'And I'd kill him,' he said, and sat back in his chair. 'I'd kill him.'

The waiter stood beside the table and looked to both of us in turn, awaiting instruction.

'It's been absolutely lovely, Mr Swanson,' I said, 'but I really think we ought to get the bill.'

Having paid for lunch with a Platinum Amex, Jim left me. It had been my intention to excuse myself as he grappled with the sudden mysteries of the portable card reader, to go to the toilet and lock myself in a cubicle and wait until he was gone, if necessary until the restaurant closed and the lights were turned off. In the event, however, the process of paying seemed to sober him up (I peered at the receipt after his exit, and the amount quoted would certainly have brought me to my senses), and he shook my hand. He even made some coherent excuse about having to return to the office for a client meeting, and he was out of the restaurant without further incident. The subsequent events of that afternoon were quite exceptional for Mr Swanson, but I was not to discover them for some days.

I myself went outside and spent some time down by the wharf to steady my nerve with blasts of salty air, which provided a glorious relief from the muggy stillness of the metropolis. As I stood there, I tried to decide whether or not a client had just threatened my life. How serious had Jim Swanson been? Had he been talking figuratively? Had he simply been overwhelmed by drink and emotion? I shook my head. It was ridiculous to take such a threat seriously. I had designed his bathroom. I remembered suddenly the model train collectors' periodical hidden away in the stack of magazines in his downstairs loo. No one should fear an enthusiast of model railways. But then perhaps all crimes of passion are ridiculous. Murder always seems to come as a surprise to the victim. One never hears of the neighbours who, when interviewed by the newspapers, say of the recently detected serial killer, 'God, he was a violent lunatic. We always thought he was just the type to bludgeon nurses.' As I mused upon his threat, I gazed out to sea, where dark stormclouds were gathering over the Thames.

It is a little-known fact that the events of 9/11 directly occasioned a handful of divorces. These did not come about as a result of post–traumatic stress, survivor's guilt or metaphysical angst, but rather by the more traditional method of infidelity revealed. A small number of men and women working in the towers were conducting affairs in downtown hotels during their morning break. When they surfaced from rooms with curtains drawn to find fifty missed calls on their mobiles, blissfully unaware of the changes in the world beyond, they phoned their wives and husbands. 'Oh, thank God. Oh, thank God, Steve, are you all right?' 'Yes, yes of course, I'm fine, I'm in the office. What's the matter?' One can only imagine the strange mix of emotions that must result from knowing that by a miracle one's spouse is safe, but also that they are a bit of a lying arsehole.

But these divorces are the exception. Generally the important events in western lives, at least since the fall of the Berlin Wall, happen in spite of world events and not because of them. At any given time, your country is probably at war with somebody, there are revolutions and counter-revolutions in places where they grow the beans for your coffee, but the births and deaths and loves that shape the course of one's existence pass through the great life of nations like bubble-wrapped parcels through the post. We are lucky really to have enjoyed this solipsism, this freedom to make our own little stories away from the crushing momentum of the grand narrative. Our grandparents' generation did not have it. No doubt it will end in a decade or two; the seas will rise or the oil will run out and we'll be eating powdered eggs and thinking wistfully of bananas and killing each other in droves. But for the moment, it is generally pleasant to have lived one's life decoupled from history.

I did not know it as I walked away from lunch, but the distant wake of world events was about to capsize my little boat. In the end, Jim Swanson was right – economics don't care if you get them or not. I certainly didn't get them, but they still triggered the series of events which was to precipitate my personal disaster. The day after my meeting with Mr Swanson, on the final day of his employment, the BBC website informed me that the next morning would bring a terrible storm.

# 15

A WARM FRONT WAS ON THE MARCH. IT WAS COMING ACROSS the Atlantic like a wave of bombers bound for London, and the jagged spirals hanging across the cheerful green map indicated that when it came, the wrath of the gods would be unleashed. I set the first part of my plan into action that very evening.

One small potential problem presented itself, in that Cee had returned unexpectedly for the night from Buckinghamshire. She had a few errands that required personal attendance, and had also informed me, rather ominously, that she needed to talk to me about something. At first I thought this might be a genuine disaster – if she was still there I could not leave the house early enough to catch Jim on his way to work without her noticing, and my being out of bed before 10 a.m. would, in the absence of fire or impending nuclear war, have been inexplicable. A delay of even one day would be fatal, for there might not be another summer storm of such ferocity, and if I disabled Jim's vehicle more than a few hours in advance of the deed his insurers were liable to provide a replacement. To my great relief, however, she explained on the phone that she had meetings and a site visit the next morning, and would be leaving at the crack of dawn.

She looked peculiarly beautiful and happy from her

trip, and I told her so. Strangely, the compliment seemed to make her uncomfortable. Since the discovery of the identity of my pursuer I had been rigorously accurate in accounting to Cee for the dates, times and durations of my meetings with Mrs Swanson, so I was easy on that score, and I was not even particularly concerned with the bestiary of my past transgressions; mostly I was irritated at her timing, and determined that she should not derail my plans with the mock-seriousness of a marital debate. She kept asking me if I had been ill, if I was all right, and it was all I could do to bat the questions away. The thought of my own morning meeting with Jim Swanson in the bowels of the city transfixed me, body and soul.

I offered to cook, and slipped one of Cee's sleeping pills into her wine at supper. It was not, I must confess, the first occasion on which I had had to resort to this expediency, although in the past it was a question of romantic convenience. Cee had always had trouble sleeping, but she held chemical assistance in the same regard as a crippled young sprinter might have held his wheelchair; there was a resentment, as if the pills themselves were the source of weakness and not the condition they were designed to alleviate. In this sense, and given that Cee could really have used the sleep, I considered that rather than feeling any misgivings over my actions I should pat myself on the back for assuring my wife a good night's rest. Cee conked out at ten thirty, conversation unhad, and I decided to set out on my mission at 2 a.m., judging this to be the darkest time of the summer night.

To calm myself I retired to spend some time with my collection. I did not sleep, but sat awake with my books in the hot night. I was intensely aware as I left the house of the possibility of being followed. I had no idea on what basis my wife had contracted with the weird mother she had placed on my tail, but I imagined that the profession required a certain flexibility with regard to hours. Although, of course, adulterous liaisons were far more likely to take place during daylight than their legitimate counterparts. If I was too smart to be caught out in adultery, I had no intention of being implicated in a murder. I spent some time surveying the street from behind the curtains of our bedroom window, and having satisfied myself there were no unusually slovenly Volvos lurking at the kerb, I made my way down. I turned on the Fulham Road, and took a deliberate detour down one of the quiet side streets all the way back to the King's Road. It was this unmolested trip which convinced me that I was not being followed.

I took the night bus along the Embankment, and hopped out well before we reached Vincent Square, not wishing to be recorded on camera anywhere in the vicinity. I walked for ten minutes on foot, the large penknife and the packet of sugar in my pocket requiring me to hoist my trousers at regular intervals. When I reached Vincent Square, I hovered in the shadows under one of the trees, aware that waiting at the spot increased the likelihood of discovery but unsure as to how to proceed. From across the square I could make out the shape of my victim; the odious bulk of the yellow jeep, resting now in the stillness beneath the shadows of a sycamore tree.

Seeing the car in the darkness, I felt an abridged version of the sensation of hatred that I had felt when I saw Mr Swanson on the steps of the hospital. There is an implicit selfishness in the ownership of such a car which seemed perfectly to accord with my view of the City – the raised bonnet and engine block means that in an accident with a pedestrian, the impact point will be the torso (or, for a child, the head) rather than the lower leg, dramatically reducing their chance of survival. The fuel consumption is twice that of an economical runaround, needlessly exacerbating the greenhouse effect, and the raised chassis, four-wheel drive and vague militarism of the conception of a car never destined to go beyond the M25 all speak of a fantasy machismo played out at the expense of your fellow man. It gave me great pleasure to have Jim Swanson's grotesque mascot at my mercy.

I had very little idea how one goes about disabling a motor vehicle. My first thought was to put sugar in the petrol tank, but to my embarrassment when I approached the thing I could not figure out how to remove the cap from the Cayenne's tank. My only other option was to slash the tyres, something that was to me a phrase rather than a practical experience. 'Slash' I felt implied a lateral cut across the rubber, but my first attempt at that almost caused me to cut off my fingers as the four-inch blade rebounded from the thick tread. My heart was beating fast, and I heard a voice calling out the name of a dog or a cat on the open turf of the cricket pitch. I froze until some time after the calling had stopped, crouching down behind the car's rear wheel in the shadows, and was almost on the point of giving the thing up when I noticed the strip of tender material between the thick moulded rubber of the tyre and the metal of the hubcap. I put the tip of my blade against it, and slammed the back of the knife with the heel of my hand. To my surprise, the blade sank into the soft black flesh, and the great beast settled on to the rim with a sigh of defeat. I had to put one foot on the deflated tyre and pull with all my might to convince the rubber to relinquish my blade.

I performed the same operation on the other back tyre, and on the two cars either side of Mr Swanson's, and for good measure decided to do one other further down the street, to scatter my destruction a little less discriminately. The final car I singled out for my attentions was a sleek, well-fed Mercedes dozing in the hot night beneath a tree on the opposite side of the street from the houses. I walked up to it quite casually, sticking close to the cover of the railings, aware as I went of the one or two windows still lit even in these silent hours of the long dawn. With my task so close to conclusion, I was even able to appreciate this facsimile of rural peace, the dew on the grass of the cricket field, the first birds singing in the leafy-cool branches. The illegality of my activities heightened my connection with this natural world – I was a thing of the night, creeping to a purpose beyond the warm firelight of society. As I approached the unsuspecting Merc, I saw that it had a small Chelsea FC coat of arms hanging from the rear-view mirror, which increased my pleasure at the thought of dispatching the wheels (it was not that I support another team, I just hate the kind of people who like football). I was beginning to congratulate myself even as I lined up my blow.

I positioned myself behind the rear wheel, and braced for a good swing down into the rubber. When I placed my hand on the boot, however, the car sank slightly on its suspension, and what had moments before been a slumbering victim became suddenly an insane carnival of defences, as lights flashed and an ear-splitting wail rent the night air. The birds roosting in the tree took fright, and rose as one to flee across the grass. Within seconds, the lights in the top bedroom across the way came on behind the curtains. I gave the car a single kick, which almost caused me to overbalance as my leather-shod foot slipped harmlessly off the bodywork, and then ran away from the car to the mouth of one of the tributary roads leading on to the square. The Mercedes continued its histrionics for almost a minute, but by the time anyone arrived to offer succour or discover my crime I was already well on my way to a clean escape, slipping down to the banks of the Thames. I hailed a taxi several minutes' walk up towards Embankment, and gave him an address ten minutes' walk from my own home. I put the sugar back in the kitchen cupboard with the self-raising flour before I went up to bed. Once there I heard the first distant peals of thunder.

Cee awoke at 5 a.m. Already late for her meetings at the stately home, she cursed herself for her somnolence and drove off without breakfast. The subject of the proposed 'talk' was never raised.

I waited for Jim Swanson at a café on the Vauxhall Bridge Road, positioned just beside one of the roads leading on to the square. When I first arrived I had a brief moment of panic that he might take a taxi rather than the Underground to get to work, but I remembered our lunch, and how he had told me he didn't like paying for things you could get for free. I felt quite confident that Jim Swanson, the millionaire banker, would rather pay for a daily tube pass whilst his car was in the garage than shell out for a £15 taxi ride, assuming it could not be legitimately expensed. Would he telephone the police to report the vandalism? Perhaps, but he would not stay to meet them. It would be a point of pride for him not to let the crime disrupt his routine.

The rain was heavy, a deluge after the drought, and I could not risk missing him beneath the cover of the elements, so I kept my eyes fixed on the point where I expected him to emerge. Helpfully there was a lamppost on that corner, and I had calculated (by standing next to it myself and measuring off my nipples) a benchmark of Mr Swanson's approximate height to help me to identify him on his approach. I also kept a lookout for the distinctive umbrella advertising the mortgage specialist, and for the Burberry raincoat I had noted in his downstairs cupboard.

I was aware that bankers began their days rather earlier than was my wont, and I was at the café by six thirty. I had miscalculated twice over, first as the café did not open until seven, and secondly as the streets were virtually deserted. I needed the assistance of my fellow man to pull off my tragedy. If Mr Swanson left for work before the morning rush hour, the incident would not be written off as a terrible accident on an overcrowded platform, it would simply be his interior decorator shoving him under a train, as seen on CCTV. I waited in a state of high anxiety beneath the awning of a dark restaurant until seven, when the café opened, and then positioned myself at a small Formica table with a cup of coffee and a view of the corner. My anxiety that he might come too early was just on the point of turning to anxiety that he would not come at all when a dark-haired figure wearing a beige raincoat ploughed with his purple umbrella past the lamppost at nipple height.

By this time it was seven thirty, well into the beginning of the morning rush, and despite the torrential rain the pavements were full of commuters struggling to keep their own umbrellas up against the wind, or simply sprinting as they headed for the tube. Jim Swanson was heading down the street at a rate of knots with the wind behind him. I rose from my table and left the café calmly, not wanting to give the staff or the other patrons anything memorable that might find its way into a little police notebook, and I had to run a little to catch him up. I lost him for a moment in the steady, steaming herd of bodies that worked its way down towards the ticket barriers. It was chaos in the little lobby of the tube station, as the habitual cyclists and walkers queued to buy tickets and charge their Oyster cards. A long grumbling line had formed behind each kiosk, and I did not know if Mr Swanson would be among them. I felt my heart rate rising in desperation as all the faces came up stranger. There was elation when I glimpsed again his tough little face as he stood in the ticket hall shaking out his umbrella, already set to the accomplishment of the grim task that was never to be done, on the day that ought never to come. Elation, and also a slight sense of misgiving.

I shrugged it off and plunged through the barrier. I jostled my way through the firm backs between us as we climbed down the dank concrete steps to the platform, treading on heels and poked by umbrellas as I went. I flattened myself against the wall on one side and shoved my way through, the back of my coat brushing against adverts for new musicals, clothing stores, adventure films, with the bright smiles of their models and stars defaced by marker pens and chewing gum.

I made it down on to the platform a few bodies behind him. He had only to turn around now to see my face, and the whole thing would be off. I felt the crush of men and women around me. Jim passed along the platform behind the stiff wet wall of backs, and took his place where the ranks were thinnest. I plunged after him, and was able to take up position just behind. A drip of cold water formed on my nose, but it was almost impossible to raise my arms to wipe it away, such was the compression of bodies. The crowd smelt like a pack of wet dogs, water in hair and wool and pooling on concrete. The heat on the platform caused steam to rise from our bodies, and moisture hung in the low curve of the tunnel. Despite the press of humanity, there was no panic – the prevailing air was one of resignation, a kind of suspension of the right of complaint (this would no doubt be resumed again later in the morning at offices throughout the city). Toes shuffled on the yellow line that demarcated safe distance from the tracks. The careful jostling of fresh entrants was directed back against the walls, away from the first rank facing the open track. This was how the English had gathered together in the trenches of the Somme, all of them resigned, all of them patiently waiting at the line. These were the ranks of office workers crossing the Thames, whom Eliot was surprised to find undone by death, packed into the deep tunnels. The tannoy was our sergeant major, cautioning against the slipperiness of the steps, and announcing the approach of the next northbound service.

I was looking at the back of Jim Swanson's head. Despite the umbrella, his attempts at self-preservation had been no match for the elemental forces whirling around him. His hair and the shoulders of his summer coat were soaked. As I stared at the back of his head, a curious optical effect began to exert itself upon my vision. It seemed that with each blink of my eyes, the focus of the picture before me intensified. First, it was the back of his head and the wetness of his hair. Blink. It was the way the water had penetrated his hair, leaving strands bound together into individual slivers with pointed tips like leaves of grass, between which appeared the paleness of the scalp, from which grew the little bulbs of drips. Blink. It was the tiny stubble stumps at the base of his neck, where the skin met the collar, which showed the time since his last haircut, and the pores in the skin between them, glistening with the tiniest accumulation of moisture. With each blink, the level of detail grew, and as it did so the reality of Jim Swanson encroached a little further on my intentions.

The sergeant major announced that the next north-bound train would be along in one minute. The ranks shuffled their feet, picked up their bags and closed their soggy papers, ready for the off. A French teacher shouted at her charges, a bedraggled posse of schoolchildren on a summer school trip. Somewhere in the tunnels, the first rumbling of the rails could be heard, announcing the approach of Mr Swanson's demise. I steeled myself to push, and as I did so I tried to keep my eyes open, tried to keep them fixed on the back of Mr Swanson's skull, knowing that another blink might bring him into full being. The rails sang, and the man in front of me edged slightly forward, ready to press his way on, and I braced myself to push, but just at that moment a droplet of water descended from my hairline, breached the defences of my eyebrows and sank itself into my left cornea. The front of the train emerged from the darkness of the tunnel, the driver with his hand held down on the dead man's lever. I tensed my shoulders and brought up my palms. And I blinked. The train arrived in front of us, the doors slid open. Mr Swanson stood back to allow those passengers who wished to do so to exit, and then boarded the train, his diminutive figure lost in the press. I stayed on the platform, and then fought my way back up against the new entrants towards the surface and the light.

It was the renewed evidence of the haircut that did it. I found that the tragic imperative, love, devotion and a need to restore some sense of value to the world, all were inadequate in the face of Jim Swanson's recent haircut, where the barber had shaved with a razor the troublesome hair around the base of his collar. Strange to say but I had not, until that very moment, considered the murder from Mr Swanson's point of view. Specifically that he might, in fact, prefer not to be murdered. Was it a failure of the nerve, or some restoration of sanity? Well, both, for as I stood on the steps beneath the portico of a neighbouring house waiting for my hammering heart to slow, I felt both relieved and tumultuous, happy not to have killed Mr Swanson but ashamed that I had failed to live up to the seriousness of my love. It was the absence of the heat too. Somehow the heat had raised my passions and softened logic until it could accommodate the whole of my murderous proposal, and with the rain now washing over the city, the legitimacy of the murder was washed away like the dust in the gutters.

The strange thing about this incident, in retrospect, is that I had sought to create a tragedy of the wrong era. I had thought that I could raise myself in partnership with Claudia as an Elizabethan hero, a man engaged in a titanic struggle with the forces of character. I had thought that, at the very least, I might make it over the line as a Brechtian symbol, compelled to murder by class conflict and capitalist envy.

It had never occurred to me that the climax towards which I moved might be classical in nature. The true nature of Greek tragedy is the mockery made by fate of human intention. As I climbed up from the wet staircase of the Underground like a solitary figure emerging from Hades, I thought that I had pardoned Jim Swanson, pardoned us both at the height of act five. There was no way of knowing that my pardon was merely a reprieve, coming some time after the interval, when the audience are still licking at their expensive ice creams. But the ancient tragedies are always inevitable.

# 16

IT SEEMED ALMOST LIKE A PUNISHMENT FOR MY FAILURE when Claudia called me the next day to inform me in rather cold terms that our session for later that week was to be cancelled. My first reaction was fear that Jim might have pressured her into cutting off contact with me altogether. This was consistent both with his stated intention to push her into the book club, and also with the celestial retribution due me for my failure of nerve. I felt panic at the prospect of her absence. When I pushed her for a reason, she resisted. When at last I threatened to come round in person to view the downstairs rumpus room (now completed), and more precisely to demand an explanation, she relented, and told me something quite astonishing. Jim had been fired from the bank.

It appears that he went for a walk after our meeting. I do not know exactly where he went during that half-hour, but I like to imagine him wandering across the grand artificial spaces of Canary Wharf plaza, walking amongst the crowds of businessmen and women, feeling for once different from them. Feeling perhaps a little out of control.

Wherever he went, it is a matter of public record that he returned to his desk at three thirty. On the way in he greeted his secretary, who later admitted at the hearing that he had bumped into the side of his door when entering his office. He sat down before the bank of screens that were arrayed around his desk, and began a frenzy of trading. He made fifteen million dollars of bets on wheat futures, almost twice his authorized daily trading limit. At 5.40 p.m., he appears to have become conscious of the inadvisability of his actions, for at this point the FSA noted that he made a further barrage of trades in an attempt to unwind his positions. The keystrokes recorded on his computer terminal noted a trade being made every 7.5 seconds. The FSA analysis of these keystrokes was enough to prove that the trades were deliberate, and not the result of some innocent accident such as leaning on the keyboard.

He returned to his wife, and Claudia told me that that night he seemed perfectly calm – he was as sweet and kind to her as usual, a great testament to his character given the fact that at that moment he must have been sobering up to the fact that in deliberately exceeding his credit limits he might well have ended his career. He returned to work the next morning and traded his way out of the positions for a small profit before confessing his lapse to his superiors. The bank suspended him immediately pending internal investigation and a report to the FSA. The regulatory hearing was two weeks later, and he was given a £30,000 fine and a two-year ban from trading. It was that successful attempt to correct his mistake which earned him the ban. The FSA said that had he confessed immediately he might have simply been reprimanded, but the calculated concealment of the unauthorized trades meant that he had to be punished with a suspension of his trading licence. At thirty years old, after a boozy lunch, his career was over.

The detail that most sticks with me did not come from

the newspapers (the story received unusual prominence due to the prevailing climate of banker-baiting), or the FSA's report, or even from Claudia's cold account. Rather it was something told to me by another former client who happened to work at the same bank. Apparently the bank's canteen was run by an independent contractor, and rather than paying money at the tills the operator had set up nifty little machines that worked like charge cards and which brooked no refunds. Jim being the organized man he was, he would stock up his charge card with £150 at the beginning of each month. Our lunch occurred on 3 September, which left him with over a hundred pounds of credit on the card. When he was asked to collect his things and leave the building, it was only mid-morning, and the kitchen was not yet open for lunch. He went down to the canteen and purchased from the limited selection available at the snack bar two crates of peanut M&M's. These were apparently one of the few non-perishable items capable of being carried from the building (the alternative being several large pallets of soft drinks). Claudia had told me he didn't come home until late that night. She assumed he had been out wandering the streets. My client told me that he had been working late himself, and when he left the building at eleven that same night, the square was empty and cold. Jim Swanson was still sitting on the bench under the stainless-steel-and-glass canopy of the bus shelter. Alone and still, he was looking out through the harsh lights of Canary Wharf plaza to where the seagulls wheeled and cried over the black sea, eating sweets. I never told Claudia the story. Bit late for these sorts of scruples, one might say, but I thought it would be a betrayal of trust.

Her account of the events leading up to his fateful afternoon's trading suggested that her new froideur towards me was motivated by a degree of blame for driving Jim to drink. If this was the case I deemed it a monstrous displacement of her own guilt, and I almost told her so. There is, however, no worse time to call a woman a hypocrite than on the occasion she knows it to be true, and I did not want to aggravate her. I told her I was sorry for their calamity and that I would call her back to rearrange. She asked me not to call her and not to come round, as my presence was unlikely to be conducive to the recovery of Jim's spirits. She asked if the remaining building works could be temporarily suspended, or rather she dressed up her order that they should be as a request. The fact was that they could not be suspended without great difficulty and expense, as the various decorators and craftsmen necessary for their completion and contracted by ourselves had blocked out time, but again I held my tongue. She told me that she would email me at some unspecified juncture, when things at home had improved. She thanked me for the time we had spent together and hung up. The neatness and formality with which she accomplished all this appalled me. It gave a sudden glare of subjectivity to my memory of each of our cherished meetings. I felt as if I had progressed towards the warm scene of my happiness from a great distance and over many weeks, only to find that the set was composed of cut-outs, visibly two-dimensional from any angle but that of my own approach.

I spent the rest of that afternoon trying to discover the exact details of Jim's suspension. It was a practical task that provided a distraction from my feelings of betrayal. I got a clearer picture from talking to our mutual acquaintance at the bank and from googling Jim in the financial press, which had the story within hours.

Over the course of the next few days, I found myself

enslaved by my various means of communication. The respite from the heat provided by the storm lasted barely twenty-four hours, and the sun descended upon London with renewed vigour. My mobile phone, my email, my Facebook, I came to watch their minutest shifts. The arrival of a fresh message in any of these media provided me with a few moments of relief, a shady spot where I could rest for as long as I could prevent myself from checking it. I had already taken to opening my inbox with a sheet of paper over one half of the computer screen, so that the presence of the new message would be visible whilst the sender and content remained hidden. Then the discovery that it was not from Claudia would plunge me back into febrile suspense, a condition exacerbated by the new disappointment. I stood with my thumb poised over the call button on my phone, the mouse quivering above the send icon on my email, half praying that some momentary short circuit deep in the bundles of my white matter might cause a spasm of pressure to release me from my indecision. But Claudia's injunction was reinforced by the pathetic certainty that she would contact me herself, and the instinctive legacy of years of seduction, which told me that to call first was to forfeit power. I did not call her.

At the same time Cee returned from the job in Buckinghamshire and informed me that although she would still be making regular trips up to monitor the works, she was essentially home for good. Whatever degree of success I had had in concealing my emotional state from Cee over the preceding weeks of her absence was entirely forfeit. Her own manner was strained and civil, but I hardly noticed it. It was so hot that she had said she could not bear to be in the same bed as me, and had taken to sleeping in the spare bedroom, surrounded by a little entourage of fans. Still I could not hide my agitation from her, nor my obsessive checking and rechecking of various inboxes. I was too distracted to care about what she knew or what she didn't. One evening as we sat opposite one another at the kitchen table in prolonged silence, my phone on vibrate in my pocket, she asked me what I was thinking. I told her I wasn't thinking of anything. She said she just wanted to know what was going on in my head. That she felt she wasn't allowed in there any more. I told her I wasn't thinking of anything. She got up and put the plates in the sink and when I came up to the spare room to say goodnight she was lying on the bed with her eyes closed.

The next day I felt I couldn't spend a moment longer in the house. The spare bed was mercifully empty when I awoke, and I left the house early. I went for a walk in Green Park, where the first of the leaves were beginning to fall. I walked back across Regent Street and into my old Soho haunts, but the long hot summer had dried out the wallows of my nostalgia. There was no relief from my present turmoil to be found in the familiar buildings and street names.

I called up Mr Rees's PA and asked her where Laura was buried. I told her I had been out of the country for the funeral and wished to pay my respects. I took a cab out to Hammersmith cemetery and found her grave. The recently laid sod stood out in a yellowing rectangle in the suffering earth. The roots had been too shallow to survive the heat, and the grass was dead. The deluge had pounded the flowers into mulch in their plastic sheaths, and the heat had made them sweet with rot. The newness of the headstone, black marble with gold lettering, gave it a showroom vulgarity. I was surprised to find myself crying, thinking of the rise and fall of her chest when she fell asleep in the hotel room. She always slept curled over in the white sheets, and the air conditioning brought the fair hairs up on her arms. It was easiest to like her when she was asleep. If the hotel had caught fire whilst she was awake I probably would have left her screaming at a window, but I would have run back into the inferno to retrieve her sleeping form.

When I walked back to the gate, I caught the eye of a middle-aged man in a suit sitting on a bench in the sunshine. A plastic bag containing a sandwich and a bottle of fizzy drink sat beside him. He had been quietly crying too, and he gave me a nervous little smile of recognition. He looked nice. His sensible black lace-ups were dusty from the path. I did not want to sully his grief, which was no doubt earned by long love, with my own, which was compounded by guilt at my mistreatment of the deceased, so I did not smile back and hurried down to the high street.

That evening when I returned home, the lights were on in the dining room but the curtains were drawn. Cee was in the kitchen. The speakers were silent, and in her stillness at the dining-room table she made me start.

'Hello, darling,' I said.

'Hello,' she said politely.

There was something disconcerting in her immobility. She sat in her habitual place at the kitchen table, but it was a habit founded on practical necessity – she did our accounts there, read her magazines, made her phone calls and checked her laptop. On this occasion she was simply sitting in front of a bare table. Her laptop was closed and unplugged on the chair beside her.

'Would you like a cup of tea?'

'No, thank you.'

'How was your day? What have you been up to?'

'Nothing special. I was catching up on all the stuff that fell behind whilst I was away. I sent out our quarterly newsletter.'

'Nothing special? Why, that's only the most eagerly awaited interior design-related quarterly publication in all of England. What was the news?'

'Elton Hall, the sponsorship thing. The fact that we're still in business, I suppose. I think that's quite impressive.'

'It certainly is. It certainly is.'

She was staring at me impassively. I smiled, and she smiled back faintly, and looked down at her hands, which were folded in her lap.

'It is impressive,' I said.

'Things have been very tight lately. We're fortunate to have some very loyal clients.'

I nodded and smiled again, and went to fill up the kettle.

'Something odd did happen actually,' she said to my back.

'Oh yes?'

'Yes.'

'What was that?'

'Well, I sent out the newsletter the way we usually do. You know, a group email to our entire client book.'

'Yes.'

'And there were a few bounce-backs. There always are – you know, people moving on or closing down their accounts, or designating us as junk mail.'

'Yes. So flattering, to go in the file with all the missives promising increased girth.'

'And as I was going through deleting them I noticed one from Hutchings Bank.'

'Yes?'

'Yes. Did you know he had been fired?'

'Who? No. No, I don't think he has been fired. I think he has been suspended, some sort of regulatory thing, a technical thing.'

'I phoned the bank. They informed me he doesn't work there any more. Do you know how long it has been since he worked there?'

'No.'

'Almost three weeks.'

'OK.'

'OK? Do you know how much the Swansons have outstanding on their account?'

'No.'

'Thirty-three thousand pounds. You promised me, you *promised* me it wasn't much, and I knew you were lying.'

'Well, if you already knew, why on earth do you feel the need to ask?'

'Because one of us has to!' she said, her voice suddenly raised. 'One of us has to keep this bloody business going!' She stopped and took a breath. It shook her as it filled her lungs. 'You have no idea how much they owe. Or you do, but you don't care. And you seem to know that their sole source of income has now been cut off, but it doesn't seem to trouble you in the least. Nor do you feel the need to share the fact with your wife and business partner. I mean, what the hell do you talk about in these tuition sessions? Don't tell me it's all so high-minded that in two hours a week you can't find one opportunity to mention the fucking bill.'

Cee almost never swears. She's not very good at it. She was brought up not to, and as a result there's always the briefest of pauses just before she drops the f-bomb that indicates a conscious rhetorical decision. She sounds like a teenager being deliberately rebellious, and the calculation strips the imprecation of its impact – if you're sanguine enough to think about word choice, you're not as angry as the choice implies. On this occasion, however, it just came out. It told me we had entered uncharted territory. High white spots of fury had alighted on her cheeks, a mirrored pattern in the skin like the wings of a butterfly sat on the bridge of her nose. She trembled almost imperceptibly as she looked at me.

'I . . . Look, I'm sorry, but I didn't think it was the right time to force the issue. I mean, the man's just lost his job . . .'

She stared at me.

'And I really am sorry I didn't tell you, of course I am, but I just, I didn't want to worry you, you've had so much else on your plate . . .'

She shook her head in disgust at this excuse. Actually, listening to it coming out of my mouth I felt slightly disgusted with myself.

'I'm going over there now to sort this out.'

'What? We can't just barge over there, it's six thirty in the evening, and I really don't think he'll be in a fit state to talk money. I'm seeing Mrs Swanson again on Thursday, I can talk to her then. I promise I'll get it all sorted out, if you just—'

'I think you've had quite long enough to sort this out on your own. You are obviously incapable of making a rational decision where the two of them are concerned.'

She looked at me, daring me to contradict her. I was desperate that the confrontation should not take place. I racked my brains for some sort of credible excuse that would prevent her, or some new line of discussion that might delay her long enough for her temper to cool. I even considered provoking her, so that we might play our screaming match as a home fixture. But I could think of nothing to say. No diversions, no inventions, not even an insult. I was a rabbit in the headlights of truth. My mouth opened, and closed. The click of the button informed me that the kettle had boiled. After a few seconds Cee rose from where she sat at the table and grabbed her keys from the sideboard. I followed her out of the room at a jog, and she did not wait for me as she strode to the car. She had started the engine before I had got the passenger-side door open, and she did not look at me when she began to reverse, implying it was pure luck I had managed to secure my place in the car before it began moving.

We drove in silence. When we reached the Embankment, Cee leaned forward and turned on the radio. I had used the car for a drive down to Hay-on-Wye, and it was manually tuned to Radio 4 (I can never quite figure out how to use the saved stations). She gave a little click of frustration with her tongue, pressed the buttons for a few seconds and then switched the thing off. We turned into Vincent Square and parked outside the Swansons' house, just behind the yellow Cayenne (back in service). Neither of us moved. We sat and listened to the tick of the motor.

'You've made your point,' I said.

Cee looked quickly in the rear-view mirror and stepped out on to the pavement. She walked straight up to the Swansons' door and rang the bell. I waited a couple of paces behind her. When Claudia opened the door she did not register any surprise. Indeed it was almost as if my wife, or someone else like her, had been entirely expected.

'Hello? How are you . . .'

'Good evening, Mrs Swanson. Do you mind if we come in for a moment?'

'No, no, of course, not at all. Jim is just upstairs . . .'

She held the door open for us and we both moved through into the hall.

'Do you mind if we speak with both of you?' Cee said.

'He's . . . he's not very well at the moment,' Claudia answered. She did not look at me once. She and Cee might have been the only people in the room.

'This will only take a moment.'

Claudia paused, and I could see her deciding whether or not to send us packing. I suspected her politeness and sense of social decorum would be unfailing, right up to the point where she felt that Jim required her protection. At that juncture, she might well punch Cee's lights out. After a few moments she must have decided that denying the request would be more embarrassing for him than accepting it would be painful.

'Why don't you come through into the kitchen? I'll go and see how he's feeling.'

The two of us went through into the kitchen and stood in silence as Claudia climbed the stairs. Cee looked around her and sniffed. I could tell that the sniff was intended to convey criticism of my continuing management of the Swansons' decoration, but I did not rise to it. I felt too unsettled, to have Cee here in the kitchen where so many of my intimate conversations had taken place. When Jim Swanson came into the room, he looked a different man from the confident young husband who had greeted me on my first visit and asked me to justify my fees and profession. His skin was sallow, and his shoulders slightly slumped.

'Hello, Mr Swanson,' Cee said, extending her hand.

'Hi,' he said.

'First, let me apologize for this intrusion. It would never

have been necessary at all if Matthew hadn't completely neglected your account, and for that I am sorry.'

'That's OK,' Jim said.

'This is rather awkward so I think it's probably best simply to deal with it directly,' Cee said, her voice taking on the headmistressy tone that she used for recalcitrant suppliers and airline staff. 'I have been auditing the company books and we have identified a number of client accounts with unusually large outstanding balances. We're seeking to have those settled as a matter of urgency.'

Jim leaned back and sighed involuntarily. Despite everything, I think it gave him some pleasure to see my posh wife sweating in her effort to grub some coins from the back of the sofa.

'So urgent that you both come round?'

'We were on our way out for the evening.'

Mr Swanson took leisurely note of our comfortable clothes. Cee jutted her jaw.

'I get you,' he said. 'How much do I owe?'

'About thirty-three thousand pounds.'

'How much exactly?'

'Oh, well, I don't . . . Wait.' Cee scrabbled in her handbag and produced a folded piece of printed paper. 'Thirty-three thousand, one hundred and fifty-seven pounds and ninety-two pence.'

Jim nodded and ran his hand through his hair. 'Look, I'm not trying to mess you about, but our cashflow is a bit tight just now. I can pay you now if you really need it, but if you leave us the invoice and give me a few days to get things in order I'd really appreciate it.'

'That's fine. We absolutely understand. We'll expect the transfer some time the week after next,' I said.

'No, I'm terribly sorry, but that's not fine. If you could

arrange to transfer the money today I would be most grateful.'

'That's not necessary,' I said.

'It is entirely necessary,' Cee said.

'No!' I shouted.

All three of them looked at me. Jim Swanson looked delighted by our disunity. It was the one thing he felt he had to wave over us. Cee's look informed me that I had finally broken the contract that underpinned our marriage. I had embarrassed her in public. As significant as the consequences of this breach would be, it was Claudia who really drew me. She stared at me without apparent emotion, and after a second's silence she gave the slightest shake of the head, a tiny and desperate gesture invisible to anyone but myself. I understood. I was not to behave in a way which might imply to her husband an emotional attachment deeper than that which ought to exist between service provider and friendly clients. It was the first time in our entire courtship that either of us had patted the elephant. It was the only acknowledgement of conscious complicity I had ever received from her. I felt a brief and bitter pleasure that she had finally been forced to recognize my rights to her conspiracy, and to share in the troubles which supporting the deceit had brought upon me. It was my recompense for the weeks of abandonment, and the humiliation I had felt at the ease with which she detached herself. To have power over her felt rejuvenating. It was a second glance at Jim that dispelled this mean little thrill. He had not perhaps grasped the full implications of my outburst, but he had glimpsed the shape of the thing moving about under the bedclothes. The look of satisfaction was frozen, balanced precariously in his eyes.

'I'm sorry,' I said. 'Things have been quite stressful for us recently. We have had a number of clients fail to pay.

In this case the outstanding fees are partly my fault as I have not been as efficient as I would like in pursuing settlement. Given this oversight on my part I didn't think it entirely fair to require immediate payment. However, I do see that given the circumstances it would be better if you could settle the full amount now.'

'Do you take cheques?' Jim said. The familiar fact of being asked for money seemed to revive him somewhat.

I looked to Cee. 'Yes,' she said, 'a cheque will be fine.'

'Can I ask you not to cash it till the day after tomorrow? I'm moving some money around and I don't want it bouncing.'

He bent over to write the cheque out on the breakfast bar in the kitchen. Claudia hurried to fetch him a pen from the cup on the side in the hall. Meanwhile Cee stood beside him, her hands clasped at the waist, studiously looking away from the cheque, as if to emphasize the fact that he was still trusted to get it right, and not to write Charlie Chaplin on the signature line. The first pen did not work, and after several attempts Cee delved in her own handbag at the same time as Claudia ran back to the cup in the hall. Jim just stood there, looking at the cheque, still blank but now faintly scored by his efforts. Cee eventually found a pen at the same time as Claudia returned with another biro from the hall. The two were presented to him at once, and for an excruciating moment they hovered at attention in front of him as he tried to decide which one to pick. In the end he took Claudia's, and Cee's wand dropped from the air. He wrote out carefully, thirty-three thousand one hundred and fifty-seven pounds, and looked up.

'And ninety-two pence?'

'Oh, don't worry about the pence . . .'

'Best to get it absolutely right.'

He bent back down again, and said as he wrote, 'And ninety . . . two . . . pence.'

He wrote the word 'only' in his surprisingly neat little hand, signed and passed the cheque over to Cee. She folded it without looking and placed it in her handbag.

With the cheque in her purse, something seemed to go out of Cee. She slumped a little, and looked around her as if the Swansons were guests at a cocktail party with whom conversation had reached its natural conclusion. Jim Swanson looked like a man at the end of his tether. All the certainty had gone out of him. Even with Claudia there at his side I felt pity for him, not muddied with condescension but derived from the shared possibility presented by his suffering. Without his job, he did not know who to be. Looking at his tired face, I thought of my own reflection in the shaving mirror at the election-night dinner party, when it was revealed to me that I was not a writer. I pitied him for having been stripped of his identity, and I wanted to tear up the cheque, and for the four of us to sit down and confess to all our tangled attachments.

It was Claudia who put a gentle arm around her husband, and asked if there was anything else she could do for us. Cee thanked her and said no, and apologized for the intrusion and for any . . . awkwardness. Claudia said she quite understood and we shouldn't be embarrassed, it was amazing how many little experiences like this they had had since Jim lost his job. News certainly does travel fast. That was the first and only time that the fact of his sacking was mentioned. Cee said we would leave them to their evening. When I walked past Claudia, she did not look at me. I desperately wanted to connect with her, to exchange a single look of apology. She kept her eyes fixed firmly on the ground. I was enraged with Cee, for turning her against me. Jim stayed where he was in the kitchen and did not see us out.

'Have fun at your party,' Claudia said on the steps.

'What?' Cee asked.

'You said you were going out for the evening.'

'Oh yes, of course, we—'

But Claudia had slammed the door shut on us.

'I'll drive,' were the only words spoken as we stepped out on to the pavement, and my wife did not protest.

# 17

WHEN YOU HAVE MISTREATED SOMEONE OVER A LONG
period, it is difficult to feel towards them that purgative
rage which allows for a full sluicing of one's resentment.
Whatever they do, they are never quite in the wrong
enough to justify a full-on bollocking, and because
of this the little moments of anger, instead of being
released by expression, tend to die inside and drift to
the bottom, accumulating at the core of one's soul,
until the pressure of other dead little emotions drifting
down from above compresses them and makes them into
something quite different, something black and sticky
and combustible.

As I drove back home with Cee in the seat beside me,
I was aware that for the first time since I had become
unfaithful I was utterly filled with righteous rage towards
her. My conscience was for once completely cowed by
the strength of the emotion, and did not dare point out
the hypocrisy. Her silence fed my anger. When the car
came to a stop at each set of lights, I could feel the silent
pulse of her presence even as my eyes stayed fixed on
the car in front. She was looking out the window at the
river. Her arms were folded across her chest. Something
was mounting inside of her too. Inside each one of us an
almighty self-justification was building, and the force of

it extended beyond our bodies, like the gravitational field of a planet. A car pulled out in front of me just before the Albert Bridge, and I slammed on the brakes, and held my hand down on the horn. Cee flinched a little in her seat, and I thought for a moment she might open the door on her side and simply get out into the traffic.

When we eventually pulled into our drive, she unplugged her belt and opened the car door without a word before the car had even stopped. She slammed it whilst I was still fumbling with the handle on my side. I called out her name. She broke into a half-run as she reached the stairs in front of our door. The keys were already in her hand, but her hands shook as she tried to enter them into the lock. I came up behind her just as she managed to get the door open, and she tried to slam it in my face as she fell through into the hall. I blocked it with my forearm, pain shooting up through my shoulder as the heft of the wood on the hinge dealt me a heavy blow. I bundled through behind her and took her shoulders, and she hit me across the face. Still holding her fast by the lapel I spun round and slammed the door on the quiet and respectable Chelsea street. Then I pushed her up against the wall. She slapped me again, harder this time, hard enough to turn my head. I put my hands inside the top of her shirt and ripped the material open. She struggled but I kept her pinned with the weight of my body against the wall. I kissed her and one of us bled as I mashed my lips against hers. I caught one of her hands and forced it down against the wall. She was still hitting me, but my legs were opened on either side of hers, and she did not bring her knee up. She did not cry out, but her breathing was heavy and ragged with the struggle and the smothering kiss. She bit my neck, and I yelled and let go of her wrist long enough to get my hands under her skirt. I pulled her pants and her tights down as far as the tops of her thighs. It was probably the last moment she would have been able to fight me off so I stopped and guided her down to the floor more gently.

Her anger had changed into excitement at the violence, and she pulled me down on top of her. I held myself over her with one arm straight as we both fumbled at my fly. There was a sense that if we were forced to pause for even a second to consider what we were doing, we would stop. I pushed inside her, she gasped involuntarily and gripped me through the fabric of my trousers, and we fucked hard enough to hurt one another. I pushed my hand between our chests and yanked one of her cups aside and ground her breast between my fingers. It made her cry out in anger, and she scored my flesh. There was no pause or change in our rhythm, we just fucked hard on the floor until I came inside her and rolled off to lie panting on my back, looking up at the hall lights. One of the bulbs had gone. Cee had asked me to fix it weeks ago, but I kept forgetting.

We lay there panting, catching our breath, but neither one of us spoke. For my own part, I had no idea what was the state of relations between us. A little frightened by the violence of what had just occurred, I wanted her to speak first to confirm she was all right. I was the man who could not stand to see a woman hit. Outside in the street, a group of teenagers passed, and their laughter and raised voices made me suddenly conscious of the strangeness of our position. Cee must have felt it too, for she sat up against the wall. She made no attempt to correct her dishevelment, but I could feel her looking at me. I zipped myself up though my shirt was still open, and clumsily turned myself around on the carpet, putting my own back against the wall with my knees up in front of me. We looked at each other across the warm cream interval.

'Are you OK?' I said.

'Yes. I'm fine.'

There was another pause.

'I'm leaving you,' she said.

It was said quite without emotion. It was a bald statement of fact.

'I know . . . I know you think I'm having an affair with Claudia Swanson,' I said, 'but I'm not, I swear it. You can ask your private dick.'

She looked at me with a mixture of surprise and pity.

'My what? I'm not . . . I'm leaving you because I don't love you any more. I'm in love with someone else. I'm in love with Hugo. I have been for months. I was just . . . working up the courage to tell you.'

The factual import of this statement entered my understanding in the usual way. My wife of ten years had been fucking someone and was now going to leave me for him. But in being understood, the phrase seemed to divest itself entirely of its practical implications. I simply could not feel what it meant.

'You're leaving me for Hugo? But . . . I don't even like him. He's a dickhead.'

'I know you think that. It's a large part of his appeal. Or it was at first anyway.'

'So you're going to him to get back at me.'

'Christ. Christ, Matthew, you're so fucking arrogant. You honestly think I'd break up two marriages and go to live with another man just to spite you? Do you even have any idea how self-centred that sounds?'

'And what about the other marriage? Does Magda know about this?'

'I . . . I don't want Magda to be unhappy. But I want

myself to be unhappy even less. And I am unhappy. With you. You make me unhappy, and Hugo makes me happy, and that's as far as I'm letting myself think.'

'Did this start in Buckinghamshire? Or has it been going on longer?'

'Longer.'

'How much longer?'

'Just longer.'

'Is it a money thing? Is it because he has more money than me?'

Cee laughed, a little theatrically, and put her head in her hands. 'No! It's not because he has more money than you. It is because he *makes* more money than you.'

'What's that supposed to mean?'

'You don't do anything, Matt. You don't . . . you're not a man. When I met you, you were a writer. That was who you were. That was what you did. Now what do you do? You go into your little study, and you open your old books, and you look at them, and you close them again, and you buy new ones. And you pick out colour samples and you fuck lonely women. That's what you do. And the worst thing is, you think that makes you better than other people. The not doing anything, the refusal to engage, you think that makes you better. Hugo, OK, he can be crass, and he's not as clever as you, but Christ, he goes out there and he takes things in his hands and he makes things different.'

After this statement, Cee fell silent. She was crying now, the tears muddying her eyeliner. She did not cry with abandon, but with impatience at her own weakness. It helped her regain her equilibrium. She reached into her handbag and dug out a packet of cigarettes. She lit one, and tossed the pack across the hall to me. I took one out and did the same. We sat for a while like that on the floor

in the hall, still half naked, smoking with our heads leaning back and our throats exposed, tapping the ash on our
perfect cream carpet.

'When did you start buying your own cigarettes?' I
asked.

'I don't know. When did things start getting so stressful?'

The answer made me smile. Something about the
reference to my own infidelities had completely taken the
wind from my sails, and I lay now becalmed. Stunned
perhaps by how much of what she said was the truth.

'I'm sorry,' I said, 'about cheating on you.'

'I'm sorry too.'

'And I'm sorry for calling you fat.'

'You didn't call me fat.'

'Really? Must have been in my head,' I said, and smiled
at her.

She looked at me for a moment, deciding whether or not
to laugh, and laughed. She chose that particular moment
to look incredibly beautiful. It was perhaps because she
was a mess. Over the years I had seen her less and less
without make-up, which was applied in the bathroom
with the doors closed before I got up and removed in the
same fashion after the lights in the bedroom were down.
As she no longer got drunk or did drugs, I hardly ever
saw her looking anything less than perfectly turned out.
With her eyeliner smudged and her clothes awry and her
hair sticking with sweat to her forehead, her eyes shining,
she looked young again. I was struck suddenly by a kind
of pre-emptive nostalgia, a sense of how I would feel in
the months to come, looking back on the first third of my
life and on the wife and lover with whom I had shared it.
I wondered suddenly whether I would have Claudia there
to look back on it with me.

'I wasn't fucking her, you know.'

'Who?'

'Claudia Swanson.'

Cee shrugged. 'OK. But you care about her. And that was much more humiliating for me tonight. That was the final straw. To turn on your wife on behalf of some spoilt girl you have a crush on.'

The reference to Claudia brought our little truce to an end. Cee stood up, and looked at herself in the hall mirror. She buttoned her dishevelled blouse and straightened her skirt, and took a make-up wipe from her handbag to deal with her panda eyes. I watched her from the hall floor. With each little adjustment, she seemed to grow further away from me. By the end, she had become a complete stranger. She was quite neat. She had gone further from me in those few moments before the mirror than she had in the last ten years of our marriage. She was no longer my wife.

She left the hall for the kitchen. When she turned to go, there was a dark patch on the back of her skirt where I had leaked out of her. When she came back in from the kitchen she had a Dustbuster in her hand, which she used to hoover up the ash from the cigarettes. When she had finished, she set it down on the side and looked me in the eye in the silence.

'I don't think you should stay here tonight. I think you should go to a hotel.'

'Is he going to come over?'

'That's not your business any more.'

'Does Magda know?'

'Not everything. I would imagine she knows as much as I did about you. But she will by tomorrow. Do you want me to pack your bag?'

She said this almost gently. Cee had always done my

packing. I forgot things if I did it myself – cufflinks, toothpaste, passports.

'No. I can do it,' I said, and I walked out of the hall, up the stairs. I stood for a few moments on the landing, and the sound of music came from the kitchen. It was La Roux playing loud, and I suddenly had the strange realization that it was no longer music from my house that I was listening to, but music coming through the walls as if from the neighbour's stereo. The iPod was no longer mine, the Bose speakers were no longer mine, the wife and the kitchen were no longer mine. My notions of divorce were surprisingly uninformed given the conduct of my marriage, but I felt quite certain that Cee would keep the house. I felt like a guest, and an unwelcome one at that, as I climbed the stairs to our bedroom. A cable TV man who has missed a few appointments maybe, or someone come to read the meter.

I went into her bedroom and took three clean shirts from the wardrobe. I unplugged the mobile charger from beside the bed and slung it into the bag along with a spare set of contact lenses. There was a split on the inside of my lip, either from kissing or from Cee striking me, and it kept drawing my tongue. I went down to my study and removed three books from the shelves, the Chaucer from the display case, and the folder of letters of famous men and women from the bureau drawer. I wrapped them up in the shirts, folding the arms across the front and tying them off to make a careful package. Then I stacked them one on top of the other in the bag, slung it across my shoulder and went downstairs. The kitchen door was shut, and I did not look in on Cee to say goodbye.

When I got outside on the pavement, the door closed behind me, and I realized I had nowhere to go. I had never had nowhere to go before. I felt terribly exposed and embarrassed at being like this in the street. I could not imagine what I would do if one of my neighbours walked past and wanted to make small talk. I checked my phone for inspiration, and there on the screen, waiting for me, was a single missed call from Claudia.

I called her mobile and it rang through. The sound of her carefree tones on the voicemail mocked my present distress. I wanted to ring straight back and to keep on ringing, to call and call her mobile and the house phone and even Jim's phone until I got her voice, her voice at any price. By a great effort of will I managed to restrain myself, and strode down Old Church Street to the Fulham Road. I stood by the flower stall on the corner, the sweet organic scent of the blossoms soothing in the hot night. The florist was packing up her wares, tipping buckets of water over the pavement where the petals and earth had fallen. I kept my phone in my hand, and after five minutes of waiting the oasis of her name appeared in the desert screen.

'Hello, Matt?' She was whispering into the receiver. The sound of that whisper, the illicit associations it carried, made my heart glad.

'Where are you?'

'I'm . . . I'm in the upstairs bathroom. I told Jim I needed a shower. Why did you call me? You can't call me. I asked you not to.'

'Cee left me.'

'I'm sorry. That's terrible.'

'It's not terrible.'

'It is. What happened?'

'She left me because I defended you.'

'That's . . . it's not fair to say that. Either of those things.'

'I have to see you.'

270

'That's impossible. I can't get away. Not after tonight.'

'I have to.'

'I can't.'

'Make something up.'

'I won't lie.'

'Either you come to me or I come to you. You owe me that.'

'OK.'

'I deserve that, don't I? Don't I deserve that?'

'I said OK. Where are you?'

'I'm going to a hotel. I'll text you the address.'

'I'll come as fast as I can.'

She hung up.

# 18

I DID NOT WANT TO BE IN A PLACE I KNEW. A HOTEL IN Mayfair, in Knightsbridge, in Chelsea, on Park Lane, in Shoreditch, all these places reverberated with the noise of association – I would not be able to hear myself think clearly in any of them. I wanted somewhere outside of my life, a vantage point from which to better survey the wreckage. I hailed a cab, and when the driver asked me where I was going, the only place I could think of was the Heathrow Travel Inn. We drove up through Earl's Court, and west along the Cromwell Road. As we rose above the ground on the Hammersmith flyover, I felt relief as the anonymity of the landscape washed over me. We left old London behind. A teenage sky of purple and orange and black hung over the city. We passed on the raised motorway between ranks of buildings that did not recognize me. The derelicts with broken windows stood beside the shining new-builds with their lights and reflective glass walls. The billboards hawked products I had never bought. As we drove out of west London, the black canopy of the A40 rose on vast and ancient concrete trunks above the five-a-side football pitches built beneath the motorway. The bright bulbs shone down on them in the twilight, and the emerald of the artificial sward glittered as young men in black and red shirts leapt and lounged in their cages, their trainers in the floodlights as white as an actor's teeth. In the distance, the tower blocks of the estates stood out above the low-rise suburbs. The headlamps picked out the lettering on the road signs hung above the motorway. Heathrow terminals 1, 2, 3, five miles. I opened the window, and the sweet fumes of the traffic blended with the summer evening. I asked the driver if I could smoke a cigarette. He told me he would lose his licence.

He delivered me into the car park and I gave him money. There was no one else there. I smoked a cigarette to calm my nerves in the empty lot, listening to the sound of passing vehicles on the motorway. I killed the coal with a quick twist of my heel, and the doors opened automatically at my approach. I knew as soon as I entered the lobby that I had made the right choice in the Travel Inn. It was a place between places, a house of exiles. The neon lighting made no allowance for night or day. Opposite the clean and brightly coloured desk there stood a vending machine containing packets of toiletries – plastic toothbrushes, single sachets of shampoo, disposable razors. The only possible market for such one-use toiletries was people who had lost their luggage, or suicides who wished to make a neat corpse. A sign on a stand in the lobby welcomed delegates of a Japanese photocopier company. The floor was sticky. The whole building was flushed and smug with the rise of the cheap. People could not afford their fancy hotels any more, the accounts department were reviewing expenses, and the humbled business traveller had come crawling back. The young man at the desk looked old. He took my credit card and scanned it, and issued me a blank keycard for a room on the ground floor. I texted Claudia the room number and the address, nothing more. The door of my room was the same as the doors of the other rooms but with a different number.

The room itself contained a bed, a chair, a desk, a fridge and a television. There was nothing to suggest it would become the scene of a murder, except perhaps for its mundanity. The first thing I did upon entering was to place my bag carefully on the table and unwrap the books – the gems of my collection. I hoped that with their age, their uniqueness and their sheer expense they might allow me to establish a little outpost of history in the featureless present. Furled in my checked shirt, the first one was Daniel Defoe's *Robinson Crusoe* in the original binding. It had been my first serious purchase, acquired at auction to mark my progress into adult success. Most of my professional friends had undertaken something similar, that first luxury item bought with excess cash, the true rite of passage in a consumer nation. For my father, I think, it was being given a signet ring by my grandfather that had ushered him into manhood. In my case, I had been obliged to purchase my maturity, being suspicious of gifts. I had wanted *Robinson Crusoe* because it was the first English novel. The first English novel is the story of someone getting terribly lost. I took out the Chaucer, but left the other books in the bag.

I made myself a cup of tea with one of the complimentary teabags. I switched on the television. It shouted out and I hit mute. A laminated guide to its use sat on the bedside table beneath the remote, and I cast my eyes down it to discover how one ordered porn. *Robinson Crusoe* eyed me from the desk like Poe's raven. I opened the mean little fridge squatting beneath the desk and retrieved a miniature whisky bottle. I improved my tea. The screen showed CNN, violent things happening silently and somewhere else. The room smelled of air freshener. Cleanliness in a hotel is the measure of the efficiency with which the management removes traces of the occupants, but for a moment I felt them, the anonymous ghosts of my fellow travellers, the ones who had made the journey before and the ones who would come after. I lay on my back on the thin sheets. Outside, the light was fading. A car turned into the courtyard in front of the hotel, and its headlights passed across the ceiling as I watched. In the quiet I could hear the planes taking off and coming in to land, taking off and landing, taking off and landing. I waited for Claudia. I felt as if my entire life had evaporated in an instant, and she was the only thing tethering me to the earth. I wondered if she would consent to join me on one of those planes. Travelling anywhere. Not anywhere. Not Europe. The new world.

To distract myself, I pictured Cee as she had been at Cambridge. The thought of her came to me weirdly clean, purged of emotion. I tried to remember what it was that had made me fall in love with her. I was not as a student, nor had I ever been, a rebel. Indeed I had a natural antipathy for rebels, generally perceiving their professed rebelliousness as a pre-emptive rejection of a society they feared would not accept them. I loved authority. I was a prefect at school. I had a college tie and socks from the rugby club. I was a member of Annabel's as well as the Young Conservatives, the International Socialist Movement and the Travellers Club. My tragedy has been that I cannot find an authority that will condone my drinking, smoking, recreational drug use, philandering, wilful political extremism or occasional bouts of homosexuality. If only there were an institution that condoned or even required such habits, I would count myself perfectly happy, as I love them for themselves, and not as most people seem to for some abstract sense of pride in the defiance of societal norms. As it was, at university my proclivities constantly threatened to throw me in with men and women my social constitution despised. I guess Cee was like that when we were young. She was smart, rich, kind, well-spoken. But so naughty. She seemed to share my desire to take MDMA and have sex in the library, and yet to avoid being caught so that we might graduate with a good degree. I lost myself in picturing her, standing on a punt in the summer on the backs, water from the punt pole soaking her jeans, trying not to fall in, her head thrown back with laughter. I remembered her looking down at me once in a quiet moment, rolled in white sheets, chin on hand on elbow on bed, telling me she wished she could have met my mother and smoothing the hair from my face. That was when I fell in love with her, I think.

My only awareness of time was from the soft accumulation of darkness beyond the window, but when the knock finally came I glanced at the little red digits on the bedside table, and discovered it was almost ten o'clock.

I stood up and immediately wished I had taken the opportunity to have a shower. The mirror bolted to the wall above the desk revealed an unprepossessing sight. I still bore the signs of my tussle with Cee, and I smelt of sex and cigarettes and whisky. There were some women to whom this would appear a bonus, but Claudia Swanson was not one of them. I went to the door and opened it.

She was standing in the harsh light of the corridor with her arms folded across her chest. I stood aside to let her in and she walked quickly past me where the corridor was narrowest, and went to stand in the far corner of the room. As I came back in I saw her cast an uneasy glance at the bed. I did not want her to be uncomfortable, so I sat down on the far corner, and motioned for her to take the chair by the desk. She shook her head.

'I'm sorry I took so long. Jim wouldn't let me leave. He kept wanting to talk about things, really strange things . . .'

'That's OK.'

'I told him that my mum and dad had a fight. Do you know, that's the first lie I've ever told him?'

'How did it feel?' I asked, and she looked at me angrily.

'How do you think it felt?'

'Familiar, would be my honest guess. I don't mean this in an unpleasant way, Claudia, but it's not the first lie you've told him. You and me, we've both been lying for weeks, to ourselves, each other, everyone.'

She looked away from me, but did not answer.

'I mean, honestly, what did you think was happening? Do you think that all my clients sit down for hours every week with me and share their hopes and fears and dreams? Do you think that any adults anywhere in the world do that, unless they're . . . unless they're falling in love?'

I slumped back against the wall. The admission was all I had in me.

'I think, Matt,' she said, her voice quivering with the effort of self-control, 'that I owe you an apology. Over these past few weeks, I have finally felt like myself again. Like my old self, back when I was young, back before the miscarriage, even before Rome, when I felt so powerful, and so intelligent, and so interesting. Oh God, it was arrogant, but I swear it was generous too. I could be good to everyone back then, and I felt I could do anything for other people. I was falling in love, you see. I was falling in love with that feeling of being like my old self. And the feeling was so strong, it made me ignore what I could see happening to you. I don't know, maybe it even became so mixed up with the thought of you that I pretended I couldn't separate out the two. But the two are separate, Matt. I don't love you. I love my husband. You have brought back to me a source of pleasure I had thought was lost for ever. I am deeply, deeply ashamed of what I have done in return. I have always thought of myself as basically a good person, even when things were at their worst, and I see now I have lied to you in a way that is quite unforgivable.'

She was crying now, the tears passing silently down her cheeks. A little shell-shocked part of me remarked to the rest of my consciousness how I seem incapable of having an honest conversation with a woman unless she's in tears, but the observation failed to raise an internal smile. I just stared at her. I felt an ache forming deep in my chest, going as deep as grief.

'I understand,' I said.

'I can't ask you to forgive me . . .'

'There's nothing to forgive. You should go home now. You should go home.'

She nodded, and I stood up. I escorted her back down the corridor. We embraced in front of reception, the wetness of her tears on my cheek and, for a moment, her lips. The old young boy looked at us with mild curiosity over the top of his magazine.

I did not follow her out from the lobby. I stood and watched her cross the tarmac, and jump into a waiting taxi. I thought it was cold of her, to have told the taxi to wait. It slightly undermined for me the significance of our final conversation, knowing the meter had been ticking away outside. As the cab door closed and the driver pulled away from the kerb, something caught my eye on the other side of the forecourt. The car park was only about half full.

The cars were mostly clustered around the entrance of the motel like flies around a light in the late evening. The spaces on the road side were largely vacant, and the lights on that side were broken, casting the few cars there were in deep shadow. In the darkness, I saw a small red light moving in a solitary vehicle. It jumped and then steadied like a sniper's sight. I moved forward and pressed my face against the glass of the lobby window, cupping my hand to better see out into the darkness. There was movement in the car's dark interior. The red light was attached to some object being manipulated behind the windscreen. As my eyes adjusted to the disparity in the light, I realized I recognized the car. It was the same rusted red Volvo which had been waiting for me outside the Swansons' house in Vincent Square. The red light belonged to a camera. I barked with laughter, and pulled away from the glass. It seemed so absurd, after the evening I had had with her, that Cee had neglected to call off her dogs.

After the worry my pursuer had caused me, I thought it only fair that I had some recompense. I was going to embarrass her, and perhaps regain a modicum of the power in what had become for me a humiliating debacle. With this in mind I flung the lobby door open and strode across the car park towards her. The red light told me she was still taking photographs of Claudia's retreating taxi, and though I could not see properly into the darkened interior until I was quite close, I knew she had not seen me. I was a few feet away when she dropped the camera into her lap and fired the engine. The headlamps dazzled me. I ran the last few feet, and easily blocked the car's exit.

She drove forward a tiny bit, almost connecting with my shins. The bumper was so close to me that the lights shone out on either side of my body, and as she leaned forward over the wheel I was able to observe her face through the glass free from the obstruction of the light. Her face had been turned away from me in Vincent Square, and I realized looking at her that the ambiguity of her hidden features had greatly contributed to my unrest over the past weeks. Out there in the Indian summer, she had been my nemesis, a mysterious figure sent to pursue me like a spare conscience. In the car park, she was a tired-looking woman in her early forties, with brown curly hair and the kind of looks one passes in the street, but might notice at the end of the night in the bar. She looked absolutely panicked, which softened my feelings towards her, but hardened my resolve to talk to her. She reversed a few inches until there was a lift in the back of the car, indicating the wheels were riding up the concrete embankment that separated the tarmac of the car park from a small copse of trees in wood chippings behind. The back wheels bumped down on the other side and raised the dazzle of the headlights back into my eyes, but I knew what was behind them now. For a moment I thought she might try to ram the trees behind her and reverse up the little embankment, but she simply revved the engine. I stayed standing where I was and raised my eyebrows, my hands on my hips. The engine idled and the car did not move.

'Look, you can either come out here and talk to me, or you can run me over, or you can stay here until I call the police,' I said into the brightness. No reply came, but the engine kept turning, undecided. I could not detect any movement, but the ground was strewn with the diamond chunks of a smashed windscreen. They crunched audibly, indicating some tiny movement in the tyres, rolling forward or back.

'Really, I mean it, I just want to talk to you. Then you can go back to doing whatever the hell weird thing you're doing. Otherwise there will be an almighty fuss.'

It's an unfortunate thing, but I have found that in moments of high drama, when I most need to sound commanding, my accent and diction become incredibly posh. I'm not sure whether this is an atavistic instinct that comes with the flush of adrenalin, or whether part of me expects the natural authority of the class system to come to my aid in the face of danger, but either way I wish I could sound just a little more street when the chips are down. As it was, the threat of an almighty fuss lingered in the air.

For a few more seconds the exhaust chugged fumes into the evening, and then quite suddenly the engine was switched off. The beams fell from the air and were replaced by a series of yellow spots dancing on my retina. I walked around to the driver's side and tapped the window. She wound it down and looked up at me. She looked embarrassed and defiant.

'Are you going to get out of the car?'

'I can't. The kid's asleep,' she said in a whisper, and jerked her head back over her shoulder. Her accent was estuary English. The child was strapped in the same position as when I had first seen her, only on this occasion it was completely still, giving no indication of its potential.

'You can get in though,' she said, 'if you're quiet.'

I heard the locks pop, and skirting close to the bonnet just in case she attempted to drive away again I went round to the door. When I opened it, she was leaning over, sweeping rubbish off the seat on to the floor. Inside, the car was air-con cool. The atmosphere had the sweet, organic smell of the child behind me, of its various foods and fluids, and also of the greasy packet of chips sitting in the footwell on my side. Shuffling my feet around on the rubber mat beneath the dashboard revealed a host of other papery bundles and empty cans.

'Do you always take your baby when you stalk strangers?'

'Do you have any idea how much a sitter costs?'

We sat for a few seconds in silence. She switched off the camera, which was sitting in her lap, and replaced it carefully in a padded bag.

'You're not much cop as a private eye,' I said.

'Pardon?'

'I mean you're a little behind the times. Cee and I broke up this evening.'

'Cee? Oh, your wife. Well, that's . . . uh.' She scratched the back of her head and checked the baby in the rear-view mirror. Something about her reaction to the news made me feel the incipient unease of a loosening certainty.

'It doesn't surprise you?'

'It sucks, but it's not exactly a surprise, is it? I mean, I've been following you for a few weeks now. I would have kicked you out if you'd carried on like that. Anyway, it's none of my business.'

She gave a righteous sniff. The implication that she was floating serenely above this miasma of personal gossip was too much for me.

'Oh, come on, don't be so hard on yourself. I think if the woman who's been paying you to peep on her husband's sex life kicks him out it's entirely proper you should feel a little involved.'

She realized my mistake before I did, but the shining light of her smile revealed it before she spoke.

'Your wife doesn't pay me. I've never met your wife. Mr Swanson pays me.'

The news filled me with a sudden dread.

'How did you know I was here?'

'I didn't. Mr Swanson called me and told me to get over to his place as fast as possible. Then I followed her.'

She indicated the departed Claudia with a gesture to the motorway.

'How long have you been following me?'

'Eight weeks or so. Since Mrs Swanson had her accident. Mr Swanson thought it was weird you being there, and then trying to see her at the hospital, and apparently you were sending her dirty books. Then you coming by like that, with all that fruit. He thought you might be trying to stalk her or something.'

'We never had sex.'

'I know you didn't do anything in the house.'

'How could you possibly know that? What, were you spying through the windows?'

'No . . .' she paused for a moment and flexed her fingers on the wheel, 'just taping you. Mr Swanson asked me to set up a mike in the living room.'

I sat back in my seat and stared at the hotel opposite. The revelation threw me into complete confusion, as I tried to review our many hours of passionate conversation in the light of a hidden listener. I remembered how Claudia had discouraged my attempts to change the venue of our meetings. She had said Jim was more comfortable if he knew where she was. I thought back to the lunch I had had with him in Canary Wharf, and to the question he had asked me. Does she talk to you about the miscarriage? He must have listened to her telling me that, and so many other private things about their life together. Hour upon hour of taped confession. I pictured the man who prided himself on being his wife's confidant, on being the provider who was strong enough to help her with anything, sat at his desk in the darkness of an empty office, listening. I pictured his face as he listened to his wife talking for hour after animated hour of English literature with a university-educated stranger, a stranger who told her of nothing but the many husbands he had humiliated. The proud man who had shared the secrets of his origin only with her, listening as they poured into the ears of a hostile stranger. How much courage must it have taken for him to face me at lunch, knowing that I knew as much as I did? I felt a piercing shame fix me to the seat. I knew that if I did not do something to try to redress the damage I had caused, the shame would never completely wash away. It was instantly clear to me that if Jim Swanson ever discovered that Claudia had lied to him and come to see me on the night of his humiliation by my wife, it would be a blow from which they would not recover. It was a strange thing, but after my interview with Claudia, all I wanted was for her to come out happy, even if it meant securing Jim's happiness in the process.

'You can't tell him she came here tonight. You can't tell him about this. This has to stay between the two of us.'

She shook her head, and reached for the keys in the ignition.

'You need to get out now. It's late . . .'

'How much?'

'It's not about money,' she said. The implication was sufficiently offensive to make her sit back in her seat, and she looked at me scornfully.

'What, it's about professional reputation? You honestly think that either Claudia or I are ever going to breathe a word of this to Jim Swanson, or to anyone else for that matter?'

'It's not about——' she snapped, and her voice made the baby in the back stir in his seat, as if his slumber ran an umbilical link to his mother's mood. She moved a hand down the steering wheel and sucked in a breath, and when she turned to speak to me again she was back to a whisper.

'It's not just about money, I told you. And it's not just about the job.'

She glanced again at the child in the back. I realized then why she always had to bring him along with her. I understood.

'You don't like people cheating?'

She didn't say anything.

'You think it's . . . what? Wrong? Well, here's the strange thing, sister. I just happen to agree with you. As of right now, tonight. But let me ask you something: do you just think cheating's wrong, or do you think fidelity's right? I mean, are you so bitter that you want to spread the pain, or if just once you came across someone who really was faithful, who really did love their spouse, would that be OK with you?'

I paused, afraid for a moment that I had gone too far. But she seemed still to be listening. It was her turn to stare out through the windscreen into the darkness.

'Now, I promise you, I promise you that despite what I wanted to happen tonight, despite what I expected to happen, Claudia Swanson left that room with her vows intact. But she also lied to her husband about where she was going tonight, because she wanted to say goodbye to me and tell me I lost to my face. If you tell him she lied about that one thing, that's all it will take to end their marriage. His imagination will do the rest. And then you'll be breaking apart two people who really, truly love one another when they most need each other. Now, that's something even I've never done.'

There was a small round tin of mints in the hollow of the dashboard below the rear-view mirror. She leaned forward and took one, and popped it in her mouth. She sucked it meditatively for a few moments, and it imparted its wisdom.

'What are you going to give me?'

'What?'

'You said your piece. I believe you. You never shagged. Now, what about my time and my bonus?'

'You get a cheating bonus?'

'I get a bonus on the successful completion of any surveillance. Lying to cover up the target's movements doesn't count.'

The answer presented itself to me fully formed. There was a moral neatness to it which, after so many weeks of literature, was completely irresistible.

'Wait here,' I said.

I jumped out of the car and ran back to the hotel. I half expected to hear the engine start behind me, for blinding light to throw my long shadow down on the ground before me. It became a brief superstition, the not looking, as I trotted to the lobby doors, and sure enough when I reached them without a backward glance the car was still stood silently on the other side of the parking lot. I slipped the keycard into the lock in my room. Inside Claudia's scent still lingered. I ignored it and grabbed the *Robinson Crusoe* from beside the television. For a moment I paused and considered rifling through my overnight bag for the other two books, but as expiatory gestures went that seemed a little expensive. I weighed *The Canterbury Tales* briefly in my hands, then set it down beside the television. There was no more point in overpaying for symbolism than for anything else. Deciding that the thing was to be done on impulse or not at all I turned tail and ran back out through the lobby. The car was still there in the shadows.

I passed the book through to her before I sat back in the seat. She took it in her hands, and righted it in the air with a frown. Then she opened it and turned a few pages, as if expecting them to be layered with money.

'Not so rough! Be gentle or you'll crack the spine.'

'What am I supposed to do with an old book?'

'Sell it. Take it to a dealer. Put it on eBay. Look, I'm not telling you what to do with it, I'm telling you it's worth ten grand. At least it will be, if you can manage not to damage it by ripping the covers off. I'm betting that's a lot more than your completion bonus. Christ, if you really can't sell the thing bring it back to me and I'll take it off your hands for five.'

'You just said it was worth ten.'

'For . . . for fuck's sake, is it a deal or not?'

'Watch your language.' Instinctively she wiped first one hand and then the other down the front of her jeans. She held the book above the steering wheel in her newly cleansed fingers and stared at it. 'Jim said you were a, a what did he call it?'

'A library consultant.'

'That.' She looked at the book for a few seconds more. Then she shook her head, leaned over me and popped the glove compartment. The book vanished inside with a pair of gloves and a torch. When the compartment clicked shut, I felt a pure gratitude flood my system. It came through washing away everything, not just the residue of her revelation about the tapes, but everything: the sadness over Claudia, the guilt over Cee, and the fear for what was to become of me. I knew that this was only a temporary relief, that some or all of these things would return to me in due course. But I also figured that salving a guilty conscience with good deeds would be like waxing, as a young model wife had once described it to me – the more often you strip the hair, the less of it grows back each time.

'What do you want me to say to Jim Swanson? He knows his wife went somewhere tonight.'

'All you have to do is say you followed her all the way up the A1. She came off at the Stevenage junction but you got distracted and missed the turn. You can say . . . say you almost nodded off at the wheel. Something about how you want danger money. Driving all over the country late at night.'

She looked at me for the first time with a trace of communion. 'Tell a lot of lies, do you?'

The baby stirred in his sleep. I smiled at her, and stole one of the mints from the tin on the dash. When I got out I closed the door as quietly as I could. Standing in the warm night, I tapped the windscreen twice. She looked out, and I put my finger to my lips. She nodded. The car slipped out on to the empty road and headed for the motorway.

# 19

I RETURNED TO MY ROOM, AND LAY ON MY BACK IN THE darkness. The energy required to generate so many conflicting emotions in so short a space of time had left me briefly drained of feeling, and I was completely at peace. Free from pangs and plans that had consumed me all through the summer, I was able for the first time in what seemed like months to make a dispassionate assessment of events. One of the strangest things of all was how little I had considered the possibility that Claudia's feelings towards me might not coincide entirely with my own. I had sensed her reluctance, of course, but had ascribed it to the obstacle presented by her husband. The idea that there might be some deficit of underlying attraction never even crossed my mind. I had simply felt that I deserved her, and that had been enough. My own sense of entitlement had been monstrously nourished by repeated affirmation. It is one of those psychological conditions that do the most damage by concealing themselves from view. I thought for a moment with sadness of Laura Rees. I wondered if in fact I had played as little part in Claudia's inner life as Laura had in mine.

I put my hands behind my head, and stared up at the ceiling. The planes were still taking off and landing. I wondered how long it would take to book a flight. For years I had felt so afraid of loneliness, but being now alone I found I had my freedom for company. I still had a first edition of *Emma* in the original binding, a signed Graham Greene, the Chaucer and a file full of the letters of famous writers. I could trade them off in New York or Hong Kong for enough cash to keep me going for months, years, and buy new copies in paperback at the airport. I wondered what I would do with myself, when I got to wherever I was going. Climb a mountain. Hug a tree. Visit old friends. Lie on a beach and make sense of it all, with the new and refreshing conviction that there was sense to be made. Write letters of my own. Letters of apology, thank-you letters, letters of explanation, love letters to a past love. And after the letters . . . I thought I might have a crack at a new novel. Not a tragedy, but rather something comical and heartfelt, with an ending bittersweet and elegiac. Comforted by my illusions, forgetting the lessons of the Greeks, I drifted off to sleep.

At about 4.30 a.m., there was a call from reception telling me that a man was here to see me, a Mr Swanson, and did I want him to be told what room I was staying in. The uncertain tone in the receptionist's voice was enough to tell me that Jim was in a visibly agitated state. I told him he could come through. I dressed hurriedly. I opened the door and we shook hands without looking one another in the eye. I held the door open for him and he came into the room. We stood for a few moments in silence. I half expected him to produce a knife or a gun.

'What are you so happy about?' he asked.

'She promised me she wouldn't tell you. Your mole.'

'She called me as soon as she got here. What, you thought I'd just doze off and wait for her to file a full report in the morning?'

'Do you want a drink?' I asked.

'Yes.'

I walked up to him. He didn't move. I could have rested my chin on the top of his head. I raised my eyebrows, and indicated the minibar with a nod. He looked down, and grunted. He took a step back and leaned against the wall with his arms folded. I pulled out two miniature bottles of blended Scotch, and handed one to him. There was a little silence as we cracked the caps, and then the two of us upended our bottles into our mouths. It was impossible to drink from them without looking ridiculous. He sniffed the air, smelling her scent.

'She only stayed for a few minutes.'

'I know,' he said.

He opened the Chaucer on the table and turned through it listlessly. Sweat stood out on his forehead, the beads illuminated by light bouncing off the mirror. I realized as I watched him that he had no more idea of what he was going to do than I did myself. I had assumed he had arrived with some kind of plan, something to say or do, and the fact that there was nothing frightened me.

'Your wife's a real bitch, you know that?' he said.

At that particular moment I was feeling a rush of melancholic remorse towards Cee. Prior to our conversation in the hall I would have defended her mechanically against such an accusation out of a vague sense of duty, but in my current mood it stung.

'She's a bitch because she asked you to pay what you owe? No bonus for ex-employees, I take it?'

Jim gave a strangled laugh, which came out as more of a snarl. 'You're fucking loving this, aren't you? It's not just you, though, it's every fucking posh twat that had less coming in than me. My fucking bank manager was exactly the same. And every poor twat too. My

291

step-brother called to offer me a job with his fucking removals van, and I could hear him, hear him smiling on the fucking phone. Christ, this fucking country . . . The working class think they hate the upper classes, the upper classes hate the working classes, but what both of them hate more than anything is someone from the working classes that gets rich. You know, that fucks everybody off, because it makes the rich feel insecure about their place at the top of the pecking order, and it makes the poor think that maybe, just maybe, their shitty lives aren't the result of some great worldwide capitalist conspiracy, just maybe it's their own fucking fault for not getting out there and making something of themselves.'

It was obvious that Jim Swanson had been drinking for some time, probably since Claudia left the house. He slurred some of his words, and the drunkard's shield of grievance blocked out his mistakes, as the illusory sense of warmth blocks out the cold. His loquacity in this state was familiar from the restaurant.

'But your fate, that's different, right? That's someone else's fault?' I said.

For a moment, it was a toss-up between anger and self-pity. Jim swayed slightly as if standing on a thin ridge between the two.

'I loved her too much. That was my problem. I loved her too much,' he said, and sat down on the edge of the bed.

'That was definitely your problem. Nothing to do with being a soulless little bankster.'

'I'd rather be like that than like you. You're . . . you're an emotional fucking vampire. You saw what we had and you tried to suck the fucking warmth into your own lifeless heart. See, I know all about you, Mr de Voy. I've listened to you drone on for fucking hours. Your fucking affairs, your dead parents, ooohh, look at moi, I'm all human because my mater died. Booo.'

He did an obscene little pantomime, screwing his fists into his rheumy eyes.

'Are you finished?'

'Finished? Not even fucking close, mate. Not even close . . .'

'You don't deserve her.'

'I . . . I what?'

'I said you don't deserve her. She feels sorry for you. You're a little homunculus with no education and you bore her. Your only real chance is to keep her guilty and financially dependent. Which, since you blew your job, is going to be a lot tougher. You must have heard the tapes, heard how happy she was being able to talk to me about books. And her feelings. And all the things you could never understand—'

Mr Swanson launched himself off the bed at me and grabbed the front of my shirt. 'What the fuck are you doing?' I said, and started laughing, more with surprise than scorn. I took his wrists, trying to prise them from my lapels. He became even more incensed by my laughter, and with one hand punched me in the side of the head. It was a lame shot, a big swinging blow such as a child might land on Nanny's thigh. The pain, not intense but aggravating, made me laugh even louder. I was conscious suddenly that I could do more damage to him with my mirth than with anything else, and I kept letting him strike me without interference, bracing my forearms around my face to shield me from the worst of the blows and bellowing with laughter. The only real source of discomfort was the bruise on my wrist where Cee had hit me with the door. We were hemmed in by the bed on one side and the desk carrying the television on the other, and when he pulled back his leg to kick me he struck it on the side of the minibar, making him cry out with pain. I pointed at him, tears now streaming down my face.

That was more than Jim Swanson could bear. When I glimpsed his expression through my teary eyes, the look was one not of rage but of madness. He launched himself at me again, and his assaults were no longer funny. He was possessed suddenly of a maniacal strength, and it struck me for the first time that I might die. Had the two of us been fighting on a moor or in the streets of London (well, maybe Westminster), this might have been an acceptable outcome, but I was not prepared to die in a Travel Inn. I stopped laughing, and tried to flip him off his feet. I succeeded, but he took me down with him, clawing at my eyes.

One of us rolled over on the TV remote, and the thing sprang to life, applause filling the neutral space of the hotel room as somebody famous walked on to a stage to the warm handshake of the presenter. The sound mingled with our heavy breathing and grunting. I was regretting my laughing fit as well as my smoking habit, for I was tiring more quickly than my adversary and finding it difficult to catch my breath. Jim's whole face was twisted into a rictus of hatred, and his astonishing strength persisted. He clambered up on to my chest, and seized my throat with both hands. I tried to push his face away from me, and he bit my hand. I grabbed his balls and heaved him over with all my strength. He cried out and landed awkwardly between the chair and the bed. He fell on the remote again, changing the channel to the denouement of some kind of action movie. The room filled with the swelling strings of an orchestral climax (relayed through the television's tinny speakers) as I reached up to the desk above me to stand, and felt the monumental bulk of the Wynkyn de

Worde *Canterbury Tales*. I was on my feet whilst Jim was still coping with the legs of the chair, and I raised the great tome above my head. Jim became aware of the danger just at the wrong moment, and looked up into the blow, presenting the bridge of his nose for consideration. Ten kilos of metal-bound literature descended on him from a great height, and crushed him.

Perhaps this is always the way with murders. Having never murdered anyone before I lacked an objective measure of comparison, but I was certain from the instant of connection that I had killed him. There was something about the sound, and the give I felt beneath the weight of the weapon, that told me quite clearly that the body would no longer be a fitting repository for the soul.

From beneath the book a jet of blood pumped out on to my shoe, followed by another, and it was this that caused me to lift the lid on my misdeed and hop up on to the bed. The blood was coming from Jim's broken nose, his heart rate accelerated by adrenalin. His features bore an extraordinary look of fogeyish disbelief, the kind of expression one might expect to see on the face of a retired admiral if a chap brought his wife into the club library. His flickering eyes gazed up at me as if I had committed some grave solecism, and I found myself apologizing to him, not with remorse but with embarrassment, as he slumped suddenly backwards and began to convulse. The convulsions lasted only a few short seconds, but the altered angle of his head sent the jets of blood pumping out over the valance and the edge of the bedspread, so I retreated further up towards the pillow end, checking instinctively that the curtains of the window were closed.

I sat on the edge of the bed with my head in my hands until I had caught my breath. Mr Swanson continued to twitch spasmodically, but his eyes were open and fixed.

It occurred to me as I bounced slightly on the mattress that fate had delivered to me the intended climax of my tragedy. And yet he stubbornly refused to be anything more than what he was: a dead man on the floor by my bed. I felt a kind of hopelessness, that here at the end of my search for tragedy, with no lover and with the body of her husband lying at my feet, that higher register of feeling, the elevated plane of meaning, continued to evade me. I was in shock, of course, I had only to look at my own shaking hands to confirm it, but it was somehow clear to me that no matter how much time was interposed between myself and the event, there would be no increase in its significance. Any meaning that did accrue to it in the light of long consideration would be mere embellishment, the habit of an educated mind to doodle in the margins of history. I might understand it better. I might understand Mr Swanson's psychology, my own motives, the bone and vessel that had undone him, the physics of the fatal blow – but for all the analysis, there would be no larger meaning. I felt no fear, and no pity. More than the distant rumble of consequence, which I could hear over the thud of my heart, it was this absence that terrified me. I wanted to switch off the television to accord to both Mr Swanson and myself some measure of dignity (the action film had suffered a commercial break, and a housewife was now expressing her views on tough-to-handle stains), but the remote was still trapped beneath his body, and reaching the television itself would have required a move back down the bed. And I don't wish to sound melodramatic, but for a moment I really felt as if my mind was going!

The Chaucer, which was still in my hands, was remarkably undamaged. Mr Swanson's septum had directed the blood down and away from his forehead, where the copy had come to rest, so apart from a few flecks (which could be bleached), there was nothing to lower its value. I left the television on, and hung the *Do not disturb* sign on the door handle. I went through to reception, and booked myself in for a further three nights. Then I called up British Airways, and bought a ticket on the first available flight to South America. It was in the cab to the airport that I began to laugh, as I remembered quite suddenly that tragedy is inevitable. The tragedy of the man searching for tragedy. That was my tragedy.

That must have been about five hours ago. The supplier of photocopy toner in the next room complained about the noise of the television, apparently. When the clerk had stopped vomiting he called the police. I always find it strange that for all our grand plans, it's things like the sleep patterns of travelling salesmen that really shape our fates. If there'd been a quiet and suspenseful drama on Sky I'd be somewhere over the wine-dark waters of the Atlantic right now. I was sitting in the BA first-class lounge when they got me, chatting to rather an attractive Argentine banker. The sergeant was very polite; he let me finish my drink. Said it was the last one I'd be having for a while. Although that's not true, is it? I was acting in self-defence. That's what I told Cee when we spoke on the phone, and she believed me. Is that what you think, too? I was thinking you could photograph my wounds, if that would help. These bruises had I on St Swithin's Day.

I'm very concerned about my books too. They've been taken as evidence, and I worry the police won't treat them properly. It would be bad enough just leaving them in direct sunlight, or in a damp room, but if they start taking scrapes off the Chaucer for blood samples I intend to sue. I suppose that's in your line too. You must be used to taking on the police. Perhaps you could reiterate to them the value of the objects they have in their possession, and the inherent litigiousness of your client. I can imagine you being highly persuasive, a little threatening even when the job calls for it. I'm deeply grateful to you for everything you've done so far. You've been very silent, and so very patient. It's almost like speaking from a real stage, when the lights are in your eyes, and the auditorium is so silent that you don't know whether there's a soul in the seats or not. I can't tell what you're thinking at all. Do you feel anything for me? Does my story make you feel anything about yourself? Presumably Claudia will have heard by now as well. She'll blame herself, of course, and for the second time in her life she'll see herself as complicit in the murder of a loved one. Of course the last time she . . . she tried . . . You must get someone to her! Don't you see? She'll blame herself, you must get someone to her right now! Get out there and tell them! Tell them! Why won't you answer me? Help! Can anybody hear me out there?

# The Night Climbers
## Ivo Stourton

---

JAMES, A NEW student at Cambridge, is overwhelmed by the thrill of opportunity and startled by his own hunger for friendship. He finds himself seduced by a covert and exclusive circle of friends – the 'Tudor Night Climbers' – who scale the university's turrets after dark, transforming it into a dangerous playground of spiralling heights.

When he falls head over heels for the enigmatic Jessica, James finds himself in a fatal love triangle with the group's reckless leader, Francis. But there is soon to be much more at stake when Francis dreams up a heist that will test their very souls.

9780552773836

# Q & A: Slumdog Millionaire
## Vikas Swarup

*'This brilliant story, as colossal, vibrant and chaotic as India itself . . . is not to be missed'*
OBSERVER

A YOUNG TIFFINBOY from Mumbai, Ram Mohammad Thomas, has just got twelve questions correct on a TV quiz-show to win a cool one billion rupees. He is brutally slung in a prison cell on suspicion of cheating. Because how can a kid from the slums know who Shakeswpeare was, unless he has been pulling a fast one?

In the order of the questions on the show, Ram tells us which jaw-dropping event in his street-kid's life taught him the answer. From orphanages to brothels, gangsters to beggar-masters, and into the homes of Bollywood's rich and famous, *Slumdog Millionaire* is brimming with the chaotic comedy, heart-stopping tragedy, and tear-inducing joyfulness of modern India.

*'A rollicking read as well as being a polished, varnished, finished work of impressive craftsmanship'*
HINDUSTAN TIMES

*'Q & A is a poignant, funny, rich, beautifully written novel with an utterly original and brilliant structure at its heart'*
Meg Rosoff, author of *HOW I LIVE NOW*

NOW A MAJOR MOTION PICTURE,
filmed as *SLUMDOG MILLIONAIRE*

9780552775359

# The Fat Years
## Chan Koonchung

Truth is not an option . . .

BEIJING, SOMETIME IN the near future: a month has gone missing from official records. No one has any memory of it, and no one can care less. Except for a small circle of friends, who will stop at nothing to get to the bottom of the sinister cheerfulness and amnesia that has possessed the Chinese nation. When they kidnap a high-ranking official and force him to reveal all, what they learn – not only about their leaders, but also about their own people – stuns them to the core. It is a message that will rock the world . . .

9780552776974

# How To Forget
## Marius Brill

Do you hold on to painful memories, or do they hold on to you?

MAGICOV THE MAGNIFIDENT, Grand Illusionist, earns his living entertaining the geriatrics of Lotus House care home. But Mr Magicov (also known as Peter) envies them – they've mastered a trick that eludes him: they can forget.

There are so many things Peter yearns not to remember: the shame of an eight-year-old wrecking his life; the FBI agent who hunts him like a dog; that suitcase stuffed with a million pounds. More than anything; Peter wants to forget Kate, the expert con woman. The one he loved and left.

For renowned brain-scientist Dr Tavasligh, Peter's craving to escape makes him the perfect candidate for a bold experiment in changing minds – for ever. Faced with this opportunity, will Peter go through with it? And if he does, who will he become?

A thrilling cat-and-mouse adventure of haunted and hunted, of illusion, deceit, love, death and revenge.

9780857520715

# The Orphan Master's Son
## Adam Johnson

---

CITIZENS OF OUR beloved Democratic Republic of North Korea!
Imagine the life of an orphan boy from nowhere who is plucked
from his orphanage by the military, to be trained as a tunnel assassin,
a kidnapper, a spy.

He has no father but the State, no sweetheart but Sun Moon, the
greatest opera star who ever lived, whose face is tattooed on his
chest.

Imagine he lives in our very own country, a model of exemplary
Communism. A nation that is the envy of the world, especially the
Americans. Where the only human stories people need to hear are
those blasting our of loudspeakers to the glory of our dear Leader,
Kim Jong il.

Citizens! Who is this individual? What is his story? Who will
remember him? Pak Jun Do is his name: wrestler of sharks, envoy
to Texan barbecues, imposter extraordinaire, whose murderous
biography has only come to light through the talents and stamina of
our most patriotic interrogators.

Dry your eyes now, comrades! This is the double-life story of a hero
and martyr: the Greatest North Korean Love Story Ever Told.

'*An addictive novel of darying ingenuity, a study of sacrifice and freedom in
a citizen-eating dynasty; and a timely reminder that anonymous victims of
oppression are also human beings who love. A brave and impressive book*'

David Mitchell, author of
THE THOUSAND AUTUMNS OF JACOB DE ZOET

9780857520555

# The Boat To Redemption
## Su Tong

---

'*Restrained and merciless, Su Tong is a true literary talent*'
Anchee Min

'*A picaresque novel of immense charm*'
Colm Toibin

DISGRACED SECRETARY KU has been banished from the Party – it has been proven he does not have a fish-shaped birthmark on his bottom and is therefore not the son of a revolutionary martyr, but of a river pirate and a prostitute. Secretary Ku and his teenage son, Dongliang, leave the shore for a new life among the boat people on the Golden Sparrow River.

One day a feral little girl, Huixan, arrives looking for her mother, who has jumped to her death in the river. Huixan sows conflict wherever she goes, and soon Dongliang is in the grip of an obsession for her. He takes on Life, Fate and the Party in the only way he knows . . .

'*Su Tong is delusional almost to the point of illness, as if wearing a black lacquered jacket, stubborn but elegant*'
John Updike

9780552774543